Volcanic TROUT

A COMPLETE GUIDE TO FISHING THE TAUPO REGION

BRENDON MATHEWS

SHOAL BAY

DEDICATION

To those who generously and selflessly pass on help and information
to new generations of anglers, so that they might enjoy fishing more.

A Shoal Bay book
First published in 2003 by
Longacre Press Ltd
9 Dowling Street, Dunedin
New Zealand

Copyright © 2003 Brendon Mathews

Photographs copyright © 2003 Brendon Mathews/186AD Photography
unless otherwise credited.

Brendon Mathews asserts his moral right
to be identified as the author of this work.

The maps on pages 20 and 135 are reproduced courtesy of DOC Turangi.
Other maps are by Rochelle Mathews, Cadlink Drafting Services Ltd,
produced with permission of Land Information New Zealand from NZTopo
Online data, extracted January 2003. Crown copyright reserved.

ISBN 1-877251-27-5

Printed by Rainbow Print Ltd, Christchurch, New Zealand

Contents

Acknowledgements

This book started with a simple telephone call to David Elworthy at Shoal Bay Press. At that stage all I had was an idea but, based on some initial interest from David, I set out to produce what you see today. Thanks, David, for taking a punt and encouraging me.

I have been fortunate to have enjoyed the companionship of a number of people during the two years it took to complete the book. Many of them are talented Taupo anglers in their own right, but special mention must be made of Peter Haxell, Tom Watson and Steve Moore who endured being photographed and dragged on out-of-the-way expeditions in the quest to show off the best the region has to offer. Without them, and others, the process would have taken substantially longer and the outcome more difficult to achieve.

Throughout the book there are maps, graphs and other sources of information reproduced with the kind permission of the organisations that supplied them. Appreciation for their invaluable assistance goes to Bruce Waters and Mike Stanley at Mighty River Power; Carolyn Vavasour at Genesis Energy; Glenn Maclean, Rob McLay, John Gibbs and Mandi Goffin at DOC Turangi; Tony Fenton at Environment Waikato; Brad Scott at the Institute of Geological and Nuclear Sciences, Wairakei; Bruce Wallen at Land Information New Zealand and Paul Anderson at the National Institute for Water and Atmospheric Research. Faye Whittaker kindly allowed me to use the photos of anglers in the 1920s, who included her father and her uncle. Garth Oakden of Tongariro River Rafting made a valuable contribution by 'gifting' a memorable visit to the Tongariro Gorge. I was also incredibly fortunate to have had the support of my employer Mike Fogarty at Crown Equipment during the latter stages of the project. Thanks Mike, for being open-minded and flexible about my taking time off work at a moment's notice, even after all my holiday entitlements had been used up. I appreciate it.

My wife, Rochelle, is a very special woman and I'm lucky to be married to her. Her enormous reserves of patience for my endless obsession with Taupo and its trout are, in part, no doubt because of her own love of trout fishing. I am indebted to her, too, for her computer skills and the hard work she put into drawing the maps for the book.

My Dad, Paul, is my best mate and biggest fan. He showed me Taupo as a boy, something I am always grateful for. More than this, he has always backed me in everything I have done. As a parent there's nothing more that he could have done to give me a better foundation for adult life. In doing so he has set a standard that I hope I can meet with my own children one day. Thanks Dad, for always being there.

I have discovered that the whole exercise of producing a book consumes resources, both tangible and intangible at an amazing rate. It also involves the goodwill and co-operation of a large number of people. Thank you to everyone who gave me a push on the way through, and a special thanks to those who came along for the ride. This is the culmination of it all.

Foreword

I well remember my first, less than successful attempts to catch Taupo trout more than 25 years ago. The very thought of fishing at Taupo with all of its history and tradition proved slightly intimidating and, despite all the great angling stories, there seemed to be an awful lot of water between each fish. Every year in the course of my job as a manager of the Taupo fishery I see many anglers who are in the same situation. The old adage that 10 per cent of anglers catch 90 per cent of the fish applies as much to Taupo as to other fisheries, yet in reality it is not difficult to catch Taupo trout once you know and apply the basics.

My early angling years coincided with the publication of the last major books on how to fish at Taupo. These books became my bibles and led me down the path of success, enjoyment and ultimately into a career. Since then fishing at Taupo has changed somewhat, as new techniques, knowledge and materials have developed, part of the natural evolution of angling. That is not to say that the old ways no longer work, but such things as downriggers, jigging and the use of Booby flies are all developments in the last 20 years. Clearly it is time for a new 'bible'.

My initial contact with Brendon was a few years ago when he rang me, in the first of many phone calls, to talk about various aspects of the ecology of Lake Taupo. In trying to develop his fishing skills, he realised the importance of understanding what was going on, and his fishing is characterised by forever trying new twists to catch both rainbow and brown trout. Brendon has an intense passion for this fishery and I am not aware of any angler who has a better understanding or enjoys more success across the whole gamut of opportunities that the Taupo fishery offers.

I am delighted that Brendon has written this book. I am sure there are many anglers who will benefit from its contents and come to enjoy this great fishery as much as Brendon and I have.

Glenn Maclean

You never forget your first fish! Tania Lawrence with an absolute beauty.

Introduction

New Zealanders have long known that their small group of islands at the bottom of the South Pacific is a paradise. The spectacular, unspoiled scenery, for which this country is renowned, is virtually at the back door for many of us. For some of us, however, the main attraction of the great outdoors is the superb trout fishing on offer, and year after year international anglers come here in their thousands to experience a quality of fishing unsurpassed almost anywhere in the world. At the forefront of this reputation is the legendary Taupo fishery, with its dramatic setting in the Central Volcanic Plateau of the North Island.

The unspoilt scenery of the Tauranga-Taupo gorge. New Zealand is famous amongst international anglers for its clean, green image and its superb trout fishing. Strikes can sometimes take second place to just being there.

The first trout were liberated into the waters of Lake Taupo, New Zealand's largest lake, just over 100 years ago. With few natural predators, an enormous food supply and hundreds of kilometres of prime spawning streams and rivers flowing into the lake, they thrived. After only a few years trout weighing over 4.5kg (10lb) were abundant and the quality of the fishing for the early pioneers was outstanding. Word quickly spread from the new colony to the outside world and a legend was born. Later, renowned angling adventurer and author, Zane Grey, immortalised the region in his 1926 book *Tales of the Anglers' Eldorado, New Zealand*. His exploits on the Tongariro River and in the remote western bays have inspired generations of anglers since.

Today, with a self-sustaining population of rainbow and brown trout, the Taupo region has cemented its name as one of the world's premier wild trout fisheries. This reputation, along with ease of access to the region, has made the fishery immensely popular, attracting over 40,000 anglers each year – more than a third of the national trout fishing effort.

What follows is possibly the most complete guide yet to the entire Taupo regional fishery. Covering all the fishable waters and all legal methods, this book is geared towards the enthusiastic angler of any ability. It seeks to help you understand the fishery better, dispel the myths, share the secrets of the experts, open up new possibilities and improve your success – whether you are fly fishing, casting a spinner or fishing from a boat.

Welcome to *Volcanic Trout*, the essential guide to one of the world's most complete and famous wild trout fisheries – the Taupo region.

1. The Taupo Region

A VIOLENT AND EXPLOSIVE PAST

The Taupo region lies in the Taupo Volcanic Zone, a hot-bed of volcanic activity that starts at Mt Ruapehu in the Tongariro National Park and stretches all the way to White Island off the coast in the eastern Bay of Plenty. Situated on the edge of the Indian-Australian and Pacific plates, this zone marks a major faultline in the earth's crust and forms part of a global network of volcanoes that border the Pacific tectonic plate known as the 'Pacific Ring of Fire'. Evidence of the awesome forces of nature that have been at work in the region for more than a million years can be seen everywhere in the area bordering Taupo. The first noticeable difference is the almost lunar-looking, white 'soils' seen in excavations throughout the district, which are actually huge layers of volcanically produced pumice that in some areas are many hundreds of metres thick.

Pumice! It's everywhere and affects everything to do with the fishery.

Less than 10 kilometres north of the lake, the huge clouds of steam and the stainless steel pipes used to produce electricity from the Wairakei geothermal area are further indicators for southbound travellers that they are entering volcano country. As State Highway One descends into Taupo, a clear winter's day offers a dramatic view across Lake Taupo to the snow-covered, active volcanic peaks of Mounts Ruapehu, Ngauruhoe and Tongariro. The eruptions of Mt Ruapehu in 1995 and 1996 remind us that the area is constantly active. Start looking even more closely and

A snow-clad Mt Ruapehu is one of the active volcanoes dominating the region.

you will see the large volcanic domes that dominate the skyline around the lake edge. From Mt Tauhara behind Taupo town in the north to Pihanga, Kakaramea and Kuharua guarding Turangi in the south, the volcanic influence in the area starts to become very noticeable.

What the eye does not see immediately is 'Taupo Volcano', mainly because it doesn't look like one. It started erupting around 300,000 years ago and has done so many dozens of times since. Of those eruptions, two are known to geologists as the world's most violent, the scale of which is difficult to comprehend. The Oruanui eruption of 26,500 years ago was exceptionally large, excavating hundreds of cubic kilometres of material and depositing it over a vast area. More recently the Taupo eruption, around 1800 years ago, was especially destructive. Over a period of days and weeks it produced a complex variety of eruptions, the largest of which ejected huge columns of pumice and ash almost 50 kilometres into the atmosphere. The fallout material rained on the Waikato to the north, showered Gisborne in the east and with the help of strong winds left ash deposits 11cm thick in the Chatham Islands, 800 kilometres off the eastern coast of the South Island.

But the most destructive part of the eruption sequence was a massive pyroclastic flow. This super-heated mixture of gas, water, pumice, ash and rock fragments was the result of the gigantic eruption column collapsing on itself. Just like a huge nuclear explosion, the blast wave travelled outwards from the vent at speeds estimated by scientists to be between 600 and 900 kilometres per hour. The main reason for its huge level of destruction was not the immense heat and speed of the flow but the fact that it reached a height of nearly 1 kilometre, blasting every obstacle in its path. It flattened and destroyed mature native forests for nearly 80 kilometres in every direction, with only the upper slopes of Mt Ruapehu escaping the devastation. When the dust finally settled, a thick blanket of cream-coloured pumice and ash covered the region and much of the North Island.

The immense size of these two eruptions, combined with the quantity of material ejected, resulted in several hundred square kilometres around the vents collapsing below the surrounding land. Over time the huge calderas (collapsed craters) refilled with water which, together with vast amounts of pumice sand, joined the remains of previous lake formations to create Lake Taupo as we know it today. The towering ignimbrite cliffs that rise sheer out of the water throughout the western bays of the lake provide the only visible evidence of the Oruanui eruption. On the eastern side the exposed white cliffs near the holiday settlement of Hatepe are the remnants of the more recent Taupo eruption. A few kilometres west of this point it is thought that the resulting 'plugging' of the vent formed the popular boat fishing spots of the Horomatangi Reefs and the nearby Waitahanui Bank.

The silent witness. This large totara was felled in the 186AD eruption. Te Totara track, Huka Falls walkway.

'Out of sight, out of mind' describes the Taupo volcano for most people. But we need to remember that it is not extinct, it is only resting and, bearing in mind its history, it will certainly roar into life again one day. As a result the area is of major interest to geological science. Based at Wairakei, just north of Taupo, a team of international scientists studies the volcanic activity of the region very closely and its hugely varied eruption history is used as a model for learning about other volcanoes around the world.

Despite the scale of the previous upheaval, Lake Taupo and the tributaries flowing into it are a freak of nature that provide one of the best natural trout habitats anywhere in the world. But everything to do with the fishery, its inhabitants and their behaviour is influenced by the volcanic activity of the past and present. When fishing at Taupo, some knowledge of the effects on the fishery will make understanding it and the fishing techniques easier.

GEOGRAPHY AND CLIMATE

Located in the heart of the North Island at an altitude of 356 metres above sea level, Lake Taupo lies in a special wilderness setting, nestled between the Forest Parks of Kaimanawa in the east, Pureora in the west and the World Heritage Tongariro National Park to the south. Together the Central Plateau's lakes, forests and mountains make a significant contribution to New Zealand's international image as one of the most beautiful places on earth to visit.

The remote western bays offer spectacular scenery and excellent fishing.

The Central Volcanic Plateau is an adventure playground that offers more than just outstanding trout fishing.

The region has a pleasant, moderately warm to cool climate throughout the year because its geographical location generally protects it from extremes. The district is reasonably sunny, with over 2000 sunshine hours a year and a moderate mean annual rainfall of around 1200mm, with the bulk of this coming from a predominantly westerly direction. Average peak daily temperatures range between 10°C in the winter and 24°C in the summer. The moderate climate isn't always kind, however, and the altitude of the region, combined with its close proximity to the mountains, means that conditions can change rapidly. Accordingly anybody venturing into the area needs to be well prepared for cool or cold weather at any time of the year.

THE MODERN FACE OF TAUPO

Its location has always been one of Taupo's best assets, helping to isolate it from the wide-scale urban and industrial developments that have affected other parts of the country. During the early years of colonisation in the mid-1800s, access to the Central Plateau for the early settlers wasn't as easy as it is today, which meant that development in the region lagged behind the rest of New Zealand – a situation that still exists today. Before the completion of sealing the main state highway network in the 1950s, getting to Taupo was a serious undertaking, sometimes taking more than a day from Auckland or Wellington. Today the townships of Taupo and Turangi are no more than a comfortable five hours by car or coach from any main North Island city. Flights from most domestic airports take less than an hour.

Better access brought a significant increase in both visitors to the area and the number of people wanting to make the central North Island their home. Today the regional population is around 30,000, the bulk of whom live in Taupo at the northern end of the lake, with 5000 in Turangi

Trout fishing is big business for the regional economy.

to the south. The rest are mainly rurally based. A sophisticated local economy has grown, primarily dominated by three main industries – tourism, forestry and energy generation, both hydro-electric and geothermal. Tourism is a highly valuable industry, generating many jobs, both directly and indirectly, and earns the region a substantial income. Nationally, Taupo is the single largest trout fishing contributor to the New Zealand economy: it's big business.

The Taupo region is also a popular holiday location with many New Zealanders. The annual summer holiday season, from around Christmas until mid- to late January, attracts more than 20,000 holidaymakers from all over the country. Small holiday settlements are scattered around the lake to accommodate the influx; the most popular of these are Kinloch in the north, Hatepe, Tauranga-Taupo and Motuoapa in the east, and Pukawa, Omori and Kuratau in the south-west.

In addition to fishing, most people come to enjoy a wide range of water sports at a time when the surface waters of the lake are a pleasant 21-22°C – comparable with ocean temperatures and ideal for pleasure boating, water skiing, swimming, kayaking and sailing. In fact the region has become a year-round playground, with day and overnight tramping, mountain biking, rock-climbing, white-water rafting, snow skiing, hunting and many more pursuits on offer. Turangi, the self-described 'trout fishing capital of the world' at the southern end of the lake, is the service centre and gateway to the World Heritage Tongariro National Park, which is the main attraction for most non-fishing activities in this part of the region.

THE TONGARIRO POWER DEVELOPMENT SCHEME

For the better part of 70 years engineers have looked upon the Central Volcanic Plateau and its vast energy resources as a means of meeting the

The enormous steel pipes of the TPD emerge from beneath Mt Tihia before plunging down to the powerhouse at Tokaanu at the southern end of Lake Taupo.

ever-increasing demand for electricity. With plentiful water and abundant geothermal reserves in the region, it was only a matter of time before concerns about preserving the natural environment gave way to the pressures of economics.

As far back as the 1930s, proposals for controlling the outflow of Lake Taupo down the Waikato River had been mooted as a way of improving the production of the Karapiro Power Station further downstream and for the seven additional dams that were in the planning stages. The answer was to install control gates in 1941 across the Waikato River, less than a kilometre downstream from the outlet to Lake Taupo, which were to help even out the wide fluctuations in level that are a feature of a natural lake.

The government introduced legislation to control minimum and maximum lake operating levels and today generation company Mighty River Power operates the gates three times a day, in the morning, afternoon and evening, according to electricity demands.

As the Taupo region grew, local energy requirements resulted in the damming of the Hinemaiaia River, while the Kuratau River at the southwestern end of Lake Taupo was dammed to supply energy to the town of Taumarunui. While the introduction of the Hinemaiaia dams reduced the habitat of migrating trout, and opportunities for anglers, the Kuratau

Dam was upstream of the Champagne Pool (a natural barrier to trout migrating from Taupo) and created a new lake for the benefit of anglers.

The Tongariro Power Development scheme (TPD) was one of the most ambitious plans for large-scale power generation ever seen in New Zealand. The scheme hit the drawing boards of engineers back in the 1950s and involved diverting water from the rivers and streams draining the mountains of Tongariro National Park in the heart of the Central Volcanic Plateau. A complex network of tunnels, canals, holding lakes and two power stations were needed to complete the project.

Construction began in 1967 and when finally completed in 1979 the TPD had introduced a number of dramatic changes to the environment. The most obvious signs of the changes were reduced flows in the Tongariro River and the creation of two new lakes, Moawhango and Otamangakau. Behind Turangi, Lake Rotoaira was extensively modified to act as the final holding lake before the water flowed 6km down a tunnel under Mt Tihia to the Tokaanu Power Station and into the tailrace at the southern end of Lake Taupo. Today the scheme is operated by Genesis Energy and the TPD is an important contributor of electricity to the national grid.

Thankfully these changes haven't been all bad for anglers and in a number of cases have been of major benefit.

A major benefit of the Tongariro Power Development has been the creation of Lake Otamangakau, one of New Zealand's top trophy trout fisheries.

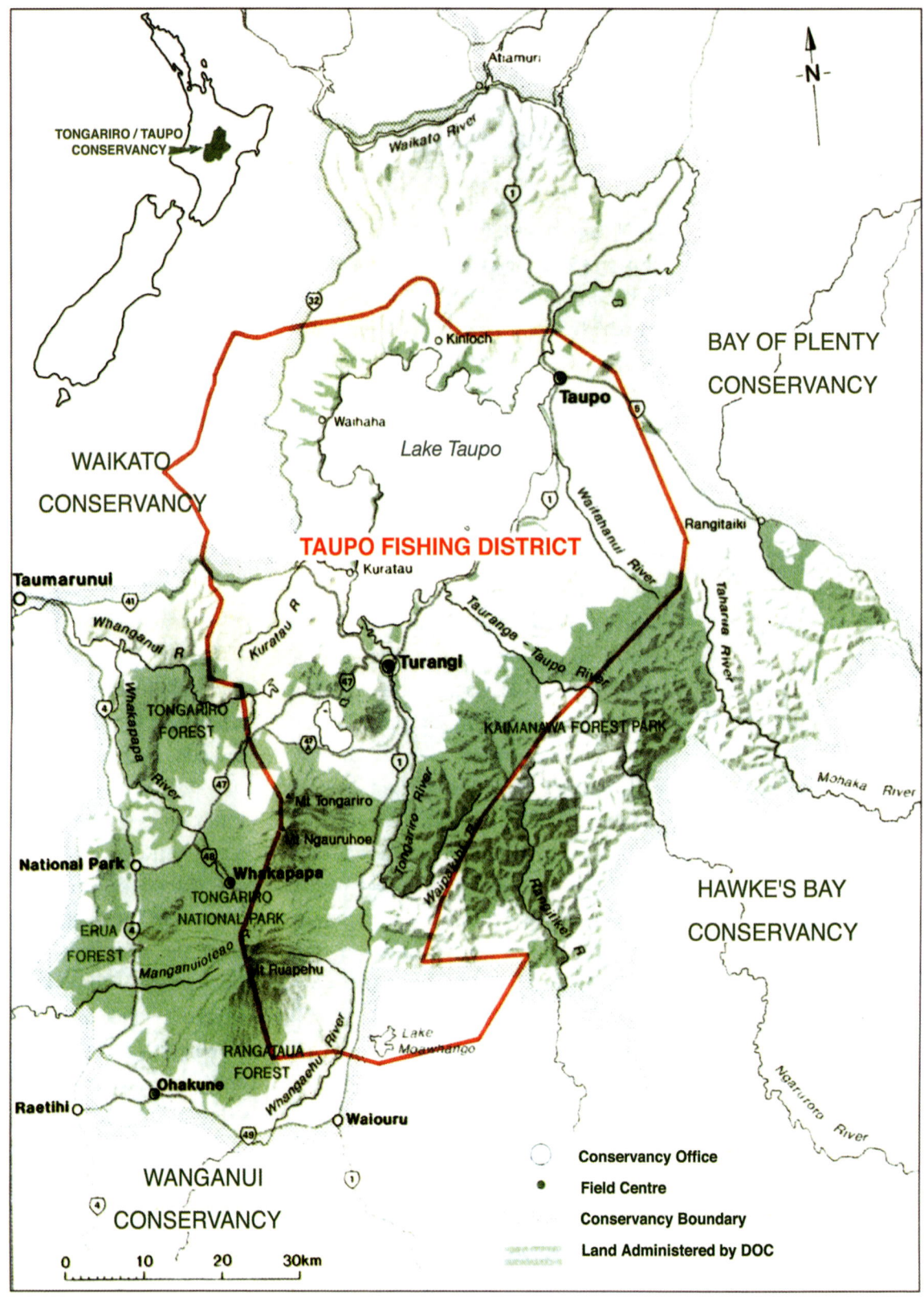

2. The Taupo Fishery

THE SEASONS: A YEAR-ROUND FISHERY

For its geographical size the Taupo region boasts a lot of fishable water, much of it virtually untouched. Why? Simply because most of it is overlooked or forgotten. Most of the anglers who fish the area are lured by the reputation of the lakes in the summer months and the open season on the eastern rivers in the winter. But some anglers don't even bother coming to the area, thinking that because they don't own a boat or haven't yet learnt how to fish with a fly rod, there is nothing here for them. The good news is that along with being what is arguably the nation's finest trophy brown trout fishery, the complete Taupo fishery is probably one of the country's best-kept secrets.

The Taupo Fishing District covers the smallest geographical area of any freshwater fishing district in New Zealand, but within its boundaries are five lakes, 13 streams and rivers, four canals and more than 32 river mouths open to angling. A 12-month season applies not only to Lake Taupo itself, but also to the river mouths and large sections of eight rivers and streams, as well as one of the canals. While the fishable western tributaries and the eastern headwaters close for the winter, they are open from the beginning of December until the end of May and offer some of the best wilderness sight fishing in New Zealand. Some of these tributaries have difficult access, but don't let that put you off. If you make the effort there is an excellent chance of catching late- and early-run rainbows and large browns, and it's quite likely you could have a whole day of fishing without seeing another angler. The same cannot be said for many so-called 'remote' fisheries in other parts of the country.

By the end of May the onset of cooler weather has driven most boat anglers off the lake and into the eastern rivers. While most of the mature

Despite its reputation for being heavily fished, the Taupo Fishing District has some of New Zealand's finest wilderness trout fishing where few other anglers are ever seen.

LICENCES AND PERMITS

The Taupo Fishing District is a stand-alone fishery administered by the Department of Conservation (DOC), in accordance with the Maori Land Amendment and Maori Land Claims Adjustment Act 1926 and sections of the Conservation Act 1987. The acts enshrine in legislation the partnership between the tribal owners of the area, Ngati Tuwharetoa, and the Crown. The 1926 act provides a 20m-wide public right-of-way around most of the shore of Lake Taupo and access for *licensed anglers on foot* on both banks of portions of specifically named tributaries. In return the Crown pays Ngati Tuwharetoa a fee in the form of a lease, being 50 per cent of the revenue of fishing licences, public boat ramp fees, fines and a few other things.

Anglers wanting to catch trout in the region require a current Taupo Fishing District licence, which must be bought before you begin to fish. You do not also need a Fish & Game licence. Licences are available from many retailers, including sports and tackle stores, dairies and service stations, Taupo or Turangi i-SITE Visitor Information Centres, and from DOC.

The Taupo licence year is from 1 July to 30 June the following year. There are many options available, including adult and junior categories for a day, a week or a whole season. Whole-season licence-holders receive a copy of an excellent DOC magazine, *Target Taupo*, three times a year. These keep anglers informed of the work being done in the fishery and include useful tips and information.

A major regulation review was undertaken in 2002 and a number of changes are planned for the 2004/2005 licence year. For the most up-to-date regulations, consult the latest copy of the Taupo Fishing Regulations available from DOC or any licence agent.

Lake Rotoaira

Lake Rotoaira is a private lake on Maori land and although it is within the Taupo Fishing District a separate permit is required from the owners *in addition* to a current Taupo licence. The Lake Rotoaira Trust Board issues these special permits, which can be bought from most sports and tackle stores in the southern part of the district. They can also be purchased from some service stations, the Turangi i-SITE Visitor Information Centre and the Tokaanu Hotel, or from the office at the Lake Rotoaira Camping Ground on the southern side of the lake on SH46.

Boat Ramp Permit

A current Lake Taupo boat ramp permit is required before using public launching ramps on the lake. There are regular checks for permits at the public ramps and out on the lake by the harbour master. If you have a small craft that is launched from a beach you won't need one, but you could get a funny look if you insist that you have launched a 6m boat this way! Public ramp permits are available for a day, a week or a year from fishing licence sellers.

Lake Taupo has a vast shoreline and there is always a good spot somewhere offering fishing opportunities, even for families.

trout in the lake migrate upstream to spawn in winter, they don't all go at once and there are still significant numbers of trout in the lake, making the most of feeding opportunities before running. Cooler temperatures in the lake mean that most of these fish are much closer to the drop-offs, which can make them easier to catch. Keen boaties who are prepared for the conditions can have vast areas of the lake to themselves, and some great fishing.

Shore-based anglers are not left out either. Spin fishing can be successful at a large number of locations around the lake edge all year round, and anglers can use spinning gear in the hydro lake systems during their open seasons, as well as in sections of some rivers and canals. Lake-edge fly anglers tend to congregate with the trout at stream and river mouths in the fly-fishing-only areas. While the mouths can provide outstanding day and night fishing all year round, lake-edge summer stalking with wet, dry and natural flies can also yield exceptional results.

Since trout move about, keeping to one method, technique or location can mean lean times for those anglers who are not willing to adjust: the more flexible you are with your approach to fishing, the more trout you are likely to encounter. As long as the method you use is legal in the place you are fishing, the only limitation is your imagination. After all, no *one* method is suitable for every situation and providing you have some knowledge of trout movements during the day and night and through the seasons, it is possible to catch fat, silver, highly conditioned trout all year round.

THE EARLY YEARS

Originally New Zealand had no salmonids (trout, char and salmon), because the warm waters of the equator acted as an effective barrier to their distribution in the southern hemisphere. With the arrival of Europeans

Huge trout were common in the early 1900s. At top, Bob Floyd with rainbows of 21½lb (10kg) and 19lb (9kg). Below, Noel Wright (left) and Albert Floyd with fish over 13lbs (6kg), 1923.

in New Zealand in the mid-1800s, the early pioneers endeavoured to recreate some of the sporting opportunities left far behind in the British Isles, one of which was angling for trout. The first successful liberations of trout into the unspoiled, sparkling clear waters of the colony occurred around the early 1870s, following imports of fertilised ova of brown trout (*Salmo trutta*) from Tasmania and rainbow trout (*Oncorhynchus mykiss*) from California. But difficulty of access to the Central Volcanic Plateau meant a delay of over 20 years before the first trout fry were introduced to Lake Taupo towards the end of the nineteenth century.

Brown trout were first released in 1887 and thrived in the cool, clear waters of the lake. A lack of competition from predators both above and below the water, combined with a huge food supply of the small indigenous fish, koaro, meant that they quickly reached gigantic proportions, some exceeding 20kg in weight. Within a few years a self-sustaining population became established, but large and numerous as the brown trout were, they proved very difficult to catch and after many failed attempts the so-called 'easy-to-catch' rainbow trout was successfully introduced in 1898.

By the early 1900s organised trout angling had begun and large rainbow and brown trout were being caught by enthusiastic anglers in the lake and rivers. Word soon spread to the outside world that there was magnificent fishing to be had and many anglers arrived on our shores to sample what was to become a truly world-class fishery. Both species of trout regularly exceeded 4.5kg (10lb) in weight, but during the second decade the demand placed on the natural food supply was so great that the population of koaro had become severely depleted. With no alternative food supply, the size and condition of the trout plummeted.

Major netting programmes were introduced to reduce the numbers of fish in the lake, the goal being to lessen the demand on the koaro so that both they and the fishery could recover. While this succeeded in the short term, the excellent rearing conditions throughout the lake's catchment meant that within a few years the existing supply of food was again near exhaustion, plunging the fishery into yet another sharp decline. Interest in an alternative food supply focused on the common smelt, an introduced fish resident in the Rotorua district since the early 1900s from the lower Waikato River. A decision was made to introduce this slender, almost transparent fish to Lake Taupo in the mid-1930s and for the next few years more releases continued until the smelt had successfully established a self-sustaining population.

Trout quickly adapted to the new food source and as a result the fishery made a sustained recovery in the early 1950s. Over 60 years have passed since the introduction of smelt and there seems little doubt that without them the fishery would not have the reputation it enjoys today.

THE TAUPO TROUT LIFE-CYCLE

One of the impressive things about the Taupo fishery is that the population of trout is self-sustaining, which means all fish are wild with no stocking done. With both browns and rainbows originating from sea-run parent stock, the trout use Lake Taupo as their 'sea' for most of their life. With plenty of spawning areas available, most of the trout run the many rivers and streams during the winter months to continue their cycle of life and death.

In the spring many thousands of tiny trout fry emerge from the pebbly gravels of the spawning streams. These natural nurseries contain prime rearing habitat for the newly hatched fry, which grow quickly, feeding on insects and other food inhabiting the waters. The arrival of the fry also coincides with the nesting of shags and other birds, which are quick to take advantage of the newly arrived bounty. When aged 6-12 months the little trout, if they have survived floods, predators and competition for food, eventually find themselves washed into the lake during the regular freshes in the tributaries. Here, a plentiful supply of smelt will constitute nearly all their diet over the next 18 to 24 months. Finally, once mature, thousands of adult fish migrate back to their stream of birth to spawn, and the cycle is complete.

Unlike salmon, not all trout die following spawning, although those that do survive face an up-hill battle to regain condition. Tired, scarred, skinny and unable to fight the strong currents in the tributaries, their only hope of survival is for a flood to push them back to the lake where they can take advantage of the ready food supply to regain condition. A dry spring and early summer can mean death for many of these trout, but once in the safety of the lake many of these fish (known as kelts or slabs) make a remarkable recovery and by the next winter most of them are again making spawning migrations.

Wild trout on spawning migrations in the Tongariro River. The regional fishery is totally self-sustaining.

Their natural colouration allows trout to blend in with their environment. They are not always as easy to see as this one!

Rainbow Trout (*Oncorhynchus mykiss*)

Taupo's rainbow trout are descended from steelhead ova imported to New Zealand in 1883 from Sonoma Creek, which flows into San Francisco Bay in California. These fish now dominate anglers' catches and account for around 98 per cent of the annual take, although comprising an estimated 85 per cent to 90 per cent of the total trout population.

Steelheads spend most of their life in the ocean and return to the rivers to spawn, much like salmon. Being land-locked, the rainbows of Lake Taupo use the lake as their ocean. While there they develop the characteristic steelhead colouration of a white belly, chrome sides and dark green shoulders. Typically the bright crimson cheeks and lateral body stripe for which the rainbow takes its name develop as the trout reach sexual maturity before spawning for the first time.

Although Lake Taupo rainbows can live for up to five years, most will be mature by the age of three, weighing around 1.7kg (4lb) in an average season. Later-maturing four-year-olds can be in the 2.5-3.5kg range, with the occasional five-year-old fish exceeding 4.5kg (10lb). Typically rainbows spawn all year round, although the main runs are winter-based and normally coincide with the first major rains in June before slowing again after October. Mortality rates from spawning account for up to 70 to 80 per cent of rainbows, and those that survive don't generally grow any larger.

A characteristic of rainbow trout is that they are very athletic fish and tend to spend a great deal of time on the move, gathering food. They also appear to be reasonably sensitive to environmental changes, which affect their feeding habits and migration patterns. In the right conditions rainbows will remain highly active throughout the day, which is a major advantage for the angler, as they can be readily caught using a variety of methods, lures and flies.

A mature rainbow trout with the deep crimson cheeks common in spawning fish.

Brown Trout (*Salmo trutta*)

The brown trout released into Lake Taupo in 1887 were from Tasmania, and were originally introduced from British sea trout stocks. Today they are the true trophy trout of the lake and comprise anywhere between 10 and 15 per cent of the total trout population. However, most anglers rarely ever see, let alone catch a brown trout and they feature in only 2 per cent of the annual catch statistics most years – hence their reputation for being difficult to catch.

Being a predominantly lake-dwelling trout, the Taupo brown is very similar in appearance and behaviour to the sea-run browns common to the South Island. Impressively thick, with spotted silver sides and copper/tan shoulders, their normal lake colouration is close to that of the rainbow, but black-spotted cheeks and a lack of tail spots are the normal giveaways for those who are unsure which species they have caught.

Many browns are mature at four years old and average 2.9kg (6½lb). They start migrating upstream to spawn four to five months before the main runs of rainbows, usually entering the rivers and streams from early January. They don't generally appear in the spawning traps until April at the earliest, and almost all fish have completed spawning by September. Brown trout tend to handle the rigours of spawning better than rainbows, with a 50-60 per cent survival rate, and once back in the lake they can continue to grow, often to very large sizes. Provided they survive spawning every year, it is possible for them to live for around 8-11 years – about twice the life expectation of rainbows. Often these trout can exceed 4.5kg (10lb) in weight and browns in excess of 6kg (13½lb) are caught most years. In 1991 Turangi fishing guide Ian Jenkins caught a huge brown in the Hydro Pool on the Tongariro weighing 8.5kg (19lb). It was one of the largest trout to come from the area in the last 50 years and is on permanent display in the shop Sporting Life in Turangi.

Predators like the white-faced heron (pictured) and the shag are some of the natural hazards for young trout.

Brown trout appear to be very deliberate in almost everything they do. They are strongly territorial and extremely cautious during the day, preferring the cover of darkness to feed on smelt and bullies in the shallow slow-moving waters of a stream or river mouth during the summer. However, there is not a lot of accurate scientific information available on the daytime habits of Taupo's lake-dwelling browns. Although radio-tagging studies are proposed, an interesting change noticed since downriggers and jigging have become more widespread is that fewer brown trout are caught than were caught with the more traditional lead lines. It is commonly believed that browns are less tolerant of extremes of temperature than rainbows which, if true, should mean that they are more readily caught in the cooler water near the thermocline, but this is not the case.

Observations of browns in the shallows by anglers and people snorkelling in the summer suggest that their apparent lethargy during the day enables them to withstand relatively high water temperatures. But until the science is in front of us we shall have to keep guessing. The good news remains that Lake Taupo has one of the most significant populations of large browns anywhere in New Zealand and the quality of the brown trout fishery is probably one of the region's best-kept secrets. Brown trout require a different approach and technique to the rainbow and although they can be taken on a variety of lures and flies, they are more easily caught using imitative patterns of food items.

Brown trout. Most anglers have never caught one in the Taupo region, but they are there if you know how to go about catching them.

3. The Ecology of the Taupo Fishery

When it comes to successful trout fishing in the lakes and rivers it is important to have an understanding of how the special ecology of each affects the quantity, variety, behaviour and distribution of its underwater inhabitants. Good information begins with a basic understanding that trout distribution is linked to water temperature, the food chain and seasonal spawning migrations.

THERMAL STRATIFICATION IN LAKE TAUPO

Lake Taupo is a large, deep lake with an average depth of around 110 metres. With an area of approximately 616 square kilometres the quantity of water it holds is measured in the tens of billions of cubic metres. Such an enormous volume of water takes a long time to warm up and cool down, which means that temperatures in the lake rarely fall below 10°C during winter or rise above 22°C in summer.

In late winter, around August, the whole lake from the surface to the bottom is essentially one temperature, approximately 10°C. When spring arrives at the end of September, the daylight hours become longer and air temperatures rise. As the surface waters of the lake begin to absorb the heat, they increase in temperature and decrease in density or become lighter. By midsummer, the temperature of the water at the surface is nearing 20°C and the warming effect in the lake extends down around 20-25 metres. It is at this point that the lake waters become separated, or stratified, into three separate horizontal layers, each a different temperature.

The flowering of the pohutukawa, New Zealand's Christmas tree, is a sure sign of summer.

The warming upper layer (epilimnion) ranges from approximately 20°C at the surface to 15°C at depth and sits on top of the middle layer or thermocline. The thermocline is where there is a rapid change in temperature over a small change in depth, typically from 15°C to 10°C in only a few metres. Below it lies the third layer (hypolimnion), at a cool 10°C. Although these three layers will vary in thickness, they have different densities and will remain separate for around nine months of the year. There is very little mixing between the layers and this has a crucial effect on the lake's ecology and the distribution of fish.

During February the surface water temperature can reach upwards of 22°C and the growing epilimnion has pushed the thermocline progressively deeper. By March the top layer has nearly doubled in size since first forming before Christmas, and by April it is more than 50 metres deep. The onset of significantly lower air temperatures in late autumn starts to have a major cooling effect on the surface waters and although the thermocline can be found well beyond 60 metres in depth, it has started to weaken substantially.

As the top layer begins to lose heat it becomes less dense again. The frosts and bitterly cold southerly winds of winter reduce the temperature in the upper layer to around 10°C and the winds also create currents that encourage mixing of the water. Usually the thermocline has disappeared by the end of July and the entire lake is back to one constant temperature, with the water mixing freely from the top to the bottom. At this point the lake is said to have 'turned over'. During the year the thermocline traps nutrients in the bottom waters of the lake and turning over forms an important function of distributing these to the surface waters, which helps to keep the food chain going. However this turn-over effect does not always occur – during 2001, for instance, the lake remained stratified for the entire year due to a relatively calm and warm winter.

In Lake Taupo zooplankton, smelt and trout display similar temperature-sensitive behaviour and seem to prefer the more comfortable 10-15°C range. Although they are able to tolerate higher temperatures for short periods, most of the immediate food chain congregate predictably many metres below the surface waters of the lake around the thermocline. Since the lake is usually stratified for nine months of the year, knowledge of the thermocline helps the thinking angler to locate large concentrations of trout much more quickly. Given the correct location, conditions and technique, this can mean a dramatically improved catch rate.

Once past the drop-off the lake-bed shelves down quickly and becomes virtually featureless.

Huka Falls, one of New Zealand's most visited tourist attractions, form an effective barrier to migrating fish.

LAKE TAUPO: ECOLOGY AND THE VOLCANIC INFLUENCE

When taking into account the violent volcanic history of the region and the large size of the lake, it is no surprise that the ecology of Lake Taupo is unique. In addition, the lake is land-locked by the Huka Falls about 4 kilometres downstream of the lake outlet into the Waikato River, which act as an effective upstream barrier to migratory fish. This means the biodiversity in the lake is limited to a few original species and those that man has introduced.

As described earlier, major eruptions formed the lake's basin and blanketed large areas of the region with a thick coating of pumice. This material forms a large component of the surrounding soil base. In between eruptions the lake gradually filled up to its present level with water from rainfall, springs, aquifers and melting snow from the Central Plateau mountains, the excess draining away down the Waikato River. At the same time, the tributaries transported eroded pumice into the lake, resulting in enormous amounts of pumice sand covering the bottom.

Of all the sources of water that feed the lake, rainfall is the single largest component. Around a third of it falls directly on the lake but the bulk flows down through pumice soils. A feature of the water from these sources is that the nutrient makeup is low in nitrogen but high in phosphorus, and thus not conducive to productive plant growth, which means that Lake Taupo is relatively free of aquatic algae and weed. It is this mix of nutrients that gives Lake Taupo its famous clear blue water.

With the exception of the Horomatangi Reefs area and a number of other underwater reefs and pinnacles scattered around the lake, the bottom is fairly flat and featureless: once past the drop-off in the many shallow bays that are a common feature of the lake, it shelves down quickly and levels out around 110-120m below the surface. In addition, Lake Taupo has a relatively wide and open shape (40km x 29km) and in some cases this enables wind waves to build up to 2 metres in height. As these near the shallow, sandy bays of the lake, wave action makes it extremely difficult for aquatic weeds to take root in the pumice sand lakebed. Combined with the nutrient mix, this means a general lack of major weed growth in many areas of the lake until the drop-off area is reached. Here the weed extends from around 8 to15m deep, where it ceases to grow any further due to lessening light. The three main well-known exceptions to this are the sheltered locations of Motuoapa Bay, Stump Bay and Tokaanu Bay in the southern end of the lake, where aquatic weed build-ups have been a common feature for more than 60 years.

So what does all this mean for boat anglers at Taupo? Low weed growth is a bonus, particularly when using techniques beyond the 15m depth, which include wire lines, downriggers and jigging. Past that point the soft pumice sand and lack of obstructions mean that the only things you are likely to hook while fishing with these methods are trout.

THE DIET OF LAKE TAUPO TROUT

Many anglers have a good understanding of the life-cycle of trout but know much less about the life-cycle, distribution and variety of its food. Basic knowledge of the daily and seasonal movements of the food sources that trout target can greatly assist in the task of identifying where trout may be located.

A Simplified Food Chain

At the start of the food chain in Lake Taupo is phytoplankton, a type of free-floating algae that belongs to the plant community. Like aquatic weed, phytoplankton does not have the right conditions for wide-scale growth in Taupo and occurs in substantially lower amounts compared with some lakes. In turn this affects the size, variety and number of the next link in the chain, zooplankton, which are mostly crustaceans. By day the bulk of these tiny animals, usually smaller than a grain of salt, normally live at depth in the open waters of the lake. Under the cover of darkness they ascend to feed on minute organic particles and phytoplankton in the surface waters.

These movements are closely followed by the third main link in the food chain. Once this was the native koaro, but the ecology of the lake was changed forever when rainbow and brown trout were introduced, severely depleting the koaro population. Their place in the food chain was largely taken by introduced smelt, which feed on zooplankton. How-ever, they too are affected by the previous links in the food chain and, while they are extremely numerous in Lake Taupo, the relatively small size and low abundance of zooplankton means that they are smaller on average than smelt in the Rotorua lakes.

Trout also follow the migration of the food chain during the course of a day and after dark can be found with the smelt in the surface waters.

Many other lake-dwelling species also make this nocturnal transition from deep in the lake, up the shelf and into the surface waters and shallows of the bays around the lake edge to feed on zooplankton and other items. Often this occurs in close proximity to a stream or river mouth and is more pronounced in the warmer months of the year when the cooler currents of the inflowing water attract bullies, koaro and koura (freshwater crayfish) at various stages of their own life-cycles. However, anglers fishing Lake Taupo should be focused on the movement of smelt, because this is the greatest component in the diet of its trout.

Smelt (*Retropinna retropinna*)

Smelt are the single most important food source for the majority of trout while they are in Lake Taupo and account for more than 80 per cent of their total diet. When the young trout first arrive in the lake during winter at about 12 months of age, they quickly adapt their feeding habits to prey on the vast supply of smelt in the open waters. Most of these trout stay out there and grow rapidly, continuing to feed on smelt almost to the exclusion of the other abundant food sources in the lake, until nearing sexual maturity. In a normal season these trout are around 1.5kg to 2kg and three years of age. Trout larger than this appear to be better able to deal with koura and some will favour these almost to the exclusion of smelt.

Smelt begin life in the sandy shallows near stream and river mouths and then move offshore to grow and feed until they are mature. They are a pelagic species and form schools for protection against mass predation. While out in the open waters of the lake they live in the thermocline

Smelt shoaling near Cherry Bay. The green specks are phytoplankton, the first link in the food chain.

during the day feeding on zooplankton, but once stratification breaks down in the winter they can be found at all depths, sometimes with large concentrations near the bottom, over 100 metres down. At approximately two years of age most smelt are 35-50mm long and begin large-scale migrations towards the shore to begin the cycle all over again. Typically this starts in late October to early November, coinciding with the return of tired, thin trout to the lake from the main spawning runs. The congregation of smelt in the shallows lasts to the end of March, and into April in some locations around the lake. After spawning most smelt die and the cycle is complete.

The shoaling of smelt at the mouths and other places can be quite incredible and at times the edge of the lake can appear to be one massive moving cloud of these small, translucent fish. This is known as 'smelting', an event eagerly awaited by many anglers. The presence of so much smelt in a confined area provides an easy meal with minimal effort, which is a bonus for kelts. It's normally the only chance these fish have of making a good recovery and consequently they dominate the catches of anglers during the day. The fat, silver maiden trout tend to be a more consistent catch in the thermocline or after dark near the mouths.

Anecdotal evidence from anglers suggests that some areas around the lake start smelting earlier than others and one place that has such a reputation is Whanganui Bay. It is unclear why this happens or why one place fishes better than others at different times. It is simply a case of finding the best spots by being on the water regularly and venturing to new locations frequently to find the action.

Rod Greenhalgh and a prime rainbow taken on a smelt imitation from the beach at Waihaha.

Common Bully (*Gobiomorphus cotidianus*)

The common bully is present in reasonable numbers in Lake Taupo and in most of the streams and rivers. Trout consume bullies readily, but they are a distant second choice to smelt, perhaps because bullies and trout generally live in different parts of the lake during the year. The gut contents from fish I have seen over the last 10 years prove that bullies are indeed rarely taken, probably making up less than 10 per cent of the total diet.

As different as bullies and smelt are, they have a lot in common. Bullies, too, begin life in the shallows near the mouths and move offshore to feed. However ,they return in midsummer when they are about three to four months of age and 20-25mm long. By the beginning of winter many of these small fish are the length of smelt (40-45mm) and during the day they hang around the drop-off in substantial numbers. Lake Taupo bullies reach maturity after two years and range in size from 50-75mm, sometimes larger. They spawn in the shallows from late winter through to just after Christmas. Male bullies can become very vulnerable to trout at this time as they defend the spawning site for

Flowering of broom often coincides with the first appearance of spawning smelt in the shallows.

An adult bully and an accepted night imitation, especially for brown trout, the black Woolly Bugger.

some months and leave it reluctantly. Unlike smelt, many bullies survive spawning and continue to grow, sometimes up to 150mm.

Bullies are well camouflaged, generally with brown and tan bands that blend reasonably well with the sandy bottom. Often they sit very still on the lakebed until disturbed and will then dart off in short, fast bursts before settling on the bottom again. In the winter most adult bullies (70mm-plus) are well down the drop-off and come into the shallows to feed at night. They are regularly taken by brown trout, which in turn become susceptible to shallow trolling or harling before dawn and after dusk.

Koura or Freshwater Crayfish (*Paranephrops planifrons*)

Koura, numerous in Lake Taupo, are an important food for large rainbows.

Koura are the last of the three main food sources in the lake for trout. There is a large population of koura in Lake Taupo and it is a widely held belief among anglers that they are responsible for the orange-coloured flesh in most trout. While it can be a factor for many large trout (over 2.5kg), most rainbow trout mature at three years of age and 1.7kg and don't eat koura, but instead get their flesh colouration from smelt. Experts believe that the quantity and relative ease of capture of smelt probably makes koura less attractive, or maybe they are just a bit too difficult for smaller trout to deal with.

For many larger trout, however, chasing smelt is an inefficient use of their energy and they switch to koura almost exclusively. The physical features of these trout include high weight and good condition, reddish pelvic fins and a distended anus. Gut inspections usually reveal only koura present, along with large pieces of pumice or stones to assist digestion and the passing of the shell remains. Although koura can grow to over 150mm in length, the majority taken by trout are 50-70mm long (not including claws), and tend to be a motley dark green/brown colour when first digested.

What a pig! This 2.8kg rainbow had 22 koura in its stomach.

Koura seem to be more concentrated around large underwater structures such as reefs and rocky areas, where they tend to live at some depth during the day. As nocturnal feeders, they ascend the drop-offs after dark into fairly shallow water around the lake edge to feed, swimming in short pulses close to the bottom. Food items include weed and the carcasses of dead bullies, smelt and trout.

Koaro (*Galaxias brevipinnis*)

Koaro used to inhabit the lake in huge numbers until predation by the newly introduced trout depleted the numbers to such an extent that by the early 1910s they were almost wiped out. However, they still exist today in reasonable numbers now that smelt are the main target.

Even though trout eat koaro infrequently now, extremely large specimens over 100mm long are a significant and frequent find in some big rainbows over 3kg I have caught jigging, particularly near rocky areas of the bottom in the south-western end of the lake around Pukawa, Omori and Kuratau. One had its entire gut filled with two of them! Since then I have tied and used with some success an enormous brown Woolly Bugger tied on a size 2, 3XL long shank hook. It doesn't seem to work with any other method except for jigging and generally only deeper than 35 metres from January to April or at night near the drop-off in winter.

Oddly enough, I have managed to catch two large koaro while jigging, and one instance stands out. I felt a bump, struck and thought that I had missed a trout. However, as I wound in to check the gear I saw a dark shape and a flash of silver, deep in the water below the boat. It appeared as though a big koaro was chasing the fly and just behind it was the unmistakable shape of a large hungry trout. I continued to wind in and could clearly see my Green Orbit fly stuck in the mouth of the koaro. What happened next stunned me. The trout promptly gobbled the koaro head first and took off for the safety of the depths. As the trout got away with its huge meal I was left trying to make sense of what I had just seen. While I don't expect a large koaro to take a fly again, it's worth knowing that they are down there and large trout will eat them, given half a chance.

Other Species

One of the earliest liberations of fish into the lake prior to trout in the late 1800s was goldfish (*Carassius auratus*), and they still exist in very low numbers around the Tokaanu swamp area. Of more interest and concern for anglers is the presence of catfish (*Ameiurus nebulosus*), which have found their way into Lake Taupo by either accidental or deliberate introduction. They are extremely hardy creatures and can survive some hours out of the water, so it's possible that they arrived lodged in a boat or a trailer from some other location. Whatever the reason, they are here to stay and exist in reasonable numbers around weedy, shallow bays, growing up to 300mm in length.

Catfish are very lethargic but will take a fly, particularly at the mouths at night. They don't fight very well and most anglers react with disgust on realising it's a catfish and not a trout they have caught. The catfish usually comes to an undignified and gruesome end. If you manage to catch a catfish, do *not* release it. Kill it quickly by cutting it up into pieces, and then bury the remains well away from the water.

It was presumed that trout might prey on juvenile catfish, which would help keep the population down, but unfortunately trout seem to avoid them as a food source.

A new development has seen DOC issue a permit for the commercial capture of catfish using fyke nets and some of the hauls have been significant. In the first week of operation around 1000kg of catfish were caught, most of them destined for dinner tables in Asia and in Auckland,

Catfish will take a fly at night at the mouths. They are a significant pest and should never be thrown back.

but it appears that the demand is not as great as first thought. It remains to be seen what impact netting will have on the population – but one fewer catfish in the lake is far better than one more and this type of venture can only be of benefit to the trout fishery.

FOOD IN THE HYDRO LAKES

How Nutrient-Rich Lakes are Different

Lake Taupo is known as a low-nutrient lake – in scientific terms it is oligotrophic. With the exception of Lake Moawhango, the rest of the lakes in the Taupo region have higher nutrient levels (they are mesotrophic), enabling productive plant growth to occur. A major feature of these lakes is the presence of extensive weed beds, which are able to support complex underwater communities. Unlike in Lake Taupo, where smelt and to a lesser extent bullies and koura are the main food items, the diet of trout in these systems is largely based on nymphs, the immature, aquatic forms of flying insects.

The largest and most common are the dragonfly (*Procordulia grayi*) and damselfly (*Xanthocnemis zealandica*) in both nymph and adult forms. Mayfly nymphs are also found in reasonable numbers in these lakes. During the various stages of their life-cycle they are taken readily by trout. Another common underwater inhabitant is from the family of midges (*Chironomus*), whose larvae are known as chironomids or bloodworms because of their red colouration. These are up to 10mm long and come in many colours, not just red, so it pays to have imitations in green, brown and yellow also.

Aquatic snails also form a significant part of the diet of trout in these systems and are an abundant food supply. Although the snails that live on underwater rocks and plants are difficult to imitate and fish properly, the species that breathe air from the surface are easy to imitate and take trout regularly. Waterboatmen (*Corixae*) exist in good numbers too, and have to breathe air from the surface, where they become a target for hungry trout. In Lake Rotoaira a small population of koaro is present.

Trout growth is greatest during the summer months when the quantity and range of food items increases dramatically. Adult forms of underwater insects enter the food chain from above the water, as do green beetles, cicadas, crickets and blowflies. Tadpoles and frogs are readily taken, as are mice in some seasons. Trout in these systems are willing and able to take advantage of additional forms of food as they come available.

FOOD in the RIVERS and STREAMS

Nymphs

The main types of nymph found in the tributaries include those from the mayfly, caddis and stonefly family. If accidentally dislodged from their underwater homes, they become part of the food chain and trout will readily consume them – even during spawning migrations. However, all species vary in size during the year, depending on when they are ready to mature, and in low and clear conditions some trout will refuse an imitation if it is too big or too small. The easiest way to determine the right pattern to use is to lift a few stones near the water's edge and see the colour and size of nymphs present. A well-prepared angler will always carry a number of patterns in different sizes to cover the range likely to be found.

Caddis

The adult stage of the caddis is a type of moth up to 35mm in length. Around dusk and in late summer evenings, the surface of the region's tributaries can literally come alive as the pupae ascend from beneath the stones and onto the surface, before skating across the water to find a rock to dry out on. The Tongariro River has a reputation for one of the best caddis hatches in the district and although the catches are mainly of little rainbows, recovering fish and early-running rainbows and browns readily take caddis off the surface waters.

Looking under stones on the water's edge is a quick way to match imitations to naturals.

Mayfly

The adult stage of the mayfly is very short, lasting only a matter of days, but significant hatches of these can occur throughout the day during the warmer months of the year. Most trout will rise to take them and during a hatch the action can be spectacular. As with the caddis, there are a few different versions of the mayfly, but so long as the imitation used is similar in size it doesn't normally matter which type it is.

Stonefly

The largest of all the tributary insects is the stonefly. They tend to prefer faster-flowing water and a rocky or bouldery bottom, both of which are common in the headwaters of the Tauranga-Taupo River and in the Tongariro Gorge. The nymphs are huge, up to 50mm long, which makes them a significant meal for a trout. During the open season in the headwaters, imitations of the nymphs in dark green and brown are proven fish takers, especially following a good fresh, when they can be dislodged from beneath large rocks. Adult stoneflies are equally large and also make a good meal, but the overwhelming presence of adult caddis means that imitations are usually ignored.

FOOD ABOVE the WATERLINE
Green Beetle

Green beetles take their name from their brilliant iridescent green colouring and are one of the regular seasonal food types available from

November to February throughout the region's waterways. Since they can't fly very well, an offshore gust on a hot sunny day can send thousands of them out onto the surface of the lakes, where trout quickly exploit them. It's not uncommon for anglers in Lake Taupo to cast to sighted fish thinking they are smelting, when in fact the fish are taking beetles. It always pays to carry a few imitations during summer.

Cicada

On a hot summer's day the song of the cicadas can be deafening, and it is the poor flying attributes of this large bug (up to 45mm long) that are of interest to anglers and fish alike. For most of their life they live in the ground at the base of trees, where they have been for up to seven years. At maturity, they come out of the ground and crawl up the nearest tree, where they shed their husks, spread out their wings and dry out.

An adult cicada emerges from its final moult, leaving the shell behind on the base of a tree. Cicadas are a favourite summer food for trout and one of the noisiest insects known to man.

A prime time to catch a trout on a dry fly is during January and February when tens of thousands of huge cicadas become a targeted food source. It's not often that a live cicada is seen on the water, though, especially since the vibrations they make attract trout for some distance. Typically the willow-lined lower reaches of the tributaries are a great place to find plenty of cicadas and large trout, including big browns that lurk beneath the overhanging branches, ready and willing to devour the next bug that drops into the water. One of the most memorable summers for cicadas was during 2001-02 when the region had plague-like numbers, which was a major bonus for anglers and trout alike.

The use of natural flies to catch trout in the Taupo region is of particular interest to anglers when cicadas are about. The techniques are covered in Chapter Eight (see page 123).

Tiny flies can catch big trout. This 3.6kg Otamangakau brown fell for a #16 Pheasant Tail nymph, a mayfly nymph imitation.

Piwakawaka, the delightful New Zealand fantail, is often encountered in the bush or near the water's edge. They appear to be very friendly, but they are more likely to be after the insects you disturb as you walk by.

Blowfly

Imitations of blowflies belong in every angler's fly box. Trout will gladly accept them, particularly in the bush-lined tributaries on a hot summer's day. Most are black but another common version is the Bluebottle. Tied in big sizes they attract a lot of attention from hungry trout.

Mice

During the summer mice become more active after dusk and their little wakes can often be seen across rivers and streams late into the evening. Trout don't waste an opportunity to eat mice, judging by the ferocity with which they are taken from the surface. Most anglers fishing a mouse imitation target the early migrations of big brown trout in the lower reaches of the large tributaries on summer evenings. However, a surprising number of comparatively little trout, as small as 1.5kg, will have a go too, such is the attraction of this big meal. 'Mousing' is a lot of fun and is one of the most exciting forms of 'dry-fly' fishing.

4. Choosing the Right Equipment

There's no doubt that the experience of fishing for trout is more enjoyable with the right equipment. Successful anglers not only have appropriate rods, reels, lines and lures or flies to catch trout with, but an array of accessories to help make the most of the fishing. There is also no substitute for good-quality equipment and while this is not the most important ingredient in successful trout fishing, in some cases it can make it much easier.

RODS, REELS AND LINES

Fly Fishing

In the early years of the fishery, anglers used salmon fishing tackle imported from Britain. The Tongariro was the main tributary being fished at the time, and since the trout back then were as big as salmon the heavy-duty gear was necessary. Large, gaudy salmon flies and spoons were used, with silk lines coated with a variety of substances to aid in sinking the tackle to the required depths where the running trout were waiting. All fishing was by the across and down technique, and upstream techniques using floating lines and nymphs did not become popular until the 1970s.

Today, heavy rods are still required when dealing with the range of highly weighted flies cast at trout during the winter months, particularly in the larger rivers, but they are certainly not essential for the rest of the fishery. An AFTMA 7 to 9 line-weight rod about 2.75m (9ft) long with floating, intermediate and fast-sinking or shooting-head lines will easily enable most anglers to fish the water productively. For those anglers who wade extensively, either in the rivers or at the mouths, a

One of my favourite rods – it's fast, light and powerful enough to tackle fish up to 6kg with ease.

longer rod of 2.89m (9ft 6in) to 3.04m (10ft) enables better casting performance, but is not essential to enjoy a good catch rate.

The reel needs to be matched to the rod and be capable of holding both the fly line and at least 100 metres of backing. Backing is just that: a spare amount of line that attaches to the back end of the fly line and is sometimes your only insurance policy against losing the lot to a strong fish.

A fly reel normally acts as a line-holding device and as such doesn't have as great a role to play as the line or rod. But the abundance of pumice sand in the region means it is fairly easy for some of it to get into the inner workings of a reel very quickly. The combination of pumice sand and grease makes a very efficient grinding paste that wears out the drags and bearings in the reel, so if you fish at Taupo regularly it is worth investing in a quality reel with a good sealed drag system.

The lower Tongariro offers some superb summer fishing, especially for large brown trout. Having the right gear improves your chances of success.

Floating lines can cast longer and offer better floating performance when treated with any of the vehicle interior plastic protectants available on the market, such as ArmourAll. It is best applied when the fly line is new, and it is also worth re-applying at regular intervals throughout the season if you fish a lot.

Spinning

A lightweight, medium-to-fast-action spinning rod of around 1.98m (6ft 6in), capable of casting a variety of 7gm (¼oz) to 14gm (½oz) lures, is ideal. Matched to a reel loaded with 150m of 3kg line, this will cover most situations likely to be encountered. In some lake-edge fishing locations, lengthy casts in the region of 40-50m are needed to reach the productive fish-holding locations and an old fly rod or long spinning rod of 2.74m (9ft) to 3.04m (10ft) is more suitable.

Harling

An old fly rod and reel is ideal for harling. Because trout hit the fly hard, a long flexible rod is more forgiving on the strike, and helps absorb any sudden loading on the line when playing an energetic fish close to the boat. A fast-sinking fly line or one colour of lead line attached to 100m of dacron makes it possible to cover the entire shallow water area in any of the bays right out to the drop-off area of 5-8m. Because harling is the slowest of all powered fishing methods the leader should be 7-10m long and of no more than 4kg breaking strain.

Trolling: Lead and Wire Lines

Typically a lead line outfit consists of a fairly stiff rod 1.8m (6ft) long and a sturdy reel with a one-way drag, capable of holding 10 colours (90m) of lead line and 100 metres of backing. While the maximum depth at usual trolling speeds of 1.5 to 2.5 knots is limited to around 15m (50ft) it is possible to fish deeper by using wire or copper lines. You'll need an extremely heavy-duty rod of the type used for sea fishing, rated for 15kg to 24kg and a large multiplying reel capable of holding up to 300m of wire. Both types of line need a trace around 3-5m long in a breaking strain of 4-6kg.

Trolling: Downrigger

The introduction of downriggers has enabled boat anglers to control the depth of fishing precisely and use sporty lightweight gear at the same time. Although it is the only method where an auxiliary item of equipment is necessary to fish successfully, the use of downriggers has become one of the most popular and productive methods of trolling. There is a variety of models, from manual lift-and-lower to electrically operated and top-of-the-line professional versions fully integrated with a depth sounder, which automatically adjust the depth of the cable to avoid snagging the bottom. Regardless of the model you choose, the maximum cable length permitted in Lake Taupo is 40m (130ft).

Jigging and using a downrigger are the most consistent methods on calm, sunny days.

Specialised equipment like this requires the use of an appropriate rod. It has to tolerate a constant high loading and be flexible enough to absorb the sudden shock when the line is first released from the clip and then tightens again on the trout, without breaking the line or ripping the hook out. Some anglers use a basic spinning rod of the type described above, which seems to perform the task reasonably well, but they tend to have a faster, stiffer action because they have been designed to cast lures. If you fish frequently it is worth investing in a purpose-built rod of the overhead reel variety, which should have a medium action designed to load correctly. Regardless of rod type, the reel should carry at least 150m of 4.5kg nylon and have a smooth drag.

Phil Hinton nets a good fish taken on the downrigger.

Jigging

For jigging, a purpose-built rod with matching reel is hard to beat. There are a number of suitable models on the market today with the typical pistol grip/overhead reel seat design. Fortunately, a properly set-up jigging outfit also doubles as a very effective downrigger rod by changing the sinker or jig for a trolling lure. The best length range is a one-piece rod of 1.67m (5ft 6in) to 1.98m (6ft 6in) with a 2-3kg (4.5-6.7lb) rated line weight. It should have eight to ten guides (including the tip) and have a medium action. A good reel is also important and many types of suitable bait-casting style reels are available. The reel should be able to hold about 150m of 4kg nylon, have a smooth drag and a 5:1 or faster line retrieval rate.

A small overhead reel loaded with ultra-thin braid and a matching light-weight rod are a great advantage for the jigging angler.

The single-most important component of the jigging outfit is the line. Since jigging enables anglers to catch trout deeper than most other methods, a new set of requirements affects success. When fishing at depths over 30m, the feeling of the take is severely limited when using nylon. This is where the various types of braided and new-generation non-stretch lines come into their own. Firstly, these lines are normally very thin compared to similar breaking-strain nylon, which makes it possible to fit more line on the reel or alternatively use a smaller, lighter reel. I use a 4.5kg (10lb) line and can fit about 125m or more on the reel, which is more than enough to take care of any fish I am likely to encounter in the lake. The thin diameter has considerable advantages when drifting as well, because lower drag allows the line to cut through the water better. The result is a more vertical line, which helps to keep the tackle in the fish-catching zone longer.

Possibly the biggest advantage of non-stretch lines is feel. The sensitivity doesn't change and unlike with nylon, where line stretch is around 30 per cent, fishing in deep water is just like fishing in shallow – everything feels the same. This also means a rod with a softer action is more suitable because it takes away some of the harshness of the non-stretch line. Also, a stiff rod isn't able to absorb the shock of a sudden change in line tension as easily, particularly when the fish is near the boat and is making desperate last runs. This can lead to problems at the terminal tackle end of the equation, causing the knots to break or the hook to rip out or even straighten in some circumstances.

FLIES, LURES AND ACCESSORIES
Fly Selection

A huge range of flies will catch trout at Taupo, and all those listed opposite are proven fish takers. However the pattern is of no importance unless it is being fished where the fish are. Sometimes the fish can get fussy, though, especially in low and clear conditions or during periods of high angling pressure. At times the trout seem to develop

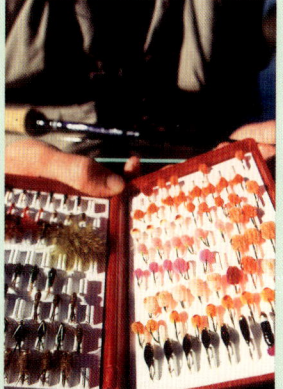
immunity to a particular pattern and it is useful to have a few different styles in a variety of sizes just in case.

Lures and Spinners

There are a number of different types of spinners and lures on the market, which all catch fish whether trolling or spinning. The most popular are the plastic Cobra type and metal Turbo in a variety of colours and sizes. The regulations allow a maximum of two hooks and while it is uncommon to use two spinners or lures, it is practical to tie a harling fly on a dropper about a metre above the choice of bottom hook. It's surprising how often the fly actually catches the fish and while any bright pattern tends to do well, always use a colour that is opposite to the lure/spinner for variation.

Jigging Accessories

Typically most Taupo jigging is done while drifting. Using a 42gm (1½oz) sinker instead of actual jigs will help to maintain good contact with the bottom where most of the trout are caught. Jigs in that weight range are quite large and few trout actually take them, but anchored jigging enables the use of jigs at the lighter end of the scale in 14gm and 28gm

A fine collection of spinners and lures for trolling or spinning. All these patterns catch trout.

A selection of general flies, jigs, sinkers and swivels for jigging.

(½oz, 1oz) and trout will take these more readily. Many types of sinkers are available but the teardrop shape with a swivel incorporated into the design is very easy to attach to the bottom of the trace. They start at 14gm (½oz) and increase by the same amount to a maximum of 84gm (3oz).

Two small standard swivels are needed when assembling the rig, but avoid at all costs the T-type swivels, which are more pain than they are worth. With the sinker or hookless jig and a two-fly rig, most fish are caught on the flies and many patterns work well. Smelt imitations are an obvious first choice, but a wide variety of wet flies will also take plenty of trout.

OTHER ESSENTIAL EQUIPMENT AND ACCESSORIES
Clothing

You should be prepared for any weather conditions throughout the year: appropriate clothing means being able to enjoy the fishing a little bit more. During the day land-based fly anglers should also try to wear clothing in neutral colours, which helps you to blend in with the environment and avoid being detected by wary trout. Typically, polypropylene undergarments are popular, along with polarfleece vests and long-sleeved sweatshirts. A wide-brimmed hat is a definite advantage and a beanie in the winter gives protection against errant flies and the cold, especially on windy days. Lastly, a good rain jacket should always be carried when fishing, particularly as the best fishing can be during nasty weather.

Success in a downpour for Peter Haxell. Be prepared for any weather, any time of the year.

Waders

Wading in the rivers and streams or anywhere near the mouths requires a good pair of full-length waders, especially as the water may be as cold as 10°C at any time of the year. During the summer months bare feet, shorts and a teeshirt are ideal attire, along with the mandatory stalking accessories and sun/bug protection, to hunt for trout in the shallows.

There are two types of wader on the market. Neoprene waders (the same material used to make wetsuits) are available in 3mm, 5mm and 7mm thickness, with in-built boots or as a stocking foot arrangement to be used in conjunction with wading boots. The latest technology has given us a new generation of breathable-material waders. These keep you dry, are very light and most of all eliminate the perspiration problem that can occur with neoprene waders, so they are ideal for long walks and summer fishing. However, the material isn't as robust as neoprene and can be holed by the blackberry bushes that infest many of the walking tracks in the area.

Other Items

It is fairly common to see fly fishermen adorned with all manner of fishing equipment, some of it essential and some not. Being prepared, though, allows more fishing time and fewer trips to the nearest tackle shop, the need for which can be a real disappointment when the fishing is hot. Top of the list are a small first aid kit, a good landing net, plenty of spare flies, lures, indicators and leader material, a hook sharpener, a variety of different fly lines, a pair of leader clippers, a measuring device, a pair of long-nose pliers and a knife. Nice to have but not necessary are scales, some simple tools, fly and line floatant, a shooting basket and a fishing vest. Night anglers will benefit greatly from a small torch or better still, a miner's-style headlamp to allow hands-free operation.

Many of these items can be combined with others to eliminate clutter in a kit bag or vest. For instance, my landing net has a set of scales built into the handle (purchased like this) and I added a crude ruler by scribing the 45cm limit into the handle, along with further 5cm incre-

Bob Wear: an angler equipped for every eventuality.

ments for the bigger trout. My fishing vest houses the net in the back pocket, with fly boxes, leader material and other small items in the front, along with a Leatherman multi-tool, which contains more implements than I normally ever need out fishing.

Polarised glasses are important when stalking trout because they reduce the glare coming off the water, helping the detection of fish. Sunscreen is necessary, even in winter, as is lip balm. Insect repellent in the form of a spray or stick is essential, especially when fishing after dusk in the tributaries or at the mouths in summer.

Remote back-country fishing requires a good pair of tramping boots along with neoprene gravel guards, which work better than the synthetic material versions, especially when wading through rivers. Be sure to take a detailed map and a compass – the weather can close in, which can make tramping along the tracks difficult, especially about the tops. Spare food and a survival blanket are also essential.

Charts and Maps

Topographical maps for the Taupo region are available from some local bookstores, sporting and fishing stores, DOC and information centres. The Topo map series T18, T19 and U18 cover the entire Taupo Fishing District licence waters. In some cases access into sections of the forest parks requires a permit, so before venturing into the unknown check with DOC or at the **i-SITE** Visitor Information Centres at Taupo or Turangi for further details.

The *Holidaymaker* regional touring map covers the lake and rivers to a good scale and shows all the main roads and network roads. Also useful is the DOC walking access pamphlet called *Taupo Walks* which is available from DOC offices in Taupo and Turangi for a small price. It gives detailed information about many short walks, some of which lead to good fishing locations around the northern lake edge close to Taupo.

Having good maps and charts will help to make your fishing expeditions more successful.

The Lake Taupo Bathymetric Chart is available from Government Bookshops, the Navy Hydrographic Division and some sports stores. A bathymetric chart used in combination with a depth sounder is one of the most useful tools a boat angler can have. While not intended for navigational purposes, a bathymetry gives a detailed look at the contours of the lakebed. It is also very useful for shorebound anglers in selecting deepwater locations close to the shore. Every serious lake angler should own and use a copy. Bathymetric charts are also available for Lake Otamangakau and Lake Rotoaira.

For navigation purposes, use the Lake Taupo Nautical Charts, NZ232 (all of Lake Taupo) and NZ2325 (western bays, Motuoapa and Tongariro Delta/Tokaanu Bay).

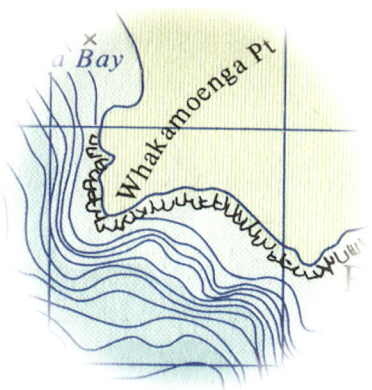

Bathymetric charts are very useful for pinpointing suitable fishing spots. The bathymetry of Whakamoenga Point shows deep water close to the shore. *Reproduced from the Lake Taupo Bathymetry courtesy of NIWA. Crown copyright reserved. **Not to be used for navigational purposes.***

Boat Fishing Accessories

Lake Taupo is very exposed to the weather and excess wind can be detrimental to successful fishing, especially for drift-fishing methods such as jigging. One of the most useful accessories a boat angler could have is a sea anchor or drogue. Looking much like the windsock seen at airports, it will slow the drift of your boat considerably in windy weather, which can keep you over the 'hot spot' for longer. It also doubles as a handy auxiliary slowing device should your vessel lose power and be heading for shore.

It's also wise to have two anchors, especially for anchored fishing at the mouths. The second anchor prevents the boat from swinging in the current, enabling an exact position to be maintained. Once out in the lake proper, at least 100 metres of anchor warp is required, especially if fishing in the western bays. Motor failure there in an on-shore breeze can be disastrous, because vast portions of the lake edge drop vertically into more than 50 metres and don't allow a short-warped anchor to dig in before the cliffs are reached.

Tackle Stores

Anglers can get a wide variety of the latest fishing equipment and regionally important lures and flies from the well-stocked tackle stores in the region. Most are located in Taupo and Turangi, although a large number are conveniently located near the main eastern tributaries. Many tackle store owners and staff have a good knowledge of the regional fishery and some are expert anglers in their own right, which means they can be a mine of information. Some service stations and dairies also have stocks of fishing equipment, mainly flies and lures, but the range tends to be limited compared to a specialist store.

There are plenty of good tackle stores in the region. Creel Tackle House in Turangi is one of the oldest.

5. Reading the Conditions

RIGHT PLACE, RIGHT TIME OR JUST PLAIN OLD LUCK?

You'll often hear successful anglers being referred to as 'lucky'. They were just in the right place at the right time. I guess to some anglers those who catch more than they do probably appear lucky, because to them it was just plain bad luck that prevented them from catching their share of fish. I don't agree. I have seen many examples of anglers fishing unsuccessfully for a few hours in an area known to contain large numbers of trout only to have a newly arrived angler hook up in the same spot almost instantly. Why? Because luck *doesn't* have a lot to do with consistently successful fishing.

Successful anglers know how to read the conditions, fish with the appropriate method and technique and, above all else, understand the behaviour of trout. All these things help an angler make good decisions about where and when to fish, which is half the battle won. Take luck out of the equation: start fishing with the *right* method, *where* the fish are and at a time *when* they are most likely to be there.

Knowing when and where to go fishing and the best method to use is an age-old problem that faces anglers every time they step out the door in pursuit of trout – and an even greater challenge at Taupo because of the wide variety of angling on offer. Many anglers have their favourite places and go there to the exclusion of others because it's what they know and they caught fish there last time. But no one place, time, method, season or lure/fly is likely to produce the same result next time or at any time – that's fishing! What happens when the conditions prohibit fishing in your usual spot, or the trout have moved?

To some extent reading the conditions and making good decisions

A *lucky* angler?

Understanding the factors that influence fish distribution is part of the secret to successful angling.

about where, when and how to go about catching trout is a very personal thing, because all anglers interpret the information they have differently. Also, good conditions for one angler may not be good for another because of differences in technique. And quite often certain conditions that make for good fishing in one place don't necessarily make for good fishing in another, and so on. With all these anomalies, it is not normally one isolated factor influencing the quality of the fishing: generally it's a combination of them.

Thankfully the task of choosing where to go and what method to use can be made easier with a small amount of planning and information gathering, along with a degree of 'gut feeling'. It is not an exact science, but there's no doubt that the well-prepared angler has a substantially greater chance of catching trout, than one who blindly turns up anywhere and just starts to fish.

HOW AND WHERE TO FIND TROUT
The 'Trout House'
One of the keys to mastering trout fishing is knowing where to find them. Many years ago when I was living in the South Island I attended one of the fly-fishing classes run by Malcolm Bell, owner of The Complete Angler in Christchurch. One of the most valuable things I have ever learned was Malcolm's concept of the 'trout house' and it changed the way I approached trout fishing for good. He suggested that trout can be reasonably predictable in their behaviour and generally favour a location for three main reasons. First, they are normally found close to a good supply of food. Second, they will be in a place that requires little effort to be near that supply of food; and third, it will be near to shelter from predators. These three requirements combine to define a 'trout house'. Malcolm strongly emphasised the necessity of looking for a 'trout house' before putting a line in the water.

Obviously this is a broad generalisation, but if you're not fishing where the majority of the fish are then it's likely your catch rate will be extremely low. Not all the water in a lake, river or stream has ideal habitat for trout and it can be easy to waste an enormous amount of time fishing in an area that's highly unlikely to produce results. There are exceptions and when environmental conditions become difficult trout will begin to sacrifice aspects of the trout house – for example, when flows in the tributaries reduce and become low and clear during long periods of fine weather. In such conditions trout houses reduce in size and number, and fish tend to build up in them, waiting for the next fresh before they move on. Often trout are forced into impossible lies as their survival instincts take over and some elements of the trout house are sacrificed. First to be forfeited is the food supply; second will be a position in a comfortable flow; but rarely will the majority of trout compromise shelter from danger. Such shelter could be the deepest part of a pool, an undercut bank, in a logjam or in the faster water at the head of a pool … the list goes on.

An ideal trout house in the Tauranga-Taupo River. The fast shallow water ahead concentrates fish in the deep water until after dark or a fresh.

When I started looking for trout houses my catch rate soared. Instead of heading straight for the named pools or known hot spots, I began searching the water for likely locations that might harbour trout instead. These are literally everywhere and yet the majority of anglers walk straight past many of them. Actively looking for places that are more likely to hold trout can have a major impact on your success too.

In-stream obstructions like logs often make perfect resting areas for running trout.

Trout Houses in Lake Taupo

The plentiful supply of food and the ability of trout to catch it with minimal effort in relative safety are major features of Lake Taupo. However, it is a vast expanse of water and being able to track down and locate significant numbers of trout can be difficult. Fortunately there are some consistent features of trout behaviour that can help your search.

Most of the trout in Lake Taupo feed on smelt, which are found in different locations and depths, depending on water temperature, the time of the year and their own life-cycle. For around nine months of the year this means most of them will be in or near the thermocline and spread over the entire lake. The thermocline is an excellent trout house, but as it extends over an area of 616 square kilometres it can be a significant challenge to find the fish within it. Remember, though, that trout will be where they can get at smelt with minimal effort. A good place to target is where the shelf of the lake, reefs or other underwater obstructions intersect the thermocline, where it is easier for both trout and angler to locate their prey.

When the thermocline breaks down in late July, both trout and smelt roam at all depths and locations around the lake, which could be out in the middle at 100 metres or more. Fishing for them successfully is close to impossible. However, between July and October a good proportion of trout are preparing to run the tributaries, and congregate near them in the shelter of the deeper water over the drop-off during the day. Typically this extends from 8 metres to 20 metres, which makes these trout vulnerable to a wide variety of techniques.

Once thermal stratification has occurred again, the inflows from rivers and streams are major attractions because they are cooler and a substantial food supply is present in the form of spawning smelt. During the day maiden trout are less likely to frequent small, shallow mouths

Two anglers at dawn. The feathered one's skills are sharply honed because it needs to eat to survive.

because of a lack of shelter from danger, but they can be found where inflows drop quickly into deep water. There are many of these locations in Lake Taupo. However, kelts returning from spawning are less concerned with danger because eating is necessary first and foremost to survive. Comparatively few of these fish are found in the thermocline, opting instead for the easy pickings at the mouths.

Under the cover of nightfall, many highly conditioned maiden trout come up from the thermocline in the vicinity of the shelf to feed in the shallows, and the fishing can be exceptional. This movement generally begins around dusk and is reversed before dawn. Typically, fishing around the sandy bays and mouths using methods such as shore fly fishing, spinning and harling, can be very productive for short periods around the change of light, especially when the lake is stratified.

Migrating Trout

Lake Taupo trout are migratory trout that have been in one of the best trout houses for most of their lives. However, if they were not completely aware of their environment while in the lake, then they surely will be once in the confines of a river or stream with plenty of anglers chasing after them. The location of trout houses can be highly varied in the tributaries and there are many places where a trout can find refuge. It is critical to read the water and make an effort to identify possible holding areas.

One of the best ways to do that is to find the first slack water or pool upstream of an area where there is no shelter from danger or where the flows are strong. Other typical locations are to the side or on the edge of the main flow, just above the bottom, behind or in front of a large obstruction and almost anywhere the effort required to maintain a position is low and safety isn't far away. These places are like staging posts where trout can be concentrated in reasonably high numbers. If the spot coincides with a particularly difficult run ahead there is a good chance that it will contain fish during the day and empty just after dark, only to be refilled with trout when the next run moves through before dawn.

For a migrating trout one of the main priorities is to get to the spawning grounds with the least use of energy and in the shortest distance possible. Sometimes that means sacrificing safety, so many trout make their main movements upstream under the cover of darkness or discoloured water from a recent flood or fresh. Often the combination of muddy-coloured water and the accompanying additional flows encourage vast numbers of trout to migrate en masse. Higher flows also benefit the angler by helping to make the fish more accessible. What could be the favoured lie for trout in normal flow conditions might become highly unsuitable in high flows. Typically, many trout can be found in relatively shallow areas – often virtually beneath an angler's feet. And it is not only high flows or dirty water that can make the difference. Sometimes a windy or overcast day will encourage trout to move during daylight.

In a big river like the Tongariro there are few things to obstruct a trout from moving through most of the pools during the day, but the high flow rate requires a large expenditure of energy, something trout are trying to conserve for spawning. Fortunately the general dynamics of flowing water dictate that velocities can be substantially lower close to the bottom, especially in a bouldery riverbed. It's not uncommon to see dozens of trout swimming upstream in the Tongariro, all very close to the bottom. One of many such places is in the pool between the Red Hut and Shag Pools, known by some as the Shag Hut Pool. Standing on the true right bank it is possible to see 10 to 20 fish an hour filing past your position in the bright daylight as they make their way upstream.

The Tongariro is a big river with few things to obstruct a trout moving through pools such as the Red Hut during the day – apart from the odd angler.

The rapids at the Bridge Pool on the Tongariro River help to concentrate trout in the quieter water in the pool below, which is part of the reason it fishes so well.

Sometimes trout are able to move reasonably freely through portions of tributaries, which means that there are occasions when the fishing action in one pool can be hot for 30 minutes and then suddenly go quiet. Normally this is a very good indication that the fish have moved through the pool and into the next pool upstream. Over a day it is fairly common for trout to have moved up many pools if the conditions are right. In the Tongariro it's possible to have good fishing at the Bridge Pool in the morning and still be chasing the run at the Hydro Pool by the end of the day.

Successful anglers shorten the odds by finding substantial numbers of trout in concentrated areas (trout houses) and will generally bypass all others when the conditions are favourable. If you are confident of your abilities as an angler and are sure you have covered all the water, there is no point standing in one spot for hours on end without success because it is possible that there are no fish there. Make the effort to go and find the fish.

Timing of the Spawning Runs

From the day it emerges from the gravels, the biological clock of a trout is on a countdown to repeat the cycle of life and death. For the majority of Taupo rainbows this is at three years of age, and for browns it is four. The onset of readiness for spawning is largely predetermined by genetics, but a range of environmental conditions can delay or advance this movement back to the trout's birthplace and make the fish more predictable when it comes to locating them before and during spawning runs. Knowledge of these factors can greatly assist anglers.

While the main spawning runs in Lake Taupo's tributaries are at their greatest during the winter months, and although runs continue throughout the year, the species you're likely to catch can vary, as can the place where you'll find them, because rainbows and browns differ in their respective migrating patterns. But they share a tendency to congregate around the mouths of the tributaries prior to running. During periods when the levels of the lake and the tributaries are above average, trout are more likely to run upstream as soon as the internal biological clock says it's time to go, provided the aspects of a trout house are present. Higher flows make the passage upstream easier, reduce their risk of being stranded in shallow water and provide better shelter from danger. In conditions like this, trout tend to make more consistent but smaller runs upstream.

Many of the streams and rivers flowing into Lake Taupo are small, though, which can mean extra danger for trout when running. This often causes migrating trout to congregate in large numbers near the mouths to wait for increased water levels or darkness before beginning a migration, especially when the lake and tributaries have been low for a long time. Consequently, lake anglers can have some good sport near the mouths – but when the rain arrives trout enter the tributaries en masse and river fishing improves. Rain isn't always necessary to encourage trout to run, though. Dirty or murky water caused by a slip upstream may provide shelter from danger and, in the case of the Hinemaiaia and Kuratau, which have hydro stations, trout run more regularly when the levels rise during generation times.

Leaving the safety and food-rich environment of the lake to spawn means a big change in the trout's habitat. Generally these fish are most vulnerable to anglers in the first few days in the tributary environment, after which they become very wary and more difficult to catch. If you are able to time your fishing to coincide with a fresh run then all the better, because it can be one of the most productive times to fish. Also bear in mind that while in the lake the eggs of a hen and the milt of a jack still continue to develop, and the longer trout wait before running,

Graphs showing the average monthly run of rainbow and brown trout in the Waipa Stream, a tributary of the Tongariro River. *Courtesy of DOC Turangi.*

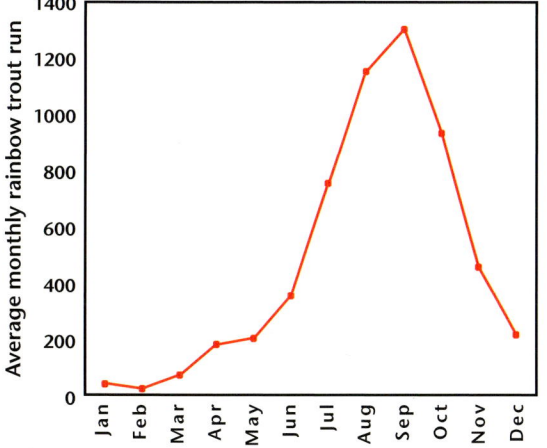

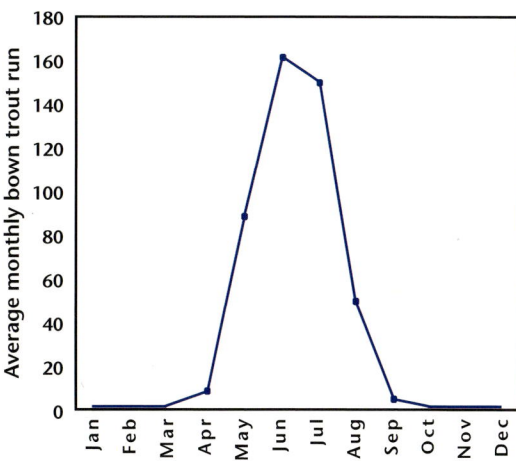

the more urgent it becomes that they reach the spawning grounds when they do run. These fish will tend to move through the lower reaches with greater speed and you may need to target locations further upstream than usual in order to find them.

Stalking Trout

Trout have an in-built survival instinct, which tells them that movement of small items in the water generally means food, and movement of large items outside the water can mean danger. To illustrate the point, next time you are in the Turangi area call into the Tongariro National Trout Centre and spend a few minutes observing trout from the underwater chamber on the Waihukahuka Stream. Watch closely and you will see them continually taking all manner of items – stones, pumice, and other debris – into their mouth for closer inspection. These are 'tasted' briefly and then swallowed or, with a flaring of the gills, forcibly ejected. Trout do this routinely as long as they remain undisturbed.

This means that the pattern of fly or lure is not the most critical part of angling – getting it in front of the trout without disturbing it is. A stealthy approach is vital to your fishing success, particularly in the winter months when large numbers of trout are in the tributaries, many of which are quite small. I consider an ability to stalk trout to be one of the most important aspects of fish-catching success.

Oddly, many people who come to fish the area opt to fish 'blind' in the hope of catching a fish. Plenty also walk up the rivers and streams in full view of the trout, sometimes wearing bright-coloured clothing, which is a sure way to send any trout into fright mode. Since we enter the trout's environment to catch them on their terms, it makes good sense that the less our presence is noticed, the less we disturb them from their normal activities, the more we will enjoy fishing success. This approach

If you can see them, you can count on it that they can see you too!

will reward the angler on all of the rivers and streams in the region, including the Tongariro.

INFLUENCE OF THE WEATHER AND OTHER CONDITIONS

The Barometer

Based on the records I have kept in the past, it would seem that baromet-ric pressure has little effect on general fishing success in Lake Taupo, especially when using deeper methods. However, the movement of the barometer appears to be a significant factor in influencing spawning migrations. During periods of low lake and tributary levels, migrating trout will sit off the mouths waiting for a 'trigger' to send them on their way upstream to the spawning grounds. A falling barometer is one of these triggers and can induce a run, sometimes up to 24 hours before the rains and increased flows actually arrive. It's common to find many anglers in the lower reaches of the eastern tributaries such as the Waitahanui, and Tauranga-Taupo as the barometer is falling. Competi-tion for the best spot at the mouths can be high, too, as keen anglers take advantage of the opportunity to get into the fish before they begin to run.

The barometer has little effect on fishing success when you are using deeper methods. Roy Bowers and a good fish taken while jigging.

A rising barometer normally coincides with clearing, more settled weather and accordingly migratory trout usually slow down their ag-gressive upstream movements. Sometimes, during long periods of low and clear flows, the next falling barometer is enough to encourage trout already in the tributaries to move further upstream in anticipation of more favourable conditions.

Time of Day or Night

Successful anglers know that trout will bite a well-presented lure or fly regardless of the time of day or night, provided that it has not been disturbed – after all, if it doesn't eat it will die. If they don't bite it is likely that there are no fish where you are fishing or they may have already been disturbed. In some cases the lure or fly you are using may be noth-ing like the food items they are concentrating on. It's a simple equation. Catching trout in the lake with deep methods such as jigging and downriggers proves the point, because these trout are less disturbed by activities going on above them, so they bite all day long. The same prin-ciple applies when fishing in the rivers.

Based on the third function of the trout house – providing shelter from danger – it is no surprise to find most trout avoid the shallow areas of the lakes and tributaries during the day and return under cover of darkness. Because of this tendency, the change of light is normally a very productive time to fish in shallower water, when trout are more active than they are during the day in these places. It's not always the case, though – it depends on where you are fishing and other factors.

Summer weather often means competition from other recreational users of Lake Taupo.

Influence of the Sun

It doesn't get much better than being out on Lake Taupo on a fine sunny day enjoying the spectacular views and calm conditions. But summer days like this mean that there could be up to 400 boats doing the same thing, and competition from water skiers and joy riders can be fairly intense in some areas, particularly near holiday settlements.

Many anglers consider that fine summer weather is perfect for fishing, and they are probably right, although it still pays to choose your strategy carefully. Generally, deeper methods such as downrigger trolling and jigging are better at this time of the year because the surface waters of the lake become very warm and many trout will be found over 30 metres down. During the day, deeper methods of fishing are not affected in the same way by the bright overhead conditions, so unless you are up early for a pre-dawn harling session, you might as well sleep in and get out around 10am to avoid the early congestion at the boat ramp. However, if you are planning to fish from the lake edge and the weather is forecast to be fine and clear, you will need to be out at first light for the best success because the fish will probably have started to head for the cover of the drop-off and down to the thermocline by dawn. During January this means a 5am start.

From July through October trout tend to be more active at all levels of the water column and can be caught readily in shallower water, from just below the surface to a depth of about 15 metres. Now bright, calm, sunny days can be a disadvantage to the boat angler because the trout are more wary of the presence of surface activity. If a moving method of shallow fishing such as trolling or harling is your choice, then you'll need to pay out more line to minimise these effects. As darkness approaches, the fishing in the shallows will start to improve as fish move in from deep water to feed.

Smelting trout at Cherry Bay. Crystal-clear water and bright sunlight can be the enemies of anglers and the friends of trout.

When the sun is high and conditions calm, you'll need to adapt your techniques to suit.

In the rivers, bright sunlight combined with low and clear flows can be the enemy of the angler and the friend of the trout. It's not uncommon for flows during the winter to drop quickly following rain, and the smaller rivers and streams can be greatly affected by bright sunlight. In these cases it is usual to have the most success from first light until the sunlight actually hits the water. Outside these times you can expect more success in pools that are very deep or in the shade, as these can hold less wary trout. Downsize everything except for the leader, which you may need to lengthen, especially when the water is very clear, the flow slower and the sun higher. This also applies at the mouths when flat, calm conditions on bright sunny days can make the fishing very difficult. Of course there are exceptions, such as when the smelt are schooling, and the fishing can be quite spectacular. Regardless of the exceptions you should always be prepared to use low-water techniques in order to be successful when the sun is high.

Influence of the Moon

One of the most controversial subjects among anglers, and especially night anglers, is the influence of the moon on angling success. The debates have raged for years. For some anglers the cycle of the moon, lunar tables and 'bite-time' tables, including the Maori fishing calendar, take on such overwhelming importance that they base their impending fishing solely on them. I don't doubt that the moon has an effect on living organisms, but how much of an effect is arguable, especially when good fishing depends on a variety of factors. Admittedly, I'm just as keen as the next person to get an advantage that will help me catch more fish, but today I look at the moon as just another source of light – much like the sun, only smaller. It doesn't get any simpler than that.

Some anglers claim to have had exceptional fishing during cloudless nights, after sticking with it when the moon has come up full and big. A

A full moon on a clear, calm night in Te Hape Bay. It's tough – but not impossible – to catch fish in conditions like this.

more consistent feature of night angling is that regardless of the moon phase, darker nights tend to bring more success than lighter nights. This raises the question, why? Perhaps the trout can see better in bright moonlight and are fussier than normal (in which case smaller flies will work better). Maybe the smelt are the culprits in being less inclined to come in close to shore for fear of being preyed upon. Or maybe the survival instincts of both the trout and smelt are factors in a lack of angling success. It is hard to know for sure, but the last suggestion would appear to be the most likely and probably explains why the deeper river mouths like the Tauranga-Taupo and the Tongariro fish much better than the shallow mouths when the moon is high and the lake is flat.

You will find information about the moon phase, rise and set times on the weather page of most daily newspapers.

The relevance of 'bite-time' tables and the Maori fishing calendar are entirely different subjects altogether. I'm sure they can have some bearing on fishing success in the ocean where there are different influences, such as tides, that can radically alter fish movements and feeding behaviour. Unfortunately, their connection to success in the freshwater environment would appear to be of little significance. At one point I made an effort either to prove or disprove the value of these various tables. Over a period of three months I meticulously maintained a record of all the factors relating to the trout I caught, both in the lake and rivers, with all the possible variations of technique and method. At the end of the exercise the number, size, condition and catch rate per hour of the trout caught in the so-called 'bite-times' was not appreciably different from those taken outside these times.

Successful angling is about finding combinations of conditions that suit the methods and techniques you are using, in the places you like to fish. For me, 'bite-time' tables of any description don't factor into the equation. Lets face it, what chance do the people who produce these tables have of predicting accurately when the fishing is likely to be good where you are, up to 12 months in advance, from an office hundreds of kilometres away from the lake – and without knowing about the other factors that relate to fishing success? Instead of spending money on things like this, it's probably better to buy an instructional fishing book that can help improve your skills as an angler.

Wind and Cloud

The effect of wind on fishing depends on a number of factors. An advantage for anglers is that wind ruffles the surface of the water and since fresh water is lighter and less dense than salt water it stirs more easily. However, strong wind can make life difficult for the angler, depending on the method being used and the location.

Fishing Lake Otamangakau. Overcast days put the odds more in favour of the angler, just.

Wind can be both an advantage and a hindrance when you are up the tributaries. It can give valuable cover to anglers, especially during periods of low flows and bright conditions, but it can also make casting incredibly challenging. Floating fly lines are made thicker to increase their buoyancy and this, combined with a bulky, wind-resistant indicator and heavily weighted flies, can make casting very difficult. One alternative is to roll cast, which is easier and would be my recommendation where this technique is suitable. On bigger water like the Tongariro it can seem almost impossible to cast a floating line in these conditions. A sinking line has a lower level of air resistance and can make things much easier. Switching techniques may save a trip to the local GP to remove an unwanted piercing from a wayward nymph.

On the lakes, very windy conditions can be extremely unpleasant, not to mention unsafe. It's worth remembering, though, that when conditions are bad in one area of Lake Taupo, they may be sheltered and suitable for fishing elsewhere. With the exception of the western bays, the rest of the lake is accessible by motor vehicle, and boat ramps are located around two-thirds of the lake edge. There's almost always somewhere to go: it's just a matter of being adaptable. It's also important to keep in mind that some methods of boat fishing can be less productive when it starts to blow, especially jigging, which requires a steady, slow drift. Motor-driven methods such as harling and trolling are not so affected by the wind.

Lake Taupo's relatively wide and open shape allows wind-generated waves to build up to 2 metres high in some extreme circumstances, which produces very dangerous conditions out on the lake. An interesting side effect of such conditions is that in the space of a few hours the constant pounding of waves into the shore helps to build sandbanks, forming

Rough conditions near Scenic Bay on an otherwise fine day.

Good cloud cover frequently means good fishing. Slip Creek is one place where you can enjoy good fishing – and sometimes you have it entirely to yourself.

new barriers to the rivers and streams, which often results in changing the direction of the flow.

Like wind, sometimes the presence of cloud cover can make a huge difference to fishing success, particularly when targeting trout in shallow water. You could be up a tributary chasing the runs of trout, standing around a mouth during the day or night, spin fishing from the shore, fly fishing from an anchored boat over a drop-off or harling. Cloudy days with little wind can fish better than no-cloud days. Better still, cloudy days with some wind are even more productive, almost regardless of your method.

Don't write off windy or cloudy days. They are not always the nicest times to be out in the elements but they can be an angler's friend and improve the fishing in places that might otherwise be unproductive.

Rain and Flooding

Increased water levels caused by rain or floods help trout to run the rivers and streams with added safety and security. Fortunately, most rainfall in the region is brief and generally results in no more than a temporary discolouring of the water in the tributaries and a small increase in flow. However, consistent rain over a 6-12-hour period in the ranges will have a much larger effect, and steady rain for more than a day is likely to result in the tributaries being high and dirty. This can have a detrimental effect on fishing success and most anglers don't bother going out, opting instead to stay indoors.

Most available angling literature suggests that the rivers and streams are considered to be fishable again when you can see your boot when standing in knee-deep water. But knowledge of the trout's survival instincts can help you find and catch them much sooner, even when the water is high and brown. The dirty water provides shelter from danger for the trout and means you may be able to find them in previously dry

Fishing in flooded rivers can be surprisingly successful.

side-streams or large eddies, behind logs and boulders, in the shallow water at the bottom end of a pool – in fact just about anywhere away from the raging current. Sometimes the fish can be found in only 30-60cm of water, often in large numbers right at your feet.

The challenge facing the angler is that although the murky water provides cover for the fish, it also makes it difficult for them to see your flies. It is essential to use highly visible flies, and going up in size and using bright colours helps to put the odds more in your favour.

WEBSITES AND ANGLERS' INFORMATION

It is hard to make the best decisions without quality information, and this is definitely the case when it comes to trout fishing. Today there is an array of information available from a number of sources. However, websites in particular are constantly changing. You will find up-to-date fishing website addresses listed at **www.volcanictrout.co.nz** – once you find the page of information required, bookmark it for future reference.

Weather Forecasts and Real-time Readings

For centuries anglers have tried to predict what the weather will be like for tomorrow's outing. Now it is no longer necessary to rely entirely on guesses or local knowledge; today there are several sophisticated sources of information.

The MetService operates a web site at **www.metservice.co.nz**, for general nationwide forecasting, and a 0900 automated telephone service with up-to-date forecasts for the area. For the Taupo area dial 0900-999-07, then press 3. This gives a five-day forecast for the region, plus a two-day prediction for conditions on Lake Taupo. The most comprehensive weather reports for Lake Taupo are provided by the Lake Taupo Volunteer Coast Guard throughout the day, at 0915, 1615, 1815 and 2015 hours, seven days a week on VHF Channel 61.

In the south-western corner of Lake Taupo at Omori an automated weather station logs a wide variety of information. This is available at **www.tokaanuskihire.co.nz/omori.htm** and contains comprehensive data relating to recent rainfall and the current temperature. It also provides information on daily highs and lows, humidity and barometer readings, wind direction and speed, along with the sun and moon rise/set times, including the phase. As well, it has a history option which collates the readings for the last 24, 48 and 72 hours, the month to date and for each month going back two years. The is one of the most useful sites for anglers, but be aware that conditions at Omori can be substantially different in other parts of the region: the readings cannot be relied on to provide an accurate indicator for the whole Taupo area.

At the opposite end of the district, about 35km north-east of Taupo town, is a rainfall recorder at Kokomoka operated by Environment Bay of Plenty, which records daily rainfall by the hour. Logging on to **www.envbop.govt.nz** gives the information in graph form. Click on **Water Levels** and a page showing the locations of all the recorder sites comes up. Then click on **Kokomoka** at the bottom of the page.

River Levels and Flows

Genesis Power operates an information service, the Genesis Tokaanu Automated Flow Phone, which gives a variety of readings taken from around the Tongariro Power Development. By dialling (07) 386-8113 and following the prompts some very useful information can be accessed. Of most interest to river anglers is the level and flow of the Tongariro River. Option 1 of the service starts by giving a reading for the Waipakihi, which is the main tributary in the upper reaches of the Tongariro River catchment. Normally the level is 0.6-0.8m and the flow 5-8m³/sec. The next two readings are of the Rangipo Dam and the Poutu Intake and aren't of much help, but the last reading is for the Major Jones Pool. During normal flow conditions the level is around 0.9m and the flow is 25-30m³/sec. It is possible to fish the river effectively up to 70m³/sec by adapting your techniques to suit. Options 2 and 3 give readings for the Whanganui and Moawhango systems and are not much use to anglers, but Option 4 gives the Lake Taupo level in metres above sea level.

It is also possible to find out the daily generating times for the Tokaanu Power Station. Call Genesis Power on (07) 386-8615, then press 4 for the control room. The generation supervisor will be able to tell you the planned start and finish times of generation for the day.

Environment Waikato has a rainfall, river-level and flow recorder situated around 6km upstream from the mouth of the Tauranga-Taupo River. The information is on the Internet at **www.ew.govt.nz**. Look up

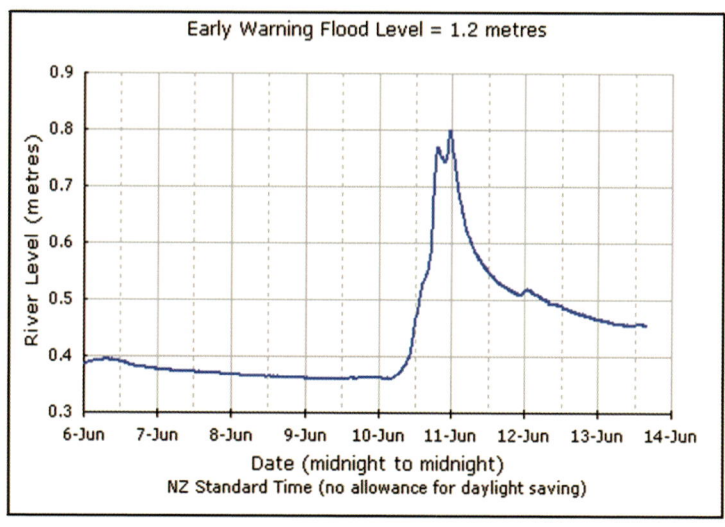

Graph of Tauranga-Taupo River levels as seen on **www.ew.govt.nz**. *Reproduced courtesy of Environment Waikato.*

Our Environment, click on **River Levels and Rainfall**, then scroll down until you reach the listing for the Tauranga-Taupo River. Click on the **Latest Reading** for a graph of the last seven days of river flows. Alternatively, a slightly different version of this information, which includes a rainfall reading, can be accessed by telephone on (083) 225-337. A small fee is charged to your telephone account for this automated service. Under normal conditions the level is 0.35-0.45m and the flow 5-9m³/sec, although the river is fishable anywhere up to 25m³/sec.

On the other side of the lake the river flows and output times for the Kuratau hydro scheme are available by contacting King Country Energy on (07) 896-0100 and asking to speak with the Duty Generation Supervisor regarding flows at Kuratau for the day. The generation times normally coincide with morning and evening meal times. Don't under any circumstance head into the gorge unless the weather has been fine for the last few days and is likely to remain that way.

Lake Levels

Lake Taupo's level is artificially maintained by the operation of the control gates underneath the bridge across the Waikato River on SH1 at Taupo. By law, only the top 1 per cent of the lake can be used for generation purposes. In practical terms this means seasonally adjusted levels between a minimum of 355.85 and a maximum of 357.25 metres above sea level. In other words, the lake can fluctuate within a 1.4m range during the year. The scheme has its critics who claim hydro generation has a detrimental effect on the lake because of widely fluctuating levels. But the reality is that if it weren't for the control gates the level of Lake Taupo would experience far greater fluctuations than it does now.

The control gates across the Waikato River. Despite popular belief, Lake Taupo's level fluctuated more before they were built than it does today.

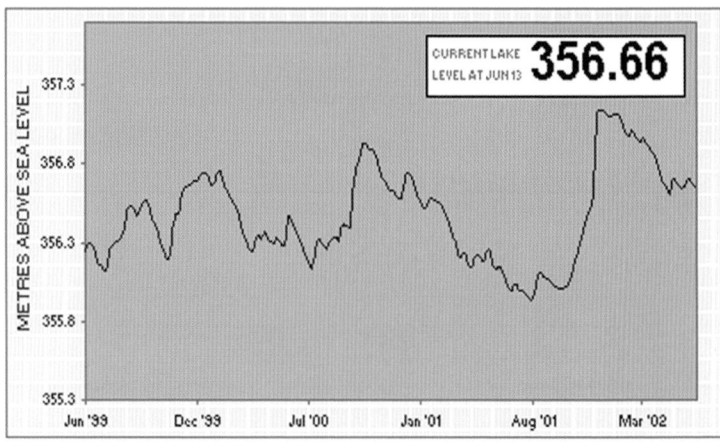

CURRENT LAKE LEVEL AT JUN 13 **356.66**

Graph of Lake Taupo levels as seen on
www.mightyriverpower.co.nz.
Reproduced courtesy of Mighty River Power.

Mighty River Power operates the control gates and the daily level of Lake Taupo is available by looking up **www.mightyriverpower.co.nz** and clicking on **Lakes and Power Stations**. Scroll down the side bar that appears and choose **Lake Levels**. A graph generator opens with Taupo as the first option. Click on the green **Graph** button and it produces a graph showing the last three years of lake levels and the current level. Lake levels can also be accessed by phoning Mighty River Power on (0800) 820-082 and following the prompts. The Genesis Tokaanu Automated Flow Phone has the same information on (07) 386-8113. Press 4 for the Lake Taupo level.

Fishing Reports

A number of fishing reports are available on the web. The Turangi tackle and outdoors store Sporting Life updates its site **www.sportinglife-turangi.co.nz** at approximately 10.30am, six days a week, with a new report and photographs to match. Turangi-based site **www.taupo.com** has a Taupo and Tongariro River report, usually updated four to five times a week. It has links to other fishing reports in the Taupo region and to the Webcam, which is based in the Taupo District Council offices on the Taupo main foreshore, looking south across the lake towards the mountains. While it's not the same as being there, when combined with the information from the weather sites at Kokomoka and Omori it gives a reasonable indication of what is happening around the lake.

6. Fishing LakeTaupo

When trout fishing began at Taupo in the early 1900s, fairly limited methods were used. Innovations over many decades since by keen anglers have earned the Taupo region a reputation for developing new ways of fishing that have gone on to become mainstream in other parts of the country. There is no sign that this process is slowing down, as new methods are constantly evolving. Technology has also come a long way and the range of highly sophisticated equipment available is larger than ever. What was once affordable only to commercial operators or anglers with deep pockets has now become accessible to almost anyone.

There have also been developments in scientific research, enabling fishery managers to make better decisions about the way the fishery functions. In a knowledge-filled world, a large amount of this data is now available to the public. Perhaps surprisingly, though, the average catch rate over the last few decades hasn't changed that much, despite all the advances. Even the gap between the 20 per cent of the most successful anglers and the rest remains largely the same. Why? The answer is probably no more complicated than simply 'fishing where the fish are' – or as is commonly the case, 'fishing where the fish *aren't*'.

Taking an open-minded approach to the opportunities available is essential, because there has never been a single best way to catch a trout in the region's waters, nor will there ever be. Being open-minded and

Lake Taupo on a picture-perfect day is hard to beat. Two boats about to round Te Oineohu Point, the southern gateway to the western bays.

flexible means using whatever is going to be the most suitable and productive method to put the lures or flies in front of trout.

The methods described in this chapter are well proven and the most common used in the Taupo region. But becoming proficient with them can take years of experience and perseverance, so don't expect results instantly. I am constantly amazed by how much I learn every season and often wonder how I ever managed to catch trout in the previous year. What happens as you become more skilled is that the odds of having a poor day reduce and the ability to catch fish more consistently increases, particularly when the conditions get tough. Trout fishing isn't an exact science, though, and sometimes all it takes is a bit of 'thinking outside the square' and not being afraid to experiment with new ideas and concepts.

Within the limits of the Taupo Fishing Regulations there are many techniques that can be successfully employed by an innovative angler. Obtain a copy of the regulations from a licence agent or from DOC Turangi, and read them thoroughly to get a good idea of what can and cannot be done. When added to over a hundred years of innovation in methods, techniques and technology, the beginning of greater success at Taupo is only the next trip away.

FISHING FROM THE SHORE
Fly Fishing

Lake-edge fly fishing is productive in most places from September through to early December, but after that the rapidly warming surface waters of the lake and development of the thermocline tend to push trout beyond the reach of even the fastest-sinking lines and longest casts. Then most fly fishing tends to become concentrated at the mouths of the tributaries, where the cool inflows attract the food chain. If the flows enter the lake at an angle along the shore, such as after a period of strong on-shore winds, the cool water may attract smelt, bullies and trout for many hundreds of metres down the beach.

A 300m fly-fishing-only area extends in a radius arc at most of the mouths, which are identified by posts like the one above. Check your licence for details.

The bonanza begins in spring and early summer as bullies and then smelt turn up in large quantities to spawn in the shallows, coinciding with the return of fish that survived spawning. These kelts are very hungry, bite readily and consequently tend to make up a significant portion of the catch. Dry- and natural-fly fishing the lake edge offers some very exciting sport too, as the green beetle makes an appearance in early summer, followed by the cicada after Christmas. Although most insects are gone by the end of March, good daytime fishing is available through to April in some places where smelt may still be spawning. The onset of cooler weather in late autumn usually sees most remaining trout move from around the shelf of the lake to follow the food supply offshore, and these fish generally don't return until just before their spawning migrations.

During winter the shallows can seem virtually devoid of fish and to all intents and purposes they are. Knowing when to target the mouths in winter is usually the most challenging decision to make because there can be few trout around for a long period of time – perhaps weeks – and then a large number can suddenly appear. Just as fast as they arrive they may disappear upstream, so reading the conditions correctly and being there at the right time takes on additional importance. This doesn't mean that it's not possible to catch good fish right throughout the year: only that fly fishing the lake edge is far more productive when significant numbers of trout have a reason to be there.

Methods and Set-up

A large percentage of lake-edge fly fishing involves using a floating or intermediate line with a rod's length of leader or less, depending on the technique or location. At the deeper locations accessible on foot, a medium to fast sinking line or shooting head is almost always the only way to get the flies in the range of the trout. Generally any of the wet fly or smelt patterns are fished with a line-stripping or hand-coiling retrieve to imitate a swimming action. However, increasing numbers of anglers now use sinking lines, with any of the large range of floating flies available, at both shallow and deep mouths and the drop-offs.

Of these the Booby fly is a particularly deadly pattern when fished with a short trace of less than 1m and an extremely slow retrieve. The polystyrene eyes or 'boobs' add significant buoyancy to the fly, and enable it to float in between retrieves. A five to 10-second pause is usually required to impart the necessary 'injured' action, whereas the Heave 'n' Leave 'fly' is simply left floating just above the bottom on a very short trace – less than 50cm. These techniques rely on the trout swimming past and noticing the fly but in some places they can be incredibly effective.

Targeting lake-edge trout with the dry fly is an underused technique at Taupo but it can also be very successful. It is mostly done during smelting, when large quantities of green beetle are about, particularly from November to January. If your smelt imitation is regularly ignored, try a dry fly instead: it can often make the difference. Usually a rod's length of 3kg trace completes the set-up.

The arrival of smelt, green beetles and cicadas brings a dramatic improvement in shoreline fishing.

Spin Fishing

Lake Taupo has about 120km of shoreline. Nearly a third of it drops vertically into the lake, mostly in the western bays, but this leaves around 80km of accessible shore, much of which is devoid of anglers. Some of the most productive water is well beyond the reach of fly-fishing techniques and using a spinning rod can often be dramatically more productive, even after dark.

Methods and Set-up

The same basic principles apply to spinning as to fly fishing: there are good and not-so-good times to fish around the lake edge. As the lake stratifies in early summer, most of the maiden trout vacate large areas of the shallow lake edge and are either at the mouths or in the thermocline many metres out of reach of most fishing methods.

My fishing mate Tom Watson and I were faced with this problem over the summer break a few years ago, when we were without the boat for the afternoon and desperate to get stuck into the trout. Tom suggested setting up our spinning rods with a jigging rig to enable longer casts. As a hybrid of spinning and jigging he called it 'spigging'. We discovered that in the right location it can put the terminal tackle in the thermocline with ease, and turn an otherwise hard day into a very successful one, particularly when using a boat is not an option. It also works well in the dark using night flies, in the places where trout come up into the shallows to feed.

Two aspects of spigging turned out to need some modification. Firstly, monofilament has inherent line-stretch characteristics over distance that can make it difficult to detect takes and set the hook. To overcome this problem we used the reels from our jigging rods, which already had zero-stretch braid loaded. Takes with braid are positive and the thin diameter gives the added bonus of longer casts. Second, as the lake continues to warm during summer, even longer casts are needed to reach the deep-lying trout. The solution was to use a long soft-action rod designed for fly fishing for salmon, also called a lure rod. At 3.4m long, it can propel a 42gm sinker and two flies around 80m offshore – three times the distance of a very good cast with a fly line and more than enough to catch trout in the thermocline.

Spigging can be a very productive technique, worth experimenting with and yet another fun way to effectively present the lures or flies to more trout.

While most spinning is done with a weighted spinner or lure cast from shore, it has the advantage of flexibility and any number of variations in technique can be employed successfully. In most places the retrieve usually begins as soon as the lure or spinner hits the water, but when spigging you should wait for the sinker to hit the bottom before beginning a slow but steady retrieve. A fly tied about 1-1.5m above a spinner or lure helps to improve the strike rate substantially, so try using any standard jigging-type flies representing smelt, bullies or koura. With the hookless jig or sinker set-up it is possible to use a second fly, which should be completely different from the other, for variation.

There is plenty of scope to be creative, so long as your variation falls within the bounds of the Taupo fishing regulations. Other options include using a running sinker set-up and any of the floating flies on the

Scott Greenhalgh with a good rainbow taken from the shore in summer with spinning equipment.

Using a running sinker rig with a floating fly like a Heave 'n' Leave Glo Bug can be a highly effective way to catch trout with spinning gear.

market, such as the Heave 'n' Leaves and the Booby. For something different, the use of a bubble float opens up new possibilities with a smelt or bully imitation and can be successful with dry or natural flies too.

Night Fishing

As the light begins to fade there is a mass migration of lake-dwelling animals up the drop-off and into the shallow bays to feed. These areas become alive with smelt, bullies, koura and trout at various times of the year, all looking for an easy meal.

During summer and early autumn the cool inflows near the mouths can be highly productive locations after dark. Plenty of kelts are always present, although better-quality maiden trout tend to make up a greater proportion of anglers' catches. It is also when brown trout are more likely to be encountered than at any other time of the day. In a complete reversal of their daylight behaviour, they become very active at night and feed extensively near the mouths in anticipation of the start of upstream migrations. These are keenly sought after for their fighting and excellent eating qualities. As well as that, they are often 3kg plus, and there's a real chance of bagging a trophy of 4.5kg (10lb) or more. Warm, overcast nights see many large browns caught at known locations around the lake when they become vulnerable to the flies and techniques of anglers who are prepared to target them.

Hooking into a trophy brown is a real possibility at night. Martin Higgs and a very large brown trout.

From June to September the chances of catching maiden trout at the mouths are extremely good after dark too, particularly if conditions in the preceding weeks have been conducive to a mass build-up of trout. Typically this effect is more pronounced at the shallower and smaller mouths when there hasn't been much in the way of rain for a while, or if the lake level is below 356.5m.

Spin fishing can also be good in the dark – even more productive than during the day. Fish are more likely to be closer to the shore than they are at any other time, so long casts are not necessary. In winter, spigging in the usual deepwater locations can be very effective, but be prepared for a much lower catch rate than in the summer. The fish available are normally large maiden rainbow trout over 2.5kg that are wintering over in the lake and have switched from a diet of smelt to feed almost exclusively on koura. Otherwise, October to April are the target months for greater success at night in the shallower parts of the lake edge, when significant numbers of trout are in close to feed on the spawning smelt and bullies.

Methods and Set-up

Fishing in the dark requires a change of flies to either dark or black versions of flies used commonly during the day, or any of the luminous range. The luminous materials used in fly-tying emit a glow based on

Stump Bay rip at the Delta. Don't spoil the fishing by wading in too far at shallow mouths.

the original strength of the absorbed light. A torch will give a glow of only low strength and duration, regardless of how long the fly is exposed to the light. When illuminated by a basic off-camera flash they can glow brightly for a considerable length of time, though, in some cases for up to 10 minutes. Luminous flies are very popular among many night anglers and take plenty of rainbows, but there is some debate over the use of luminous flies for browns, with a few anglers swearing by them and many others swearing against them. My fishing mates and I trialled a two-fly rig with both types of flies over several seasons of night fishing to let the trout decide. More than 150 large browns took the dark fly (big Woolly Buggers and Boobies), yet only eight took the luminous fly when given the choice. The results speak for themselves. If you are in doubt about one fly type or another, do what we did and vary your set-up. That way you can cover all the bases.

Regardless of the pattern, rainbows usually hit the fly at speed and the takes are very noticeable. Browns, on the other hand, often take the fly very subtly and any slight hesitation or feeling of the line stopping during the retrieve should be instantly struck. With luck, the line tightens on a big fish and then it's all on. A few words of caution: continual casting, the odd snag, poor technique and abrasion from the sharp teeth of trout all weaken the trace and reduce knot strength near the fly. Retying in the dark after landing every trout is a hassle, but not doing so could see your line breaking with the loss of a trophy trout later in the session. Many successful night anglers use a trace of 6kg-plus as insurance against this problem and I recommend this for serious night fishing.

CHOOSING THE RIGHT LOCATION
The Mouths and Bays
At the mouths the usual practice is to fish in the 'rip', which is the visible line the inflowing water makes as it converges with the lake water.

Normally it is very noticeable but sometimes at the smaller mouths it can be hard to determine precisely. With a ready supply of buoyant pumice on the shore, simply put a few large pieces into the last part of the flow before it enters the lake and watch what happens to it as the current dissipates. Quite often the currents can flow a significant distance into the lake, or make unexpected changes in direction further out.

Understanding where the flows are and how they vary in strength can make a big difference to catch rates and success. Trout, smelt and bullies are not likely to hold in the fast, direct force of the flow for long because the energy required is too great. More often than not they are slightly to one side of the flow – commonly on the inside or shoreside of the current as it enters the lake. Since most Taupo tributaries have less than $7m^3$/sec of flow and many are less than $3m^3$/sec, they usually enter the lake in bays where the water level is often no more than 3m deep, so extensive wading is not normally required. All too often anglers spoil the fishing by wading in too far, too soon, which only serves to push the trout further out. Like most forms of fishing it often pays to 'fish your feet first' before venturing out deep. Obviously if the fishing is still good while standing on the shore, you should stay there until the strikes dry up.

Sensible – and safe – wading techniques are even more critical when fishing in the dark. At dusk it's normal to start as far out as possible and progressively work back towards the shore within a few hours of nightfall. This allows the trout to come closer inshore and when undisturbed they will come right into very shallow water. The reverse applies first thing in the morning at 5am. Start by fishing from the sand, and if necessary, gradually move out as the sky lightens. More often than not the first fish will be caught within a few metres of the shore, where the water may be less than knee deep. I often stand well back with the tip of the rod virtually on the sand to ensure that the fly is retrieved right to the shore, especially when browns are about. They can be so close in that they are often hooked as the fly is being lifted up for the next cast.

Where to Go

Most of the good shoreline locations are accessible by car and then a short distance on foot or bicycle. Naturally there are exceptions, the main one being the Tongariro mouth. Although the western bays look remote, of the four main breaks in the plunging cliffs only Waihora and Whanganui bays are not accessible on foot. The latter is not because of a lack of a road or a suitable way in, but because of the unwillingness of the landowner to allow access for anglers: the only way in is by boat.

Kawakawa Bay is one of the forgotten gems, yet it can be reached via a good walking track from Nisbett Terrace in Kinloch. A parking area for up to six vehicles is located next to #36. It is a good two

Kawakawa Bay track in the western bays. There are many easy walking tracks providing access to good fishing spots.

hours' walk, or under an hour by mountain bike, but well worth the effort. There are some good stream mouths that receive very little pressure from other anglers, day or night. The three largest, the **Tutaeuaua**, **Omoho** (Chinaman's Creek) and **Otutira** (Stony Creek) streams, have good rips.

Whangamata Bay, where the track starts at Kinloch, has some good fishing too. Less than 500m west of the marina, the **Whangamata Stream** enters the lake and only 400m beyond so does the **Okaia**. Further west and a decent walk of about 1.5km from the end of Nisbett Terrace is the **Otaketake Stream** mouth, which has some of the finest day or night fishing in the northern end of the lake.

The next bay towards Taupo town is **Whakaipo**, where the **Mapara Stream** flows into the eastern edge of the bay. It is popular with anglers throughout the year, especially at night, because of the consistent fishing and close proximity to Taupo. It is found by taking either Acacia Bay or Poihipi Roads and then Mapara Road. Once the lake comes into view the access to the reserve and the stream mouth is from Whakaipo Rd. It is more of a track than a road and it splits in two near the bottom, with the left branch leading a short distance to a grass parking area. The foot track down to the mouth is less than 100m long and starts on the lake side of the fence. Climb over at the stile – right by the car.

On the eastern side of the lake a number of small stream mouths provide good fishing and although these are right beside SH1 most are overlooked in favour of the larger, well-known mouths. One such place is the mouth of the **Mangakoura Stream** (Dirty Duck Creek), which is located under the pines about 1.4km north of the Waitahanui mouth. The next virtually unknown mouth is that of the **Waitotara Stream** in Halletts Bay, south of Hatepe. There is a parking area about 150m north of the houses on the point. It is a very short walk to the lake edge and the mouth from there. Another small stream, the **Wairere**, enters the lake immediately to the south of the same houses. Its tiny mouth is well sheltered from almost all easterly winds and offers good night fishing and daytime smelting. A small parking area is located under the tall trees south of the houses.

Not more than 3km further south, between Ohoumahanga Point and Motutere, is the **Waipehi Stream** mouth. A reserve is signposted from the road, from where it is possible to drive a vehicle to the water's edge beside the mouth. It is very rocky underfoot and can make for tricky wading, although like most small stream mouths it is possible to catch fish from the shore without getting your feet wet. The last of the little mouths on the eastern shore is the **Waitetoko**, which can be accessed by driving through the campground at the southern end of Mission Bay. This vehicle access is over private land, so be courteous and respectful to ensure the privilege is available to others who come after you.

The Waipehi mouth is unusually rocky underfoot so take care when wading.

A change of fly for Peter Haxell at the Slip Creek mouth, Tokaanu Bay. Waihi village is in the background.

At the bottom end of the lake are three stream mouths between Tokaanu and Waihi Village off SH41. The first is the **Tokaanu Stream**, but access to it is over private land and permission is required at the house on the western side of the bridge. The next is **Slip Creek**, reached from the road to Waihi Village. Park at the ski lane and walk around to the point – a distance of about 300 metres. Lastly, the **Waihi Stream** enters the lake north of Waihi Village – home of the Ngati Tuwharetoa. Permission must be sought before crossing their land to get to it. Alternative access is by way of a small dinghy or canoe taken across the bay from near Braxmere Lodge.

Three more small stream mouths can be reached by taking SH41 over Waihi Hill. The first of these is at **Pukawa**, and is found in the left-hand corner of the bay after descending from the Pukawa turn-off. Less than 500 metres further along SH41 is the turnoff to Omori and Kuratau. At the bottom of the hill Omori Road crosses the stream of the same name and just before this is a short vehicle track that leads down to the **Omori** reserve, where you can park right beside the mouth. Like the Waipehi, it has a rocky bottom, which can make wading difficult, although it is not required for good fishing. Lastly, the **Whareroa Stream** mouth is located in the middle of Te Hape Bay, accessed from Whareroa Road, which is a continuation of Kuratau Hydro Road, just past the junction on SH32. A crude vehicle track leads down to the mouth at the bend in Ngati Parekaawa Drive, although the last stage of a new subdivision is due for completion in the middle of 2004, which will make access to the mouth

Success at Whakamoenga Point.

easier. Otherwise it is a 400m walk along the shore from the northern end of the lakeside reserve at the bottom of the hill.

Small stream mouths often provide very good fishing throughout the year, usually after dark. During the summer and autumn, brown trout are available and during the winter rainbows can be taken as they congregate before running. Most fishing is done with a floating line and 1.5-3m of trace because the water is normally very shallow.

Deepwater Locations

With the exception of Kuratau Spit, most of the accessible shoreline deepwater locations are outside the 300m fly-fishing-only areas at the mouths. This means there are numerous opportunities to fish with the long casting advantages of spinning equipment. The very best of these are where the lake drops into deep water close to the edge. Starting at the north end of the lake, a track to the eastern headland in Whakaipo Bay gives foot access to **Whakaipo Reef** at **Tahunatara Point**. Clockwise from there are the **Rangatira** and **Whakamoenga Points**, easily reached from the end of Acacia Bay Road. Park on the left at the end of the public access point (signposted), and follow the track for about 100 metres. A small sign for Whakamoenga Point directs walkers to the right, while the track straight ahead leads to Rangatira Point. Either walk takes less than 25 minutes one way at a leisurely pace.

In the vicinity of Taupo town, SH1 gives easy access to two virtually urban locations. The first of these is beside the **Two Mile Bay** boat ramp. Less than 150 metres west of the ramp the drop-off comes right in to the shore, making it a good location for spinning methods. Only 3km further south, **Wharewaka Point** is reached by turning off SH1 onto Wharewaka Road and following this down to the water's edge.

There are many places where the drop-off is very close to shore, such as at the southern end of Te Hape Bay.

The actual point is very rocky and the best place to fish is about 200 metres north at the reserve, where the drop-off is right at the beach. The next opportunity is at **Motutere Point**, where a long cast towards Motutaiko Island will put your terminal tackle into prime deepwater fish-holding territory. Get to it by parking at the motorcamp and wading in shallow water around the lakeshore to the western side of the point.

On the south-western shores a good sandy drop-off is located under the cliffs of Rangitukua at **Whareroa**. Turn right at the roundabout by the boat ramp and park beside the fence bordering the DOC reserve. The drop-off is closest directly in front of the fenceline, where a decent cast with a spigging rig can put your terminal tackle in about 30 metres of water. Finally, **Whakatonga Point** in Waihaha Bay shouldn't be forgotten either. Refer to Chapter Nine (see page 190).

Other Locations of Interest

There are more than 200 urban stormwater outfalls draining into the lake at various locations around the shoreline and while these are normally not noticed they can be new sources of significant inflow when the rains arrive. All manner of items are washed into the lake including worms, snails and, in summer, a wide variety of bugs, all of which can attract fish. The more notable outfalls are along the lakefront at Taupo town and these can discharge up to 2.5m^3/sec during heavy rain. If it starts to rain, or looks as though steady rain has set in, it can pay to head down to the lake edge in built-up areas. I have had some excellent fishing at outfalls, both day and night, and there's every chance of being able to fish alone because most people are indoors during nasty weather. They don't know what they are missing.

Outfalls can provide a temporary rip and bring good fishing in the summer.

BOAT RAMP LOCATIONS

Access to the lake is very good, with a number of well-positioned and signposted boat ramps around the lake. Some of them are wide enough to allow more than one boat to be launched at a time, which minimises queuing during the busy summer months.

Kinloch Marina is the closest launching point to the western bays.

Starting at the northern end of the lake, there is a private ramp and marina at Kinloch, located off Poihipi and Whangamata roads. It is open to the fee-paying public and has three lanes as well as a jetty either side, making launching and retrieving a boat of up to 7.5 metres easy, even when the lake is low. If you plan on fishing the western bays this is a perfect launching place because it cuts the run to Waihaha to around 25 minutes, compared to nearly an hour from Taupo town or any other ramp.

Moving around the lake in a clockwise direction, the next available ramp is located at Acacia Bay on Acacia Bay Road. North from there and located at the end of Alberta Street in the Acacia Bay area is the Te Moenga Bay ramp. In Taupo town on the true left bank of the Waikato River at the boat harbour is the Nukuhau ramp. It is reached from the end of Rauhoto Sreet, off Norman Smith and then Noble streets. Almost directly opposite are the motorcamp and Taupo Boat Harbour ramps, both located off Redoubt Street. All three ramps in the Taupo boat harbour are usable in all lake levels.

Next around from Taupo town, just off SH1 in Mapou Road, is the Two Mile Bay ramp. This ramp was modified in 2001 and is now useful at nearly all lake levels. Further along SH1 the Three Mile Bay ramp is found by turning right at Wharewaka Road and then right again less than 200 metres later, through the Three Mile Bay reserve and down to the ramp. Note that when the lake is really low, around 356m, this is too shallow for fibreglass boats larger than 5 metres. Further along Wharewaka Road there is a ramp of sorts at the Four Mile Bay reserve, although it is not a recognised public launching facility. It is marginal for a light alloy craft under 5 metres and is not a good option, particularly considering the low cost of a ramp permit.

About halfway along SH1 between Turangi and Taupo is the Motutere ramp, which is a popular launching place for people staying in the adjacent camp and from the holiday settlement of Hatepe. The Mission Bay ramp is located to the north of the Waitetoko Stream mouth. It is accessed through the Waitetoko campground off SH1, which is easily missed if you blink when going past so keep an eye out for it. The Oruatua ramp is located just a

few hundred metres south of the Tauranga-Taupo River off SH1 at the end of Oruatua Avenue. Less than 2km further south there are ramps at either end of Motuoapa Esplanade, at the Motuoapa Marina. A single ramp is located at the southern end at the junction of Parikarangaranga St and the other is a double ramp at the northern end, at the junction with Maniapoto Street. This ramp is signposted from SH1.

The next public ramp facility is located by taking the SH41 turn-off at Turangi and heading for Tokaanu. Turn right opposite the Shell gas station in Tokaanu and take the road that leads to the Tokaanu Marina, where there are two double ramps. Approximately 1km further along SH41 is the turn-off to Waihi. Off this road you will find the lake's southernmost ramp at Braxmere Fishing Lodge, but you'll need to speak to the proprietor about parking. (They are usually accommodating if there is space.)

The first of the ramps on the south-western shore of the lake is at Pukawa. From SH41 take the signposted turn-off for Pukawa and follow it to the beach to find the ramp. Two more ramps are located on SH41 by turning onto Omori Road, which leads to Omori and Kuratau. The Omori ramp is about 3km from the SH41 turn-off, while the Kuratau ramp and jetty can be found by continuing on Omori Rd to Kuratau, then turning right onto Waipapa Street and lastly into Pihanga Street. Finally, a public ramp is located at Whareroa, which is reached by turning off SH32 onto Kuratau Hydro Road about 2km north of the SH41 and SH32 junction. SH32 is often referred to as the Western Access road, and is in fact a useful Taupo by-pass, linking Turangi and Tokoroa.

The last boat ramp in the south-west of the lake is Whareroa.

Light boats can be launched at other locations as well. While there is no ramp, you can launch a small craft at the western end of Whakaipo Bay, which is reached by taking Mapara Road from either Acacia Bay or Poihipi roads and then Whakaipo Road. No fee is payable here, but you'll need to be able to carry your vessel to the water's edge. Similar lake access can be found inside the Tauranga-Taupo mouth, but only for lightweight vessels that can negotiate the bar. A 4-wheel-drive vehicle is recommended to avoid getting stuck in the soft shingle.

For further information relating to the Lake Taupo public launching ramps contact the Taupo Harbourmaster's Office, Landing Reserve, Taupo Boat Harbour, PO Box 256, Taupo. Phone (07) 378-7176, Fax (07) 378-2718.

Public Right-of-Way

The general public has a right-of-way 20 metres wide around most of the shore of the lake and unrestricted access where the foreshore lies in public reserve.

FISHING LAKE TAUPO BY BOAT

Harling (sub-surface to 7m)

Originally harling was a term given to drift fishing or rowing across weed beds or areas of shallow water, trailing a fly line and flies. It is an old and proven technique, which has its origins in the British Isles. Although Lake Taupo has limited weed, the extensive areas of shallow water close to shore mean this is a highly effective seasonal boat fishing method. While drifting or rowing the shallows has largely disappeared and most modern harling is done under power for convenience, the principle remains the same. Either way it is generally the slowest of all the moving boat methods.

Serious harling traditionally begins in late October at Labour Weekend and continues through to April, when the majority of anglers give it away for the winter. Some good sport can be had for pre-running trout during winter, though, particularly if it hasn't rained for a while and the lake is low. Because there is no shelter from danger for trout in shallow water locations during the day, harling is much more successful around the change of light at both ends of the day, when greater numbers of trout are present.

Often the action lasts for only 30 minutes or an hour at the most, unless conditions are overcast, windy, rainy or a combination of all three, enabling trout to remain undisturbed for longer. Also, once the thermocline has formed, the shallows can easily exceed 20°C, which encourages trout to spend less time out of their comfort zone deep in the lake. Then the most successful anglers tend to find trout on their way between the thermocline and the cool inflows of a tributary mouth. It is generally more productive to fish near the drop-off at dusk and as close to the beach as possible for 5am starts. In a place like Waitahanui Bay that could mean the difference of up to half a nautical mile (850m) in location.

Harling at dawn. It is not only a beautiful time of the day to be out on the lake, but your chances of success are greater.

Methods and Set-up

Whatever your form of propulsion – drift, row, paddle or motor – it is essential to be moving slowly, ideally at less than 1 knot. A fly rod and reel with an intermediate or fast-sinking fly line is ideal for harling, although some anglers make up dedicated lines out of a single colour of lead line attached to the backing. Generally a long trace of 5-10m of 4kg nylon is used, but some anglers use over 20m. The most productive set-up involves using two completely different flies, one about 1.5m above the other, which is a good way to cover a few options. Bright variations of smelt or bully patterns work well in the dim light of dusk and dawn, as do black flies.

Two fish on one line is a rare treat, but it is possible when you use two hooks. Gary Greenhalgh is the lucky angler.

When they are first hooked, trout are close to the surface and their normal response is to immediately leap into the air and make strong early runs. This means that it's important to set the drag on the reel correctly to ensure that the trout is well hooked on the strike. If you are unsure about the resistance needed, an easy method is to put a cup (250ml) of water into an empty 2-litre plastic milk bottle and tie to the line (before it is threaded through the rod guides). Adjust the tension on the drag so that it's just possible to pick up the bottle without the reel slipping. Too loose and the hook may not take properly; too tight and the hook could rip out or the line might break. It's a good thing to check, along with the rest of your equipment, before you go out on the water.

Trolling: Lead (5-15m) and Wire (20-35m) Lines

The use of lead and wire lines for lake fishing began in the 1960s when these methods were first allowed in Lake Taupo. However, these lines are very heavy in the water and greatly dull the fight with the fish. Nearly half a century later, the introduction and acceptance of downriggers and jigging means that most new anglers taking up boat fishing are doing so with lighter and sportier gear.

A lead line consists of a lead core and a polyester/nylon sheath, which gives the line its strength in 12kg (27lb) or 16kg (36lb) breaking strains. Lead lines are normally sold in 100-yard (90m) spools and every 10 yards is coloured differently to assist the angler in fishing at the desired depth. Each colour in the water at normal trolling speeds equates to roughly 1.3-1.5m of depth that the line sinks below the surface, so by the time all 10 colours are in the water the fishing depth is about 13-15 metres. Because of the enormous friction on the line, the amount of drag nears its maximum with eight colours in the water, which means that it is very difficult to fish any deeper than 13-15 metres, regardless of how much more line is let out. A number of anglers use 20 colours or 200 yards (180m) of lead line in an effort to fish deeper, but this causes exceptionally high levels of additional drag, actually preventing the line from sinking any further than 10 colours will.

Trolling lead or wire lines lacks flexibility but good catches can be made when the conditions suit.

Lead line trolling can be reasonably successful, particularly during winter when the trout are more spread out in the water column. However, by late November the thermocline has started to form and the fish are regularly at the 20-25m mark, which is 5-10 metres deeper than lead lines reach. Understandably, catch rates during the day take a sharp drop and remain low until after the lake turns over. It is simply a case of the trout not seeing the lures.

In days gone by, targeting those deep-holding trout meant using stainless steel or copper wire lines. Heavy-duty rods and reels are required to hold the 200 metres or more of wire needed to put the lures down to the maximum depth of 35m these lines can reach. But it is unusual to enjoy any sport with wire and most hooked trout are simply wound into the boat, which virtually renders the method a harvesting tool only.

With all the inherent difficulties and limitations of fishing with lead or wire lines, many boat anglers are selling or throwing away their old gear and changing to downriggers and jigging. Given the ease of use, flexibility, success and fun that modern equipment provides, it is widely expected that within a few decades these old methods will be rarely seen on Lake Taupo and become consigned to Taupo's boat fishing history.

Methods and Set-up

As with harling, a long 5-10m trace of 4kg nylon is typical with both lead and wire. Try tying a big, bright harling fly like a Yellow Lady, Ginger Mick or Parson's Glory off a dropper 1.5 metres above the lure for an improved catch rate.

Trolling: Downrigger (15-35m)

The use of downriggers for trout fishing around New Zealand is a relatively new development – and it was a Taupo-based initiative. Downriggers

More than one line can be used on a single downrigger.

were originally banned throughout the country and it is largely the tourism industry that anglers can thank for the change. Summers are generally very busy for charter operators, but this is a time when trout are in deeper water and beyond the range of most traditional trolling methods. Without the use of cumbersome and highly unfriendly wire lines, the catch rates used to nose-dive and many patrons returned from a charter empty-handed: not a good look when trying to attract more people to come to the region and spend money.

Lobbying by the Taupo Commercial Launchmen's Association, with the support of the Taupo Fishery Advisory Committee to DOC, resulted in a three-year trial of downrigging methods beginning in 1993. The trial ended successfully with the permanent adoption of downriggers as a legal method in the fishery and today it is one of the fastest-growing and most popular ways to troll for trout. This is hardly surprising, given the enormous advantages over traditional methods, and it has meant a big improvement in angler satisfaction.

Instead of the weight being in the line, as it is with lead and wire lines, it is in a 4.5kg lead ball on the end of a wire cable. A drum or reel holds the cable and a counter gives a readout of how far the ball has been lowered into the water. Light monofilament or braid lines are attached to the cable by pressure-release clips and the lures or spinners are lowered to the desired depth. Flexible rods loaded with tension complete the set-up. When a trout is hooked, the line pulls free from the clip and the angler is able to have a far more exciting fight than would be possible with a heavy lead or wire line.

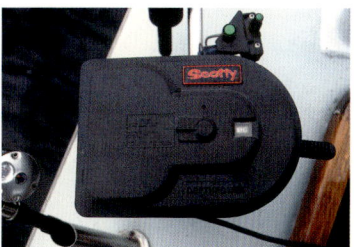

A downrigger cable drum and counter. One of the major advantages of the downrigger system is that it enables you to target a specific depth accurately.

Many types of downrigger are available, from the basic manual models all the way up to automatic electric lift-and-lower versions integrated with the depth sounder to ensure the ball doesn't hit the bottom. Regardless of the model used, the main advantage of a downrigger is that it

The downrigger: a revelation in deep trolling techniques. Make sure the line is in the clip properly and check the release tension.

enables the angler to control the depth of fishing quite simply. Cable length is limited to 40 metres in New Zealand, but drag on the cable at normal trolling speeds causes the ball to rise and reduces the fishing depth to about 35 metres.

Methods and Set-up

Special purpose-built downrigger rods are nice but not necessary and I use a jigging rod by simply replacing the sinker with a lure or spinner and removing one of the flies. Braided jigging lines work extremely well in the downrigger clips, which with intensive use can end up bruising monofilament. Some anglers make up special lines with a length of braid or dacron in the area where the clip normally clamps onto the line. The clip has a small screw for adjusting the clamping force on the line, but be careful to adjust this properly because it helps set the hook on the strike. Too loose and the hook may not set; too tight and it is possible to tow a trout around for hours and not know it.

By using a layering system, up to four lines can run off one downrigger without any problems, but most boats run only two. There is a chance of the lines tangling but this is easily avoided by using the same type of lure or spinner and making sure the lines are spaced at appropriate distances on the cable. Start with the first line off the ball and place the rod in a holder to the far side of the transom. The second line is positioned about 3 metres above the ball and the rod placed in a holder on the inside of the first rod and so on. I am yet to have a tangle using this technique, but there is some mucking around to avoid damage to the downrigger arm when retrieving the cable all the way in. Fortunately the clips are easily moved and can be quickly repositioned anywhere on the cable without the use of tools. Tangles are also avoidable by ensuring the length behind the clip is the same for all lines – generally 4-6 metres is adequate.

Another advantage of downriggers is that because the cable is almost directly below the boat, you can make sharp turns to follow the drop-off and bottom contours or to turn quickly away from the bottom and into deeper water when a fish is hooked. The chance of lines crossing and catching each other is remote because they are only a short distance from the clip. Keeping the power on reduces the possibility of tangles, but once in the safety of deeper water it is safe to stop the boat. Since the ball can't sink further than the cable length it is unlikely to snag on the bottom while you are playing a trout, which lead and wire lines can do. Always lift the ball after a fish has struck, and check the gear before starting to fish again. If the boat has been at rest the lures or spinners can easily tangle around the wire, so it pays to check them while replacing the other line back in the clip.

What is a Good Trolling Speed?

While 'fishing where the fish are' is undoubtedly the most important factor in fishing successfully, many trolling anglers are focused on finding the right speed to tow their lures or spinners through the water. Typically most trolling is done at between 2 and 4 knots, but everyone has their own ideas about the perfect speed and if you ask five different anglers you'll probably get five different answers!

The trolling speed when you are using plastic lures is different from when you are using metal ones.

The simple fact is that all lures and spinners have different actions in the water and they vary with speed. There are many brands and models available, in both plastic and metal and in different sizes and weights, so every time I troll I run the lure or spinner beside the boat and alter the engine rpm until the action seems right, usually somewhere in the mid-range. Because it can be difficult to find a speed that suits all types, it is usually more productive to use the same size and type of lure or spinner when two or more lines are being used. Mix up the colours for variety and if one seems to catch most of the fish, change the others to suit.

Jigging (15m-plus)

Jigging is a method of fishing for trout that was borrowed and adapted from saltwater fishing, where various techniques catch a wide variety of species. It is possibly one of the most misunderstood of the lake fishing techniques, yet it's probably one of the simplest. It gained acceptance and popularity in some of the deeper lakes in the Rotorua district in the early 1990s but while a number of anglers were quietly using the technique in Lake Taupo for many years it wasn't until 2001 that it made it on to the local scene properly, after some good publicity. The smooth pumice sand on most of the lakebed makes Lake Taupo almost perfect for jigging. There are some rogue snags in the lake, but most drift jigging is done over sandy drop-offs and they are unlikely to be encountered.

As a *bona fide* method of trout fishing, jigging has real advantages and attractions. With other moving-boat methods the rods are left in a holder until a trout bites, but with jigging an angler is directly involved in the complete process of catching a fish using his or her own rod. It is also the only method that is not limited by depth. This is a significant advantage when boat fishing during the day, especially from March onwards when the thermocline is often beyond 40 metres and past the maximum depth of downriggers. With the right set-up and braided, non-stretch lines it is possible to catch trout anywhere below this point – when conditions in the lake allow trout to be there. And because the motor is usually turned off, noise and fumes are eliminated, ensuring the experience is a peaceful one. These benefits have helped jigging grow in popularity.

But by far the main attraction of jigging is the catch rate. Being able to isolate trout at a given depth or area and repeatedly place the terminal tackle in front of fish means some superb fishing can be experienced. Multiple strikes are common as the flies travel through the holding zone and sometimes everyone on board can be playing a fish within moments of each other. It is also possible to catch two trout at once, particularly when using two flies, and most experienced jigging anglers I know have this happen at least once a year.

Fortunately jigging is also one of the cheapest ways to get started in boat fishing. All you need is a suitable rod and reel, some sinkers or jigs and a few flies – all costing at most a few hundred dollars. With the combined help of bathymetric and navigation charts of the lake, an angler using any type of vessel (in the right location) could be into trout less than 100 metres from the shore.

Jigging is often a fascinating new experience for anglers who have never tried it. The realisation that there are huge numbers of trout deep below the surface, combined with the simplicity and ease of the method, have most people shaking their heads in amazement. Make no mistake: jigging can be a highly successful method of fishing for trout.

Chris Power demonstrates the jigging set-up he used to fool this superb trout.

Methods and Set-up

There are several terminal tackle options open to jigging (**see page 45** for the equipment required). As the rule stood in the 2002-03 season, a maximum of two hooks are allowed, regardless of how they are attached to the line. Typically the jig or sinker is tied to the bottom of the trace with a fly about a metre above it on a 25-40cm dropper from a standard swivel. If using a sinker or hookless jig, another fly can be added to the rig a further 50cm above the first. When constructing a trace, be aware that the high catch rates typical of successful jigging can accelerate line and knot fatigue, which sometimes results in broken-off fish. To avoid these problems, ensure that the trace used is no less than 4kg in strength.

Saltwater jigging techniques involve a significant rod movement to impart a fluttering action to the jig, imitating an injured fish, or simply cranking the reel flat out to represent an escaping fish. In freshwater fishing such large movements of the rod and terminal tackle are not needed, so the term 'jigging' is used with a bit of licence. Generally it is only when anchored that actual jigs are used and all it takes is a very small movement of the wrist; a short 40-70cm movement of the rod tip will impart enough action. When drifting, the movement of the line through the water is virtually like deep harling and is all that is needed to get a strike.

Jigging requires concentration and vigilance. Many takes are easily detected when the line suddenly tightens and the rod loads up, but any slight hesitation, bump or lifting of the line is almost without exception a trout and should be quickly dealt with by a short, swift strike to set the hook.

Drifting or Anchoring?

Finding large concentrations of trout in the huge expanse of Lake Taupo can be a daunting task, but a number of factors can substantially reduce the guesswork and greatly improve the odds. Thermal stratification concentrates large numbers of trout into a small band of water for up to nine months of the year, although the actual fish-holding area at any given time remains an educated guess. Most are encountered within a few metres of the intersection between the drop-off and the thermocline, and jigging tends to work immediately if trout are present.

It is a simple process to identify just where the trout are by drifting up or down the drop-off while dragging the sinker along the bottom. Drifting up the drop-off from deep to shallow water is preferable because it allows better contact with the bottom. Some locations in the lake are better than others for this; ideally a shelf gradient of around 1:5 to 1:3 will give a good drift of three to eight minutes, depending on the wind strength, starting depth and location. Generally it should not take any

Jigging is so simple it can even be done from a kayak, and you'll still catch plenty of trout.

Always thumb the spool. It provides resistance to set the hook when a fish hits.

more or less time than this, otherwise the effectiveness of the method reduces rapidly.

After selecting a starting point, begin fishing by free-spooling the reel until you feel a mild thud as the sinker (usually 42gm/1½oz) reaches the bottom. In breezes of 5 to 10 knots the line may have to be retrieved progressively on the way up the shelf to maintain correct contact, but during windy conditions (10 to 15 knots) and quicker drifts, the sinker can easily lift off the bottom. In this case let out more line or add more weight, otherwise the catch rate can drop off quickly. If a total of 84gm (3oz) won't keep the sinker on the bottom during a drift, chances are that it is too windy, so deploy a drogue (sea anchor), drop the anchor or find somewhere else more sheltered to fish. When a drift down the drop-off is the only option it pays to take the reel out of gear and thumb the spool. This way it is possible to maintain contact with the bottom by letting more line out every few seconds, depending on the speed of the drift, while also providing some resistance on the reel during a strike to help set the hook. It also allows a few seconds to engage the reel properly once hooked up to the trout.

With little or no wind, a new approach is required, particularly when the location of the trout hasn't yet been identified. Simply motor out to the drop point, lower the line to the bottom, then free spool the reel and feed out line as you reposition the boat at the end of the hypothetical drift. Engage the reel and retrieve the line very slowly all the way back to the boat, ensuring contact with the bottom at all times. Wind or no wind, once the 'drift' is complete pull up the lines, motor back out and repeat the process. The principle always remains the same, whether or not the boat is actually moving.

Anchored jigging benefits from a few exploratory drifts to identify the location of trout. Once they are found, isolating a particular spot can result in astonishing strike rates. This is when an actual jig can be more productive than a sinker rig. Keeping in contact with the bottom is easy, so a small jig of 14gm (½oz) or 28gm (1oz) can be used, the smaller shape being more like the actual size of smelt and bullies.

Fly Fishing

There is plenty of scope for fly fishing on the lake, from an anchored or a drifting boat. Generally most of this is done in the few places where anchored fly fishing is permitted, such as at the Tongariro Delta and also at the Tokaanu Hole, where a boat is mandatory and anchoring is necessary to maintain a position in the right spot.

Anchored fly fishing is not the only option for the open-minded and resourceful boat angler, though. Drifting the wide open bays and many shallow flat areas while casting to sighted fish is seldom done, yet it can offer some spectacular fishing (reminiscent of targeting bone fish in the

The Tokaanu Hole fishes consistently well, especially for anglers who are fly fishing or jigging.

saltwater flats of the Caribbean). With it comes the very real prospect of tangling with one of Taupo's very large but elusive brown trout. During periods of stratification the cool currents from some inflowing rivers and streams can continue into the lake for a considerable distance, often well out beyond the 300m restriction. Many of Taupo's bays do not offer good shelter during the day, but from October to March plenty of trout can be found in parts of the bays, attracted by the cool water, huge schools of smelt and terrestrials such as green beetle and cicada.

Methods and Set-up

Super-fast sinking lines or shooting heads with a range of floating flies such as Boobies and Heave 'n' Leave balls are productive in anchored fly-fishing locations. However, a floating or intermediate line is better for drifting the flats – as is a good assistant on the oars. A long trace of up to 4 metres with 3kg breaking strain line is usually necessary, as well as a long cast and good stalking and spotting techniques.

Night Fishing

One of the best times to fish the lake is at night, particularly when targeting the bigger trout, which can be harder to catch during the day. Generally most night fishing from boats is confined to fly fishing at the Tauranga-Taupo mouth, the Tongariro Delta and to a lesser extent the Kuratau Spit. Outside these locations there are rarely any boats out on the lake after dark. The mouths are not the only places to look for good fishing, though, and resourceful anglers have a lot of water to choose from. Obviously the skipper needs to understand sound navigation techniques in order to travel safely but there is no good reason not to go out anywhere around the lake.

During winter when the lake has turned over and is one constant temperature (10-11°C), trout can roam wherever they like in search of food. Typically, most immature trout feed exclusively on smelt in the open waters of the lake where they are virtually impossible to find. It is not until the lake stratifies in late November or early December that these fish become much easier to locate in the thermocline, albeit still somewhere in 616 square kilometres of lake. However, of significant interest to enthusiastic night anglers is the location of some of the bigger maiden four-year-old trout weighing up to 3.5kg (less than 5 per cent of the population), maiden five-year-olds in the 3.5-5.5kg range (less than 1 per cent of the population) and some large, well-recovered previous spawners.

These big trout are usually rainbows, which need plenty of food, captured with minimal effort, in order to grow very large, and they have switched their diet from smelt to koura, large bullies and adult koaro. They live close to shore, but over the drop-off, and they can be as far down as 85m during the day. After dark these trout follow their prey to the edge of the drop-off to feed, before retiring back to the depths before dawn. It is a fairly simple food chain but understanding it can make finding the big fish a whole lot easier.

Methods and Set-up

The koura, large bullies and adult koaro eaten by very large trout are generally 70-120mm long, so don't be scared to put on an enormous imitation, either as a fly or rubber lure. You'll need it. Trout take koura from behind to avoid a confrontation with the large claws, but most commercially tied koura flies are made back to front for fly casting, which makes a solid hook-up particularly difficult. Either tie your own the right way round or, better still, buy any of the excellent range of soft plastic crayfish imitations available over the Internet.

It is essential to remember that koura, bullies and large koaro swim in short, irregular pulses very close to the sand, so imparting the right type of action to the imitations is critical. Most powered fishing methods, such as harling and trolling, cannot replicate this movement properly. The most effective methods are either drift jigging using a sinker and two flies on extra long traces, or fly fishing with a fast-sinking line or shooting head when anchored in a likely location.

Be prepared to catch only a few fish in a night – though one very large fish usually more than makes up for the low numbers. Remember, too, that big trout have big teeth and after a few good fish have been taken fatigue can set in at the terminal end of the tackle: it pays to use heavy leader material in the 6-8kg range.

Wait for at least an hour after dark before heading out onto the water, to allow time for the fish to migrate up the shelf. Alternatively, be on the

water first thing in the morning, but keep in mind that during summer the nights are shorter and the migration back to deeper water has usually already begun before you arrive at 5am.

Once the sun is on the water most of the larger trout have gone deep for the day. Target them in the dark for the best results.

CHOOSING the RIGHT LOCATION
Harling and Drift Fly Fishing

Lake Taupo has many productive harling and drift fly-fishing locations, including **Tokaanu**, **Stump**, **Motuoapa**, **Waitahanui** and **Waihaha** bays. They all have features in common, such as a reasonably consistent, flat lake bottom less than 7 metres deep, and proximity to inflowing rivers and streams. Much of the lake edge has these characteristics and identifying potential areas is as easy as studying the navigation or bathymetric charts. Bucking the trend, the **Horomatangi Reefs**, which are well offshore and nowhere near inflows, are among the lake's best shallow-water locations and produce good trout throughout the year.

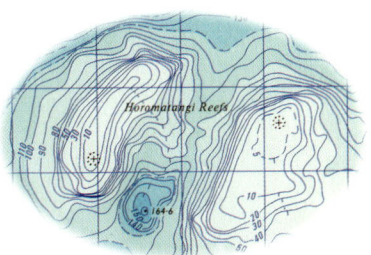

Trout can be found throughout the year at Horomatangi Reefs, and a wide variety of methods can be used to catch them. *Reproduced from the Lake Taupo Bathymetry courtesy of NIWA. Crown copyright reserved.* **Not to be used for navigational purposes.**

Most of the bays are very large and knowing where to start can make the difference between catching a few fish and catching a lot. Since smelt have not only trout as predators but shags as well, the presence of large numbers of shags searching for their next meal can be a dead give-away. There will usually be good numbers of trout close by, which can mean very productive fishing. Smelt don't swim fast and shags will often return to the same or a similar spot day after day, which is an obvious sign that there are probably significant quantities of smelt in the vicinity.

Anchored Fly Fishing

In addition to the usual anchored fly-fishing locations, boat fishing restrictions don't apply to two productive mouths in the western bays. One is the impressive **Otupoto Falls**, between Waihora and Waihaha, which is especially good in the summer; and the other is the mouth of the **Waikino Stream** in Te Papa Bay, between Waihaha and Whanganui. The Waikino can be hard to find, because unlike the Otupoto, which is visible from some distance, the flow enters the lake at water level through a fissure in the cliffs. Both locations require a careful approach and a fast-sinking line cast right into the head of the flow where the trout are concentrated, especially during stratification and smelt spawning. However, continual disturbance from eager trollers and their hooked trout usually has the effect of limiting the catch to a couple of quick fish before they all disappear.

Trolling and Jigging

Almost all trolling and jigging methods are concentrated around the edge of the lake, where trout are most easily targeted by keeping the lures or flies in close proximity to the bottom. Not all the lake edge offers productive fishing, but over the years those places that do have earned a good reputation. Typically they also receive the most angling pressure and known 'hot spots' such as **Waitahanui Bay**, **Mine Bay**, **Jerusalem Bay to Rangatira Point** (the 'Mad Mile'), **Stump Bay**, **Mission Bay**, **Te Hape Bay**, and **Waihaha Bay** can become congested with boats, especially in the summer.

However, there are less popular places that can be equally rewarding, and you can discover these for yourself. Get out the trusty Lake Taupo bathymetry and compare the underwater features of the 'named' places

The Waikino Stream enters the lake at water level through a fissure in the cliffs. There are no boat fishing restrictions.

to others around the lake shelf. When I did this I highlighted likely locations with a fluorescent marker pen and referred to them on a regular basis. As my knowledge of the shelf around the whole lake grew, I realised that suitable locations were virtually everywhere. Find at least four places – north, south, east and west of each other – and make a habit of fishing them regularly, probably for at least a season. In that time it is possible to build up an invaluable knowledge base that can be transferred to virtually any suitable location in the lake. Since conditions and fishing success vary enormously each time, this will also help to improve catch rates, because knowledge builds confidence – an invaluable asset in successful angling.

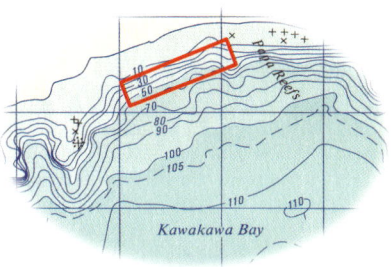

Bathymetry of Kawakawa Bay. Look for gradients such as those outlined in red, which show an area ideal for trolling and jigging. *Reproduced from the Lake Taupo Bathymetry courtesy of NIWA. Crown copyright reserved.* **Not to be used for navigational purposes.**

With jigging, a great deal of the work to identify likely locations can be completed before going out on the water by ascertaining the general direction of the wind and relating that information to a nautical or bathymetric chart. The bottom gradient and contours likely to be encountered on the drift need to be factored into the equation as well, rejecting those that are unsuitable. Fortunately, with a shoreline that stretches 120km there is always somewhere to go. Once on the water it pays to do an exploratory drift by positioning the boat at the likely finishing point, then heading to the windward starting point under power while looking at the sounder as you go. This will give you a look at the shelf profile in reverse and a good indication of its suitability before you drop the lines down.

Because jigging is so effective, a drift without a strike usually means there are no trout present and requires a change in depth or location until something works. Often a small move to either side of the original starting point (by as little as 50-100m) can make all the difference. Continue along the drop-off in that manner and if you haven't caught a fish

Trolling at Whanganui Bay.

or had a strike in an entire bay it is time to try somewhere else. With this approach it is possible to cover a lot of water very quickly and it should take no longer than an hour to cover a bay properly.

Temperature cycles in the lake affect the depth of trout and their food throughout the year though, so I usually have an exploratory jig to begin with. The information gathered helps in deciding whether to jig or troll. After stratification begins in late November or early December, the trout become more concentrated in the thermocline and I'll usually start in 30 metres and finish at the beginning of the weed beds in 15 metres of water. A basic, almost foolproof method of being regularly in the zone is to add 5 metres to the starting depth and deduct the same off the finishing depth for every month after Christmas until April. Note the depth under the boat when a hook-up occurs, and if most of the trout are being caught deeper than 35 metres the decision to jig is fairly straightforward.

During May and June the lake enters a transition period when the thermocline is still in existence (although very deep and weak) and the upper layer is rapidly cooling down, so I'll start at 50 metres and drift back to about 15 metres. When the lake is completely mixed, from July to early November, trout generally roam all over the lake at any depth and all boat fishing methods can become a bit hit and miss: jigging is no exception. The only answer is to cover plenty of water to find the trout, which often means using the downrigger and varying the depth throughout the day.

Offshore Locations

Numerous productive offshore locations exist such as the **Horomatangi** and **Whakaipo Reefs**, **Waitahanui Bank**, **Motutaiko** and **Motuwhara Islands**, as well as many underwater cones and pinnacles dotted around the lake. The islands are obviously easy to find but locating the underwater sites often requires the combined help of the bathymetric and navigation charts, some good old-fashioned navigation skills or a GPS, and a depth sounder.

Most of the deeper cones and pinnacles are more than 40 metres below the surface and need to be jigged. They are not always productive, though, and good fishing is generally to be had only when the thermocline exists at and beyond that depth, typically from early March through to the end of June.

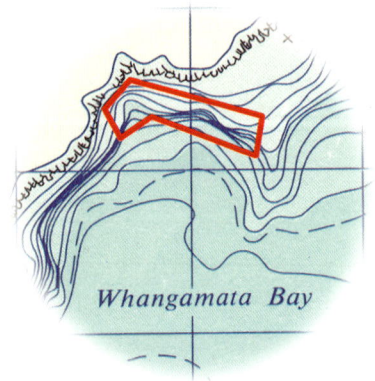

Bathymetry of Whangamata Bay. The area outlined in red has features that make it highly suitable for night jigging, especially in the left-hand corner. *Reproduced from the Lake Taupo Bathymetry courtesy of NIWA. Crown copyright reserved.* **Not to be used for navigational purposes.**

Night Fishing

If you plan to fish away from the mouths at night for some big trout, keep in mind that their prey – koura, large bullies and koaro – live in and around rocky areas at depth during the day, before migrating up the drop-off onto the sandy flats to feed after dark. However, they don't

Mt Ruapehu dominates the skyline on a beautiful spring day. The Horomatangi Reefs are visible in the centre foreground.

travel very far in a night, often less than 80 metres in one direction. The wide-open and expansive bays that are common in Lake Taupo do not generally provide suitable habitat, but the ends of the bays where the steep topography of the surrounding land meets the lakebed often do.

TECHNIQUES FOR SUCCESSFUL BOAT ANGLING

Keep the Motor Going!

When using powered fishing methods such as harling and trolling, many boat anglers instantly turn the motor off when a fish is hooked. That's fine with one line out, but with two or more lines there is usually a mad rush to start winding them in before they sink to the bottom and risk getting snagged. The resulting commotion at the back of the boat can often be a nuisance, and there is actually no reason why the boat should not continue to have good forward momentum while the hooked fish is pulling line off the reel.

Where there is one trout there are likely to be others, so keeping the motor going and the other lines in the water increases the chance of further strikes – sometimes within a few moments of the first hit. This is a regular occurrence, and to prove it I kept figures over a few seasons. The results showed that a second strike occurred within about a minute of the first hook-up about 25 per cent of the time, so it is definitely worth doing. Obviously someone needs to keep steering the boat while the angler playing the fish gets settled in. If the other rod/s pick up a fish then you may have no choice but to kill the power – but that's a good problem to have!

If turning off the motor is the only option left, it pays first to turn the boat out into deeper water, away from the drop-off. This reduces the chance of the lines or the downrigger ball from coming into contact with the bottom and either wrapping the lines or snagging the gear. It

Keep the motor going because there is a good chance of a second strike.

also gives the other anglers on board the chance to wind in with a minimum of drama at the back of the boat. Once all the gear is up and the fish safely netted, head straight back and make a return pass over the same area. You'll often get additional strikes this way.

Getting the Best from a Depth Sounder

Trout are located all over the lake at depth and it is much easier to isolate them against a shelving part of the lakebed than it is to find them in mid-water in the enormous expanse of Lake Taupo. Accordingly, knowing how deep you are fishing is crucial to successful boat fishing for trout. It can save a lot of wasted time in locating your preferred area, reduce time spent fishing in unproductive areas, or simply keep you on a 'hot spot' longer. The Lake Taupo bathymetric and navigational charts can be very helpful, but a depth sounder (or fish finder, as they are commonly known) is one of the most useful weapons in an angler's arsenal.

A depth sounder uses soundwaves to measure depth. It does this by sending a series of ultrasonic 'pings' towards the lakebed from a transducer, usually mounted on the transom of the boat. The time taken for the 'ping' to return to the transducer is calculated, converted to distance, and displayed on the screen as the depth below the boat. Solid objects such as the contour of the lakebed are interpreted as a series of strong lines, but intermittent 'returns' from mid-water are commonly seen on the screen as well and could represent a wide variety of actual objects in the water. While individual smelt don't register a return on most sounders, a large concentration of them will. And since smelt display a strong schooling tendency and are abundant in Lake Taupo, they make up most of the returns.

Most modern recreational depth sounders have a 'Fish ID' function, which displays a generic fish symbol on the screen when a strong return is recorded. However, the large quantity of smelt in the lake regularly generates false returns of 'fish' and it is not until the 'Fish ID' function is switched off that the truth emerges. To get an idea of what actual soundings can look like, try the demonstration mode without 'Fish ID' enabled. It will show a fish as a crescent or arch shape, much like a flatter, upside-down V. While this can be seen sometimes in practical use, the combined movement of the trout and boat more often show trout as bold lines of varying sizes and lengths. Smelt schools usually look like a clump of fine dots. Actually, few returns of trout are seen, although this has surprisingly little to do with catch rates. The most important information to be gained from a depth sounder is about the depth and bottom contours.

If you want to maximise your fishing time, become a better angler and catch more fish, then take the following advice:

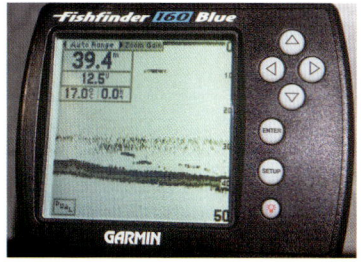

Here the short, solid lines are trout, above and below the fuzzy layer of smelt. However, it is best to use a depth sounder for its original purpose: telling you the depth and contours of the lake below the boat.

- Use the Lake Taupo bathymetric and navigational charts to identify likely fishing locations suitable to the method being used – prior to getting on the water.
- Once there, use the sounder for its original purpose: telling you the depth and contours of the lake below the boat.
- Turn the 'Fish ID' function off.
- Resist the strong temptation to drive aimlessly around looking for smelt and trout.

GPS (Global Positioning System)

A major development in the advanced technology available to anglers these days has been the GPS. Many boaties now rely on GPS as a sole means of navigation, and while it provides accurate information it is only an addition to generally accepted navigation skills such as using a chart and compass. In the ocean it is common to use GPS to find out-of-the-way fishing spots time and time again by entering the location as a 'waypoint' in the memory of the unit. But in Lake Taupo its usefulness for pinpointing good fishing spots is limited. The reason? Trout don't often stay in the same location for long and will follow the food chain to wherever it takes them. Also, after the lake stratifies in early summer the thermocline sometimes moves significantly deeper after a long period of fine, settled weather, which means targeting deeper water, and the bottom contours may not be suitable. That's why it is almost always better to look for locations suiting the methods being used instead of looking for trout and smelt.

However, GPS has some definite advantages when some of its best features are put to use. The track function and chart plotter (available on sophisticated models) make it possible to quickly cover a wide area methodically and systematically before moving on. This is particularly handy when jigging or trolling around the drop-offs because it is easy to see where you have been and return directly to the same location if it is successful. But a GPS is not essential for good fishing and in some cases can result in 'paralysis by analysis' – a debilitating condition some anglers become afflicted with when they rely too much on technology in an attempt to catch fish.

SAFETY IN BOATS

Many boaties dismiss Lake Taupo as being 'just a lake'. In some ways this is understandable, since no part of the lake is out of sight of land, there are no tides and if the motor fails there is no chance of being blown for miles and never seeing land again. For these reasons many skippers think nothing of making the trip to the western bays, a distance of around 20 nautical miles from Taupo town, yet would not contemplate the same sort of journey off the coast of New Zealand. However, as New Zealand's largest lake, Taupo is a formidable expanse of water that should command respect from those who voyage on it. A false sense of security could turn an otherwise exciting trip into a fight for survival.

The point cannot be stressed too strongly: **conditions can turn very nasty, very quickly on Lake Taupo, and when the weather changes for the worse it is one place a boatie doesn't want to be.**

Because of the size and shape of the lake, and its geographical location and altitude, conditions on the water can change rapidly. Fresh water is less dense than salt water, so when the wind blows, the surface waters stir more easily and can become rough more quickly than the sea would in similar conditions.

If you are out on Lake Taupo always be aware of the rogue easterly that often develops around midday in the summer on flat, calm, hot days. In a matter of a few minutes things can get nasty and in some cases seeking shelter is the only option. Safe anchorages are few and far between, particularly in the western bays. Of those available, Scenic Bay, The Nooks, Cherry Bay and Boat Harbour are very useful. If

Boat Harbour is one of the best anchorages in the western bays. Remember it in an emergency.

Lake Taupo is no place to be in a dinghy when the weather turns for the worse.

The Taupo Harbourmaster's Office attended more than a dozen fatalities in the 1990s and there appears to have been no let-up in the number of people losing their lives on the lake. The tragedy of most of these deaths is that they would not have happened if the victims had taken proper precautions. Unfortunately the stories of severe risk-taking are often mind-boggling to say the least. Serious mishaps on Lake Taupo are usually characterised by a number of the following factors:

- The occupants had no life jackets on board, or they had life jackets but weren't wearing them.
- They were wearing inappropriate clothing such as jeans, boots and other items that make swimming exceedingly difficult.
- They didn't tell anyone where they were going or when they would be back and as a result weren't missed for many hours, by which time it was too late.
- They had no means of communication other than perhaps a cellphone – no VHF radio or flares.
- They developed motor troubles and had no auxiliary engine.
- They ran out of fuel (all too common).
- They had no chart or compass and consequently had no idea where they were.

There is currently no legal requirement for recreational boat owners to have any formal training in the safe use of a boat, nor any kind of warrant of fitness for the vessel, so it probably comes as no surprise to learn that the avoidable tragedies on Lake Taupo are only symptomatic of a wider problem. The flow-on effects are reflected in New Zealand's appalling drowning statistics, which are among the worst per capita in the world. But while there is no regulatory constraint for recreational skippers, there is still a legal responsibility to ensure the safety of all people on board their vessel, as well as that of other lake users. For this reason alone all recreational skippers should voluntarily undertake a basic approved course before venturing onto the water anywhere.

Contact the Coastguard Boating Education Service on 0800 40 80 90 or online at www.cbes.co.nz for information about the location and dates of a course near you.

you're unable to reach any of these in time it is sometimes possible to get a vessel inside the mouths of the Waihaha and Waihora for shelter, depending on its draft and the lake level.

Other things to be mindful of include navigation lights. If you are venturing out at night or likely to return after dark, ensure that your vessel displays the correct lights. Usually that means an all-round white light, including port (red) and starboard (green) sidelights for most vessels. Check with your local boat dealer to see if your vessel complies.

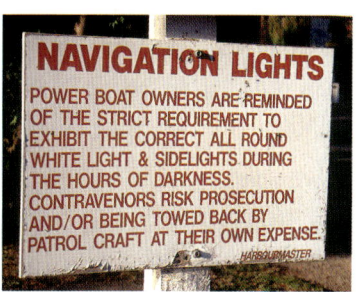

Play your part in water safety by following safe practices as prescribed by Coastguard and the Maritime Safety Authority. Always be a safe skipper.

LAKE OTAMANGAKAU

(incl. Te Whaiau and Wairehu Canals)

Season: 1 October to 30 June.
Methods: All legal Taupo methods.
Size / Bag Limit: 45cm minimum / 3 trout.
Anglers' right-of-way: 20m wide around lake shore and either side of the canals.
Map (1:50,000): 260-T19-Tongariro.

N.B. This information is in accordance with the Taupo Fishing Regulations 1984 (incorporating amendments to 30 June 2000).

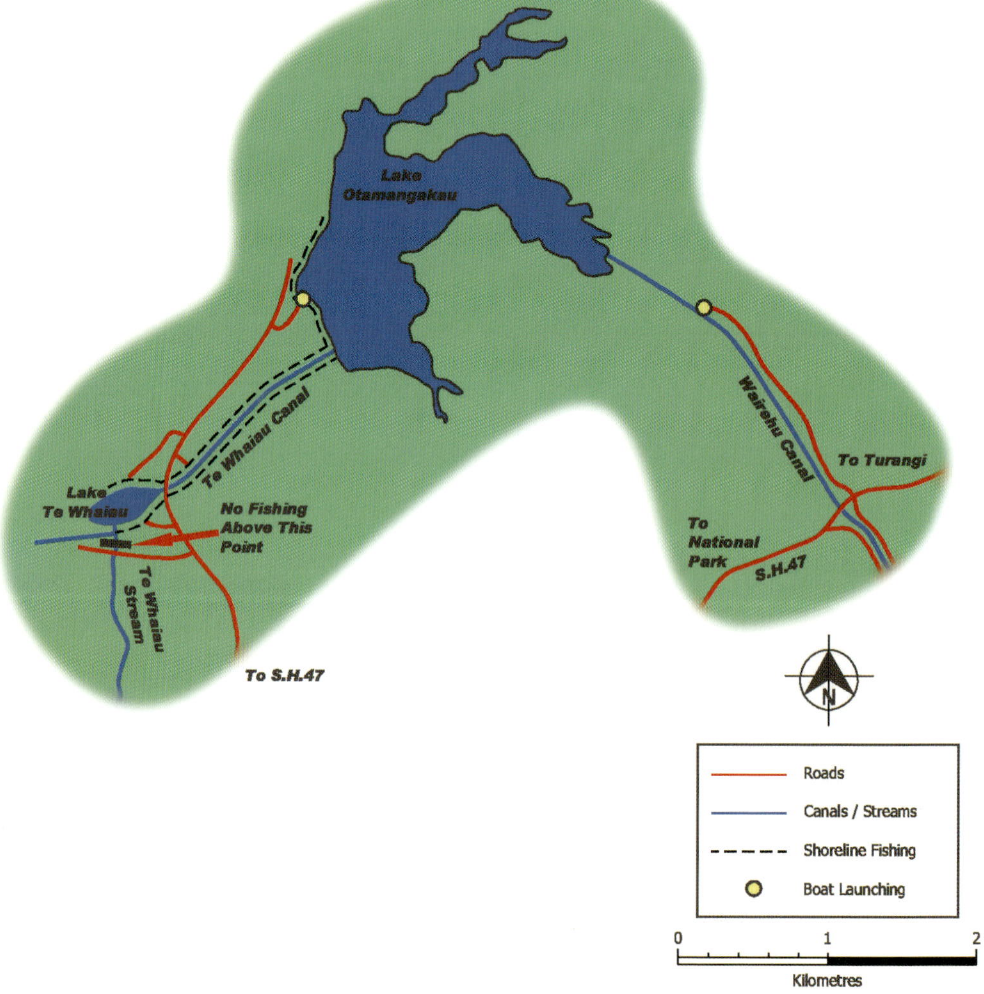

Lake
Otamangakau

Wairehu Canal

To Turangi

Te Whaiau Canal

Lake
Te Whaiau

No Fishing
Above This
Point

To
National
Park

S.H.47

Te Whaiau
Stream

To S.H.47

N

——	Roads
——	Canals / Streams
- - -	Shoreline Fishing
◉	Boat Launching

0   1   2

Kilometres

7. Fishing the Small Lakes and Canals

LAKE OTAMANGAKAU

Since the original swamp was flooded by the TPD in the early 1970s, this small, shallow and highly productive lake has become one of New Zealand's premier stillwater trophy trout fisheries. In that time it has also gained a nickname, 'The Big O', because of a reputation for having big trout that are notoriously difficult to catch. In some anglers' minds the 'O' stands for zero in numbers of trout caught in a day, which can often be the case. But don't let that stop you from returning, as perseverance is the key to success here.

The main inflows come from the TPD western diversion, which includes water from the Whanganui and Whakapapa systems, along with other rivers and streams draining the Tongariro National Park on the same side. To a lesser extent the Te Whaiau and Waipa streams also make a contribution and together they form Lake Te Whaiau, the first major part of the Otamangakau system. The water is then carried through the Te Whaiau Canal and into Lake Otamangakau before exiting down the Wairehu Canal. This steady supply of cool water throughout the year provides more than enough of the nutrients required for productive plant growth. Because the lake is so shallow light can penetrate to the bottom easily, encouraging photosynthesis and the development of extensive weed beds which have become a major feature of the fishery. These weed beds provide a rich supply of food, which is the main reason Otamangakau trout grow so large.

The lake has rainbow and brown trout, with rainbows accounting for around 60 per cent of the overall population. The rainbows have the highest average weight in the region and only Lake Taupo's impressive

Water from the western slopes of the Tongariro National Park provides valuable flows to Lake Otamangakau.

Otamangakau has a reputation as being tough because of low catch rates, but it is a stunning part of the country to be in – and the big trout are worth it.

fish have a higher average weight than the browns found here. Typically, the attraction for anglers is not the high average weight but the prospect of landing a trophy rainbow over 4.5kg (10lb). Without doubt Lake Otamangakau provides the best chance in the region to do so. In the 1980s some fish taken were over 8kg (17¾lb) although it is unlikely trout of this size will be seen again soon.

One of the other major attractions of the fishery is that unlike Lake Taupo-run fish, rainbows in Lake Otamangakau survive spawning well and it is these fish that make up the majority of trophy specimens. The spawning run fluctuates substantially from year to year because of the small population, but in the last few years the numbers running through the DOC trap on the Te Whaiau have averaged around 2500 trout.

All Taupo Fishing District methods are legal here, but the depth of the lake and the presence of extensive weed beds limit the practicality of many of them.

Access

Lake Otamangakau is an easy 15 minutes' drive from Turangi, by taking SH41 and turning onto SH47 before Tokaanu. For those with boats there are two good ramps available. The first is on the Wairehu Canal and is reached by taking the Wairehu Control Gate road on the right just before SH47 crosses the canal, 18km from Turangi. The second is the main ramp, which is located near where Te Whaiau Canal meets Lake Otamangakau. It is reached by taking the signposted turn-off 4km further along SH47 from the Wairehu Canal bridge.

The best foot access is also from the Te Whaiau end of the lake, although even this is not always easy. Lake Te Whaiau, the Te Whaiau Canal and some sections on the western side of Lake Otamangakau are your best bet for shore fishing.

Fishing with a friend. The hydro canals offer something a little different.

Fishing 'The Big O'

Shoreline angling is possible at various locations around the lake edge but it is swampy in many places, which can make moving around difficult. From the shore, fly fishing is usually best with a floating or intermediate line, but anglers unfamiliar with fly fishing can use spinning gear quite successfully. A simple cast into the channels and gaps in the weed beds with either a small dark spinner or a bubble float and flies can attract the attention of trout cruising in search of food. However, because you are land-based you could find it difficult to extract a stubborn fish from the weeds, so be prepared to have some challenges with a good trout.

Having a boat or canoe or a float tube is a major advantage. You have considerably more flexibility and access to the channels between the weed beds where fish are commonly found cruising. Generally the most productive method is fly fishing with a floating line and indicator, much as you would when nymphing in the rivers. A 3-4m low-visibility leader of around 3kg and imitations of the various food groups present complete the set-up.

Cruising trout tend to follow a set routine in the pursuit of prey and they can become a relatively easy target for the thinking angler. Once a fish has been spotted it is worth spending some time observing its movements. When the fish moves away, cast the line and let the flies settle. As the fish comes back into view and is nearing the flies, give the line a small pull. Even a small movement is enough to entice the trout to have a closer look, and with any luck it will take one of your flies. This sort of fishing can be highly exciting but also incredibly frustrating, especially if your flies are regularly ignored. It is a case of finding what the trout are responding to on the day and changing patterns until something works. Shorten the odds by always using two different flies.

Usually the best chance of success is during overcast and windy conditions. Obviously spotting trout is virtually impossible, so either slowly twitch the imitations back towards the boat or simply leave them there for a cruising trout to intercept in its travels. The takes can be very subtle and it pays to keep a good eye on the fly line or indicator at all times and strike at the slightest hint of movement. Spinning can also be productive, especially when the lake is at its coolest, which is at the start and end of the season.

Regardless of the method, fishing from a vessel is usually easier when anchored on a weed bed beside any of the channels because it gives you more control of your fishing position. Metal anchors are cumbersome and noisy to deploy, which can be counter-productive to good fishing, so instead try using a plastic milk bottle 'anchor' filled with sand. When lowered quietly into the weed it provides all the stopping power needed. But its main advantage is that it doesn't get caught up

David Alexander with a 2.7kg brown on a wet and wild December morning.

in and disturb the vital growth of the weed, and this also makes it a piece of cake to retrieve.

Summer can be one of the most exciting times to fish at Lake Otamangakau. This is when dry-fly and natural-fly fishing come into their own with the arrival of terrestrial insects. The sight of a buzzing cicada on the water during the heat of the day is enough to get trout (and many anglers) really excited. I have seen trout completely ignore imitations right in front of them, only to swim 5 metres to take a live cicada that has just crash-landed on the surface. The pulling power of these insects is amazing.

As late autumn and early winter approach, many of the maturing trout start to 'pair up' prior to their spawning migrations. These trout are in excellent condition and the best time to get them is following good rainfall in the Tongariro National Park. This attracts the trout to come up from Otamangakau, through Te Whaiau Canal and into Lake Te Whaiau before running Te Whaiau Stream.

During the day a Tongariro-style nymphing rig with a couple of small Glo Bugs works well and at night a luminous fly on an intermediate line has produced the goods.

TE WHAIAU CANAL

Te Whaiau canal is relatively short, about 1km long, but it can see some successful fishing, especially late in the season when migrating trout make the short journey up from Lake Otamangakau. Steep banks and plenty of vegetation means that casting a fly line can be difficult, though not impossible, and a nymphing set-up with a short 1-1.5m trace is all that is needed. Simply cast upstream and drift the nymphs down the middle of the canal. Spin fishing with a bubble float using the same rig makes casting easier and can help less experienced anglers to catch some good trout.

Congratulations! Success for Daryl French at Te Whaiau Canal.

All legal fishing methods are allowed but fishing from a boat is prohibited.

WAIREHU CANAL

Of all the canals, this is the longest and the least productive. Connecting Lake Otamangakau to Lake Rotoaira, it is stepped along its 6km length and the only trout available above the last weir at the Rotoaira end are those that have found their way down from Lake Otamangakau. The canal also suffers when minimum flow requirements in the western diversion of the TPD force the Wairehu Gate to close. This usually happens in a very dry summer. Obviously closing the gate is detrimental to the fish, but if it has not happened for a few seasons good weed beds develop and stalking the edges of the canal with a dry fly can be good fun during the summer months. The trout are not usually very large, though – 0.5kg is a big one.

LAKE ROTOAIRA

The second-largest lake in the Taupo region, Lake Rotoaira is a shallow lake situated in a natural depression south of Turangi, in between Mt Pihanga and Mt Tongariro.

Prior to the TPD this lake had its main source of water from small tributaries draining the slopes of Mt Tongariro and the Wairehu Stream. The only outlet was via the Poutu Stream, which is one of the major tributaries of the Tongariro River. The lake had extensive modifications as part of the TPD and now the Wairehu Canal brings in water from Lake Otamangakau, while at the eastern end, where the natural outlet of Lake Rotoaira is situated, inflows from the Tongariro River and Lake Moawhango arrive into the Rotoaira Channel via the Poutu Canal.

Lake Rotoaira is closed from 1 July until 1 September. The Rotoaira Channel section, from the lake to the Poutu drum gate, is not open again until 1 December, because trout use this for spawning.

Access

Lake Rotoaira is around 20 minutes by car from Turangi by taking SH1 south and turning onto SH46 at Rangipo. From here it is less than 10km to the Lake Rotoaira campground, where the main boat ramp is located. Alternatively, you can get to it in a similar length of time by turning off SH41 on to SH47 at the Tokaanu Junction. The first boat ramp is at the foot of the saddle on SH47, 12km from Turangi. It is not specifically signposted but it can be found by turning off at the sign that reads 'Opataka Historic Place – Site of Two Maori Dwellings'. This road leads around to the outlet of the Tokaanu Tunnel. Turn left onto the gravel as you reach the outlet and continue along it for about 200 metres to a boat ramp on the right. You'll need to

Lake Rotoaira is only minutes from Turangi, the 'Trout Fishing Capital of the World', but its fishery is unique.

look for it because it is not immediately obvious to first-timers. It's also very steep – you'll need a 4WD vehicle.

Be aware that during generation periods the currents in the channel can be reasonably strong, so have the anchor at the ready and make sure the motor starts before you push the boat off the trailer.

Another popular shore-fishing location is the inlet area of the Wairehu Canal, which is reached off SH47 at the Wairehu bridge by turning down either of the gravel roads running alongside the canal. This 5km-journey to the lake can be comfortably negotiated in a standard road vehicle. Access to the Poutu drum gate is not signposted but it can be reached by turning down a sealed road located off SH46 approximately 4.5km from the SH1 and SH46 junction. Another 1km further along SH46 a signpost points to the beginning of the Rotoaira Channel.

Fishing the Lake

Lake Rotoaira has a healthy population of medium-sized rainbow trout in the 1-1.5kg range, which are known as being the scrappiest fighters in the district. It is also one of the most productive fisheries in the region and after Lake Kuratau is probably the pick of the lakes when it comes to catch rates. Rotoaira has its dedicated followers and for some anglers the bag limit of 10 trout is the main attraction.

A peaceful evening on Lake Rotoaira.

Although the lake was formed naturally and is not technically a hydro lake like Lakes Otamangakau and Kuratau, large areas of weed are a dominant feature around the edges and the food chain is similar. What makes it different is that a small population of koaro is present. This means the trout are used to feeding on small fish and many of the smelt flies and trolling lures that work well in Lake Taupo work well here too.

Shore-based anglers tend to concentrate at the few places that are easily accessible: the inlet of the Wairehu Canal, the outlet for Tokaanu

LAKE ROTOAIRA

(incl. Rotoaira Channel)

Season: 1 September to 30 June (1 December to 30 June in Rotoaira Channel).
Methods: All legal Taupo methods.
Size / Bag Limit: 35cm minimum / 10 trout.
Note: Anglers are required to hold both a current Taupo Fishing District Licence and Lake Rotoaira Fishing Permit before commencing fishing.
Map (1:50,000): 260-T19-Tongariro.

N.B. This information is in accordance with the Taupo Fishing Regulations 1984 (incorporating amendments to 30 June 2000).

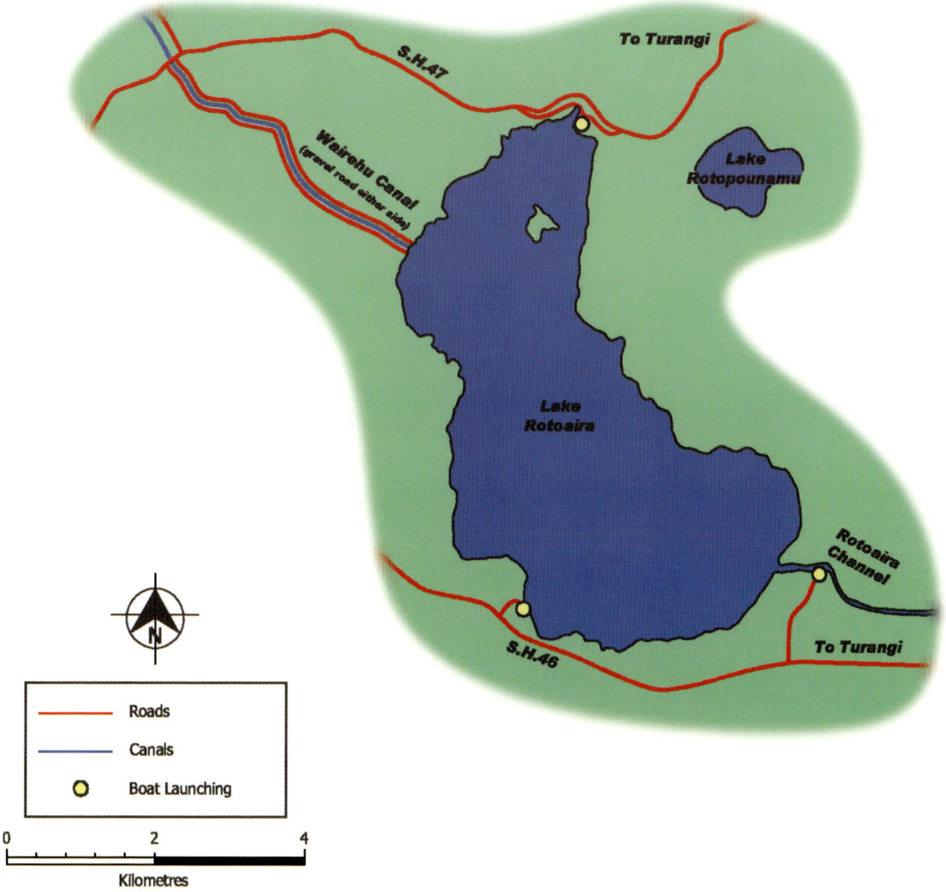

S.H.47

To Turangi

Wairehu Canal
(gravel road either side)

Lake
Rotopounamu

Lake
Rotoaira

Rotoaira
Channel

S.H.46

To Turangi

N

— Roads
— Canals
○ Boat Launching

0   2   4
Kilometres

A good rip (just visible on the right) develops at the outlet when generation begins at Tokaanu.

and the beginning and end of the Rotoaira Channel. Some good fishing can be had in these locations, particularly at dawn and dusk to coincide with generation at Tokaanu. This causes a good current to develop, which has the effect of concentrating trout in a small area where the visible rips form. Fly fishing or casting a spinner can be very productive, as can night fishing.

Beyond the drop-off the average depth of Rotoaira is about 13m and the contours are remarkably even. All Taupo methods are legal, but in reality only shallow methods such as spinning, drift-fly fishing, harling and lead-line trolling are practical from a boat. Having a small boat or canoe makes access very easy to all parts of the lake, including over 1km of the Rotoaira Channel – a place where the trout are rarely disturbed. In the summer months fish congregate here in good numbers and the fishing can be excellent.

Opening day on 1 September is usually eagerly anticipated and regular catches of 20 or more fish are common. Typically the lake fishes best up to Christmas and again from April onwards, when cooler temperatures make the trout more active during the day.

ROTOAIRA CHANNEL

Like Lake Rotoaira itself, the channel existed before the TPD and is not technically a hydro canal. However, major modification to the outlet was needed to accommodate the new influx of water from the eastern diversion and now the Rotoaira Channel serves a dual role as both an inlet and outlet. The Poutu drum gate helps to regulate both the inflow and outflow, so at times the channel can have flows coming and going. This is not a problem and does not affect the very good fishing on offer during the open season from 1 December to 30 June.

The usual place to fish is in the vicinity of the drum gate, but a small vessel is the best way of accessing the entire length of the channel. All methods catch fish, especially on opening day, but dry and natural fly are good choices, along with small spinners cast from the boat.

The Poutu Canal east of the drum gate is permanently closed to angling. Because the Rotoaira Channel is part of the Lake Rotoaira system, a Lake Rotoaira permit is required to fish it, in addition to a current Taupo licence.

LAKE KURATAU

As is the case with a number of Lake Taupo tributaries, the presence of a sizeable waterfall on the Kuratau River has always prevented migrating trout from accessing the upper reaches of the river. The waterfall at the Champagne Pool is as far as they can go, but when the hydro lake was developed in the 1950s above this point, the dam flooded the old riverbed and created a new fishery for anglers. This lake, along with

Lake Rotoaira, is a regular location for fly-fishing tournaments in the region.

Kuratau is less than 3km long and 500 metres across at its widest point (similar in size to Lake Otamangakau), and it has always been the poor cousin to all the other stillwaters in the district because of the quality of the trout present. However, it can provide some exceptionally good sport for high numbers of rainbow and brown trout, normally around 30-40cm in length with the odd fish over 50cm and 1.7kg.

The western end of the lake is where the two tributaries, the Kuratau River and Mangaongoki Stream, join. A shallow delta has formed here and the remains of dead and decaying trees protruding from the waterline make it an eerie setting, particularly on a foggy morning. The drowning of the old river meant that this is not the only part of the lake with underwater obstructions present, and trout have an uncanny ability to find these when they are hooked, resulting in many of them escaping. It is these slowly rotting trees combined with natural leaching of tannins from the forest in the upper catchment area that give the lake water its distinctive light tea colour.

Access

Lake Kuratau is around 24km or 20 minutes' drive from Turangi. Turn off SH41 at the Kuratau Junction and take SH32 for 2km before turning onto Kuratau Hydro Rd, the road to Whareroa. About 4km down is a 90° left bend in the road. Go straight ahead and immediately to the right is a gate and short track through the paddock down to the launching ramp.

Lake Kuratau is an unusual place to fish. Trees drowned by the new lake present hazards both above and below the water.

LAKE KURATAU

(incl. Upper Kuratau River and Mangaongoki Stream)

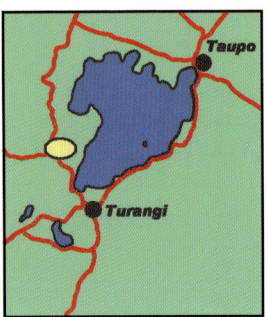

Season: 1 October to 30 June.
Methods: All legal Taupo methods.
Size / Bag Limit: 30cm minimum / 3 trout.
Anglers'right-of-way: 20m wide on both banks from the mouth upstream 16km from Lake Taupo (incl. Lake Kuratau).
Map (1:50,000): 260-T18-Kuratau, T19-Tongariro.

N.B. This information is in accordance with the Taupo Fishing Regulations 1984 (incorporating amendments to 30 June 2000).

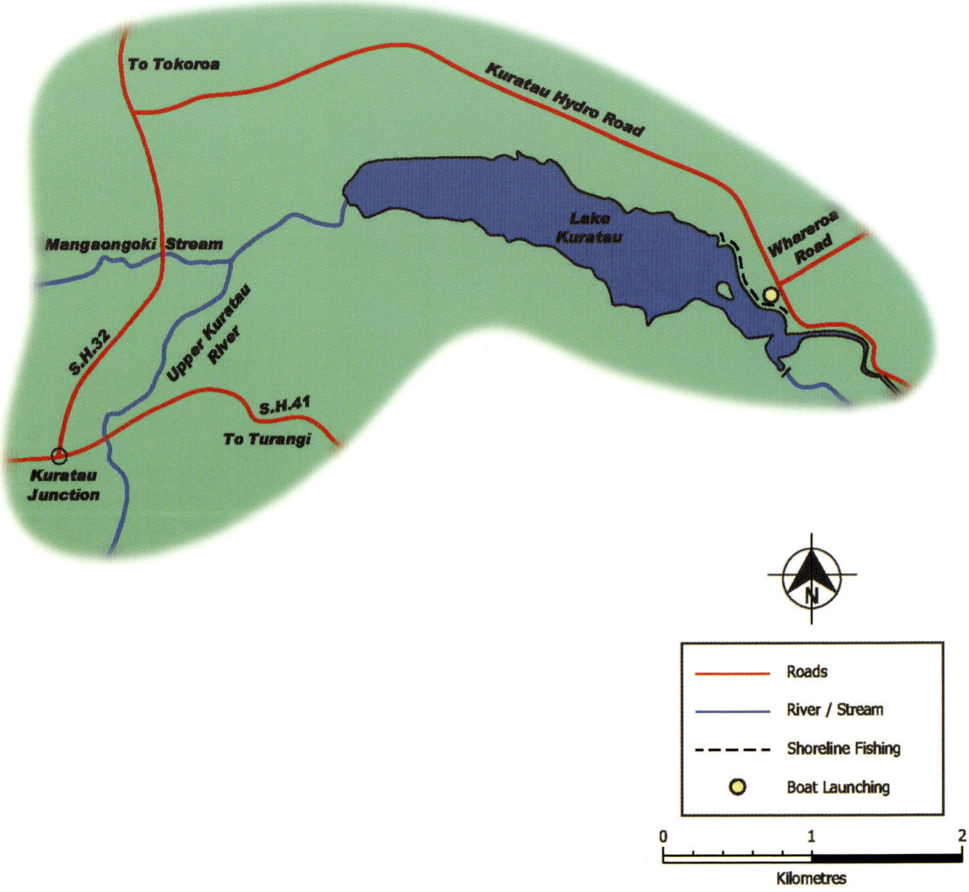

To Tokoroa

Kuratau Hydro Road

Mangaongoki Stream

Lake Kuratau

Whareroa Road

S.H.32

Upper Kuratau River

S.H.41

To Turangi

Kuratau Junction

N

——	Roads
——	River / Stream
- - -	Shoreline Fishing
⊙	Boat Launching

0   1   2

Kilometres

The ledge near the boat ramp at Lake Kuratau is a favourite spot for many anglers.

This is also the main shoreline fishing area, giving anglers around 500m of fishable lake edge until the heavy growth of flax and raupo halt any further progress. Beyond this point a boat, canoe or float tube is the only real option. Irrespective of that, a right-of-way exists giving a 20m-wide strip around the entire lake for anglers on foot.

Fishing the Lake

The pattern or method used doesn't seem to make much difference to Kuratau trout because almost anything cast into the water is hammered by the first fish that sees it. To illustrate the point, one November afternoon I was driving to Whareroa when I saw a good rise happening on the lake. I wasn't intending to fish but I made my way to the water's edge to watch the action anyway. The green beetles were flying and the trout were gorging on them. I couldn't stand it any longer and in desperation (I didn't have any dry flies with me) I retrieved my fly rod from the car. It was set up with the double Glo Bug rig I had been using on the rivers during the morning, but that didn't seem to matter. Less than a minute after casting the line onto the lake and leaving it there, the indicator bobbed and a rainbow trout was on. Over the next 30 minutes four more trout fell to that unlikely rig. This is what Lake Kuratau can be like.

The best months are from opening day in October to early summer, and of particular interest is the arrival of the green beetle in November and December. During summer an imitation or natural cicada is one of the best ways of getting a trout once the sun is up, but warm water temperatures in the lake can mean lethargic fish. Predictably these fish are found closer to the inflows at the head of the lake. In the early and later parts of the day they are more active and can be found around the edges. The cool water of the tributaries also offers a sanctuary for trout and can be extremely productive, but they are difficult to reach on foot.

The fish aren't big but they are pretty.

As water temperatures drop, the trout become more widespread during the day, and from April through to the closing at the end of June any kind of spinner or sub-surface fished fly will take trout, although standard stillwater patterns are usually the most productive.

While the fish here are not particularly large (minimum size limit is 30cm), they put up a spectacular fight and behave like larger fish when hooked. It is a great place to take people new to the sport or to fill in some time if the conditions are not good elsewhere. It beats catching nothing and can brighten up an otherwise blank day.

HINEMAIAIA B LAKE

There are three dams on the Hinemaiaia River, which are run by Trust Power for the supply of electricity to the local Taupo grid. The two upper lakes, Hinemaiaia A ('HA') and Hinemaiaia C ('HC'), lie in the Lake Taupo Forest and a permit to access the area is required. This is normally only granted to beneficiaries of the trust that owns the forest. The upper lake, HA, received liberations of brook trout or char (*Salvelinus fontinalis*) over 50 years ago and they are still there today, although very small in size and number. Brook trout are also found, along with numerous small rainbow trout in the other lakes.

Access

The lower lake is reached from the end of the road leading up the true left from the SH1 bridge over the Hinemaiaia River. Once the dam is reached a rough track continues on the true left for a distance of about 500 metres from where it is possible to carry a small vessel to the water's edge.

While impractical, it is worth knowing the Taupo fishing district right-of-way provisions cover the entire Hinemaiaia B Lake, and allow access on foot to a 20m-wide strip around the shore.

Fishing the Lake

'HB' lies in a steep-sided gorge, and while it offers spectacular scenery, wading is not easy and using a float tube, canoe or small dinghy is the safest way to get to the best water. It has a productive fishery for small rainbows up to 1kg and the occasional brook trout around 0.5kg. While the brookies are difficult to catch (I've never caught one myself), the rainbows respond readily to all legal methods.

Most stillwater lake techniques are just as productive as they are in the other small lakes in the district, although the scrappy rainbows will hit a spinner without too many problems. Using a dry fly on summer evenings is a proven method of taking huge numbers of fish in a short time, as is dawn and dusk harling with small Woolly Buggers or killer-style flies such as Mrs Simpson or Hamill's Killer. Alternatively, a dead-drifted pair of nymphs will take fish virtually any time.

HINEMAIAIA 'B' LAKE

Taupo
Turangi

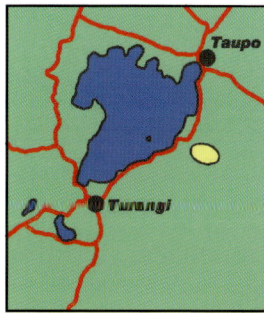

Season: 1 December to 31 May.
Methods: All legal Taupo methods.
Size / Bag Limit: 45cm minimum / 3 trout.
Anglers' right-of-way: 20m wide around lake shore.
Map (1:50,000): 260-U18-Taupo.

N.B. This information is in accordance with the Taupo Fishing Regulations 1984 (incorporating amendments to 30 June 2000).

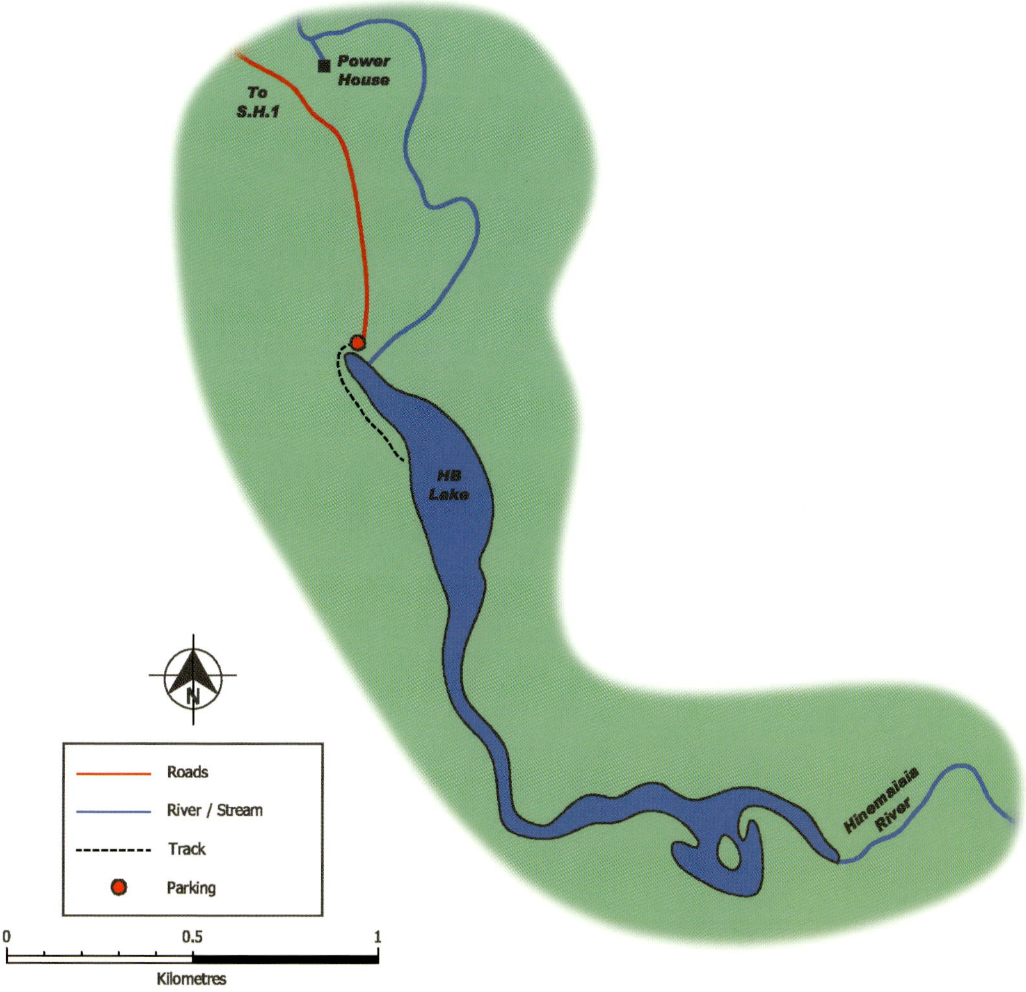

Power House
To S.H.1
HB Lake
Hinemaiaia River
N
Roads
River / Stream
Track
Parking
0
0.5
1
Kilometres

LAKE ROTONGAIO

This tiny lake is well hidden from view, tucked behind Rotongaio Bay, a couple of kilometres south of Waitahanui. Lake Rotongaio is legally fishable, but it lies on Maori land and unless you are a member of the local tribe it is highly unlikely that access will be granted.

A spring feeds the lake, which is only separated from Lake Taupo by a large pumice-sand bank. There is an outlet to the lake and this is an excellent location for catching large brown trout at night in the summer months. A number of people, myself included, believe that these huge trout make regular sorties into Lake Rotongaio after dark to feed on the abundant frog population. Whatever the attraction, when the conditions are right, browns are there in good numbers and definitely worth the effort.

Access to the outlet

Park in Northcroft Street, off SH1 at the southern end of Waitahanui, and walk through the right-of-way that leads to the lakeshore. From here the outlet is a decent walk south for around 1.5km on soft sand. Like many of the less well-known fishing locations, the fact that you can't drive a car down to it means you will probably have it to yourself.

LAKE MOAWHANGO

Situated on NZ Defence Force land near Waiouru, 85km south of Turangi, Lake Moawhango is the southernmost part of the TPD. It was created to supplement the upper reaches of the Tongariro River and provide increased generating capacity at the underground Rangipo Power Station before the water is taken through to Lake Rotoaira and down to Tokaanu for generation a second time. There is a low, self-sustaining population of small trout, but the fishery suffers badly from wildly fluctuating lake levels (over 17 metres). This prohibits the formation of a stable plant base and insect growth suffers accordingly.

Access

Although this lake is included in the Taupo Fishing District, features on the licence and has no closed season, no right-of-way currently exists and permission is required from the NZ Defence Force at Waiouru for access. It is usually refused, which is understandable considering the large number of armaments in and around the lake. I've yet to meet any angler willing to risk his or her safety just to catch a trout, and until the situation changes Lake Moawhango is likely to remain off limits to the general public.

8. Fishing the Rivers and Streams: Methods and Techniques

FLY FISHING

Fly fishing, using either a floating or a sinking line, is the only method permitted for most of the Taupo region's rivers and streams. With a floating line the cast is normally made upstream and the flies drift down naturally with the current, past the suspected lie of the trout. Nymphing, the most common method, involves the use of imitation nymphs or underwater drifting food. The other version using a floating line is known as dry-fly fishing, a productive summer technique that generally involves using imitations of flying insects. The regulations also provide anglers with the unusual benefit of being able to use a natural fly throughout the district, which can be an incredibly deadly technique when done correctly. Fly fishing with a sinking line, otherwise known as wetlining, is also a popular and effective method of catching trout, especially in a big river such as the Tongariro, though the method has its devotees in the other tributaries too.

While dry-fly and natural-fly fishing are seasonal, all other methods can be used effectively throughout the year and there is no need to be an expert caster to catch a lot of fish. In most rivers and streams a competent cast of 10-15 metres will put the fly in front of more fish than most anglers catch in a year, and it is only on a large river such as the Tongariro that a longer cast of more than 20 metres might be required. Even there, most of the fish I catch are within 10 metres of where I am standing.

Floating and sinking-line techniques require completely different approaches to fishing though – and the angler still has to be fishing where the fish are. Whatever method you are using, if you arrive at the river's

Nymph-fishing techniques account for most of trout taken but other methods can be just as effective.

An admiring audience. Nymphing at the Birch pool, which is reached from the Tongariro National Trout Centre.

edge to a pool empty of anglers, always resist the temptation to wade in as deep as possible, before you have fished the water closest to you. It is also easy to fall into the trap of fishing where everyone else is. After all they must know what they are doing, otherwise they wouldn't be there in the first place, right? Not necessarily. It is surprising just how much water in a river or stream is left virtually untouched. Instead of following the crowd, concentrate on looking for the elements of a trout house. You should be able to identify likely holding areas quickly and be very successful in catching fish from them.

UPSTREAM NYMPH

When trout are running on their way to the spawning grounds, two of their main instincts are to get there with the least effort possible, and in complete safety. This means that migrating trout are almost always on or near the bottom of the river, well out of the fast flow of the current, and they are unlikely to move far to intercept a potential food item, especially during the winter. Accordingly, a number of factors need to be taken into consideration when attempting to catch trout with this method.

Much of the technique in any upstream fly fishing with floating lines involves having sufficient line control to achieve a natural drag-free drift. Nymphing is no different. Rivers and streams rarely flow at the same speed across a pool or through the water column, so a drag-free drift can be difficult to achieve, especially when casting across a big pool. An experienced angler can correct and adjust the line during a drift by using a technique known as mending, but this demands a great deal of effort. A much easier way to fish is to cast more directly upstream, which will generally result in the line drifting more naturally back towards you, and this is by far the best approach. Most pools appear at first glance to offer very little opportunity to fish like this, particularly when other anglers are present, but on closer inspection you will find it is usually possible.

Sometimes the final cast and laying of the line onto the water doesn't turn the flies over properly, particularly in windy conditions or when using heavy flies. During the drift this can create a section of slack line offering no resistance between the end of the fly line and the fly, which means a trout can take the fly and spit it out without the angler knowing. A good way to avoid this is to straighten the line immediately it hits the water. A couple of quick strips or pulls will usually ensure that the flies trail the fly line on the journey down the river. Then any slight hesitation at the business end will be seen instantly and you can strike. The other advantage of this is that the fly will normally lodge in the corner of the mouth and be very difficult for the trout to eject. More strikes and solid hook-ups result.

Upstream floating-line methods generally mean approaching the pool or fishing location from the bottom and working up to the top, methodically covering the likely fish-holding areas in the process. The drift should start as far ahead (upstream) of the angler as possible. This will give the flies time to sink to the required depth, maximising the opportunity to catch trout on the bottom. Typically the drift is finished when the line has come back level with the angler, although many anglers continue the drift below their position for some distance by feeding out extra line. Using this technique can result in fish lost on the strike because of the angle between the trout and angler, so you should either move to a position further down to target those trout or find somewhere else more suitable.

Methods and Set-up

Leader Length

When arriving at water's edge it is important to determine the length of leader material needed to effectively get the flies down to the bottom. Obviously the faster and deeper the water being fished, the longer the leader will need to be. Too short and the flies won't be drifting close enough to the bottom; too long and you may not be able to detect a strike before the trout spits the fly out.

Achieving a happy medium is relatively straightforward if you use a simple calculation. Multipy the depth of the pool by 1.3 to give you an appropriate length for your leader; for example a pool that appears to be 3 metres deep would need a trace that is about 4 metres long. This works surprisingly well and in most of the Taupo tributaries this will put the flies near the bottom with weighted nymphs and you will be in with a chance to catch a trout. Note that the ratio depends on the speed of the drift and the size of the pool. If the leader length is right and the flies are the correct weight, they should start to contact the bottom during the last third of the drift, a tell-tale sign being the indicator bobbing. An adjustment either way needs to be made if it does this too early or not at all, until a balance is achieved. Sometimes all that is needed is a change in the weight of the flies being used.

While initially all this might seem rather time-consuming, a well-prepared angler will quickly reap the rewards of a good set-up with a better catch rate. Keep in mind when attempting to measure out the leader length that most fly rods are around 2.7m (9ft) long – a handy benchmark. In fact it is common to hear anglers discussing leader length as a proportion of a fly rod: describing it, for example, as a rod length, a rod and a half or even two rods long.

Nymphing with the correct leader length and weighted flies means hooking up on the bottom occasionally, and in some places – such as the Hinemaiaia – a lot. All nymphing anglers need to be prepared to lose a lot of flies and leader material in the quest to catch a trout. It is not uncommon to get through 20 to 30 nymphs in a few days of solid fishing. I often do, and if I didn't I wouldn't catch as many fish.

The Strike Indicator

Trout normally take drifting nymphs passively and because the line is usually limp to enable a drag-free drift, the contact between trout and angler is initially somewhat delayed. Catching trout this way is relatively straightforward, but in order for a good strike to be made you normally need some assistance in detecting the take. A small synthetic yarn indicator can be attached to the end of the floating line and when this dips under the water it is a fair bet that your fly is either in a trout's mouth or snagged on the bottom. Always assume that it is a fish and strike immediately.

Nymphing usually means approaching the likely part of the pool from downstream.

Don't always wait for the indicator to disappear, though, as sometimes the only outward sign that a trout is on the other end is that the indicator just isn't right. By that I mean sometimes it may stop, move slightly upstream or to one side and in some cases it may even take off downstream. Be alert to any change in the normal natural drift of the indicator and strike quickly. There is a chance that it could be just because the nymphs are snagged on the bottom, but there is an equally good chance that you have a trout.

Strike indicators do become waterlogged and by the end of the day they may not float very well. Always buy pre-treated indicators or treat your own using any of the range of fly floatants available from tackle stores.

DRY FLY

The late Joe Frost was legendary for his exploits on the Tongariro over a number of decades from the early 1920s and is regarded by many as the pioneer of dry-fly fishing in the region. He knew that the dry fly was not only a valid method on Taupo's running trout, but that in the right conditions it often out-fished other methods. Overseas it is well known that summer-run steelhead trout respond eagerly to a properly fished dry fly, and since Taupo's rainbows come from the same type of parent stock they can be readily tempted to rise to a dry fly during late spring, summer and early autumn upstream migrations.

These days few anglers take the opportunity to fish for trout in the Taupo tributaries using this method, which is a pity. In late spring and early summer insect activity around the district increases and the dry-fly fishing can be exceptional. A variety of insects can be imitated, including mayfly, caddis, green and brown beetle, grasshoppers and cicadas, all of which are active at various times of the day. There can be spectacular caddis and mayfly hatches on the tributaries, especially at dusk when the water seems to be boiling as fingerlings, spent trout and some early or late runners feast on the huge numbers of these creatures available. As the light begins to fade in the early evening, the splashes and plops of rising fish become more frequent and skating a caddis pattern across the pool on a floating line can bring strikes at every cast. No longer can the takes be seen, but the jolt of the fish on the end of the line can be felt.

Terrestrials and in-stream insects are not the only imitations that catch trout. Large rainbows and even larger browns readily take imitations of rodents such as mice, and small rats. At dusk in the summer, an imitation mouse fished on a floating line in the wetline style of across and down can produce incredible results. It is particularly good for large brown trout in the lower reaches of the Tongariro, Kuratau and Waihaha rivers.

Personally I regard the dry fly as an integral part of successful angling for running trout. Typically, it is November when I catch my first trout

Synthetic or woollen yarn indicators are the only ones permitted in fly-fishing-only waters.

on a dry fly, at a time when there are huge quantities of migrating trout in the rivers and streams. Often the dry-fly fishing continues for many months, in some years providing excellent sport into autumn. The latest I have caught a trout on the dry fly was in early April. That fresh-run 1.5kg rainbow hen was taken in 2002 on a cicada pattern in the Tongariro and although it was an exceptional year for cicadas, it shows what is possible by taking advantage of the conditions.

Methods and Set-up

Dry-fly fishing is similar to nymphing in that you need a drag-free drift, except in the case of caddis and mouse fishing. Fishing the caddis is a relatively simple technique. Standing above the known lie of the trout, cast the line across and slightly downstream. Keep the rod tip high and the line tight so the caddis imitation will skip or skate across the water like a real one.

Mousing uses a similar technique. Large browns usually hang around beneath the riverbank or near to obstructions and this is the place to target them. Again using a floating line, cast the line across to the other side of the river if possible, well above the suspected lie: 5-10 metres is about right. Immediately mend the line by throwing a decent-sized loop downstream, but keep the tension off the line as it drifts down, by feeding out more line. Tighten the line at the point where you think the trout is, so the mouse imitation will 'swim' across and slightly down the river. This will immediately attract the attention of any large trout in the area. The take is in the form of a lunge at the imitation, and can be virtually heart-stopping.

In normal dry-fly fishing, once the fly has been taken it is important to wait a few seconds for the trout to close its mouth and turn down before you strike – otherwise you can pull the fly straight out without connecting. Most anglers count to three before tightening – something

An ideal situation for dry-fly fishing is downstream of overhanging trees.

A good selection of dry flies – and a good result.

that is particularly hard to do when fishing the caddis or mouse and the fish is downstream of your position on a tight line. Resist the temptation to strike too soon and, if anything, lower the rod to give the fish more slack line. This can be a difficult technique to get your head around when you're on the water, but it must be learned, otherwise your efforts are likely to come to nothing.

Dry flies are obviously designed to float, but not all float as well as they should, especially after a few casts. Always treat new flies with floatant before using. Treating the leader as well will help in achieving a drag-free drift in faster water.

NATURAL FLY

The use of a natural fly (an actual insect used as bait) has been legal for many years in the Taupo Fishing District, yet most anglers are either unaware of this or are unwilling to take up the opportunity. While the use of a natural fly relates to above-water insects only, the method can be used in all fishing waters where an imitation would normally be used. It is almost without exception a summer-only activity because you are limited by the availability of suitable insects. Not all insects make good natural fly bait. Cicadas are the most practical to use, because of their size, and large blowflies or bluebottles can also be useful.

Methods and Set-up

Cicadas can be present in huge numbers one year and then be quite sparse the next. They live underground most of their lives and usually begin emerging out of the ground in early January, climbing up the nearest tree to dry out. Catching cicadas isn't always easy, but by investing in a child's butterfly net and following the noise to find them, a dozen or more can be caught within a few minutes. Keep them in a dark container with holes in the lid and use them within a few hours, otherwise they tend to become very lethargic and are not much use. The better they are cared for, the better the result.

The cicada is the best and most practical natural fly to use.

Attaching them to a hook is another challenge. After a fair amount of trial and error with superglue, a fishing mate of mine, Steve Moore, managed to get hold of an excellent product over the Internet called Bait Stick (**www.baitstick.com**). Take a standard #8 fly hook and bind some thin wool or chenille along the length of the shank, returning once to complete the job. This gives the special glue a larger surface area to hold the cicada on to. Apply a small amount to the wool and gently press the hook onto the cicada's abdomen.

When it comes to actually fishing, most insects are not designed for the stresses encountered during casting. This means the method lends itself to places like the lower reaches of the rivers and streams and the hydro lakes, where frequent casting is not needed. A cicada makes a lot of commotion when on the surface of the water, which is like ringing the dinner bell for trout, and it doesn't take long to get the attention of fish in the immediate vicinity. This means that if the offering has not been taken within a few minutes, it is likely that there are no trout present or you are doing something wrong.

DOWNSTREAM WET FLY

Traditional wet-fly fishing uses comparatively tiny flies, commonly known as 'wee-wets', which represent the latter stage of a nymph's life-cycle – just before it leaves the water to fly. At Taupo this method is rarely used and the term 'wet fly' can be slightly misleading. Here fly fishing with a sinking line for migrating trout is different because it has its origins in salmon angling overseas. It is known as wetlining. It is a very simple method and one of the easiest ways to catch a trout on a fly in the rivers, which also means it is the method of choice for many beginners. Another advantage of wetlining is that the irregular currents found in most pools are of little importance to successful fishing and the

Tom Watson wet-fly fishing the Breakfast Pool. The Tongariro is a big river and it suits sinking fly line techniques.

concept of the drag-free drift doesn't enter into the equation. Yet another bonus is that sinking lines are generally much thinner in diameter than floating lines, so they are easier to cast. This makes wetlining the preferred method on windy days, when nymphing can be extremely challenging.

Methods and Set-up

For Taupo-style wetlining, large Matuka, Rabbit and Woolly Bugger-type flies (#2-8) of various colours are commonly fished on relatively short (1.5-2.5m) leaders. This standard set-up is cast across the river and carried downstream with the current, sinking as it goes, before the line is drawn tight to allow the flies to swing across the noses of trout lying on the bottom. Once the line has straightened below the angler it is retrieved back to the feet by stripping or hand coiling and the process is repeated. Trout generally hit the fly as it begins to accelerate across the pool from the far bank once tension has been applied to the line during the swing. With a tight line, strikes are easily detected because contact with the fish is immediate, usually brutal and often highly exciting. Leaders need to be 4-6kg to handle the sudden load.

Sinking lines are available in various sink-rate options, generally rated as Type 1-7, which normally indicate the inches per second that the line will sink in still water. A Type 1 is usually sub-surface or intermediate, and although not normally used in Taupo tributaries it is a good option at the mouths. Most sinking lines used in the rivers and streams are Type 4-7. There are also different versions, such as the shooting head, which is only 10 metres of actual fly line and designed for distance casting. In the last few years some manufacturers have introduced a shooting-head line incorporating a floating fly line back section. This is particularly useful on a big river such as the Tongariro where the use of a shooting

Peter Haxell demonstrates the technique of using a shooting head with a floating back section in the Red Hut Pool, Tongariro River.

basket to hold the backing line is awkward, but without it the backing can get caught in the large boulders lining the riverbed. A floating back section does away with this hassle and makes it easier to employ advanced wetlining techniques.

Wetlining is a downstream method, so the pool or fishing location is approached from the top and casts are made to cover the likely area methodically before proceeding to fish further down the pool. Typically wetliners will take a couple of steps down after every two or three casts, ensuring that the entire pool is fished thoroughly. It is important to be fishing the flies very close to the bottom, and on the swing the line should be just starting to touch the riverbed. If it's not, a faster-sinking line may be needed, or try casting the line across and up to get deeper, or simply find somewhere else more suitable. Conversely, if the line is too heavy for the water, either cast it on a more downstream angle or find a deeper pool.

SPIN FISHING

While most of the rivers and streams in the district are for fly fishing only, there are some parts of the catchment area where spinning methods are permitted. Often a spinning set-up is more flexible, enabling a longer cast to reach the fish, and it can also mean being able to fish in places where a lack of room to back-cast makes fly fishing virtually impossible.

Methods and Set-up

Usual spinning methods are similar to wet-fly fishing in that the cast is made across the pool and the lure allowed to sink before swinging back across and being retrieved to the feet. It is also possible to use a bubble float with nymphs, dry or natural flies and wet flies. If using dry or natural flies, fly floatant added to the last 10 metres of line helps to achieve a drag-free drift. Cast upstream in the normal dry-fly or nymphing style. Other variations include using a running sinker and floating flies as described earlier (see page 70). They are useful additions to the arsenal, particularly in the calmer parts of the tributaries.

NIGHT FISHING

Few anglers fish in the tributaries after dark: they are either back at their accommodation for the evening or at the tributary mouths until midnight. However, fishing in the rivers and streams in the dark is an opportunity to have some excellent fishing without the crowds, and often in complete solitude. There are always fish to be caught right throughout the season, too. From January to May large browns make significant movements upstream at night, and during the year runs of migrating rainbows are there for the catching.

It is also worth fishing immediately inside the mouths, especially when strong winds bring sizeable waves crashing into the shore, preventing good fishing in the lake. It is common for trout to move into the tributaries at night in these conditions, so the fishing can be very productive in the first few hundred metres, where you are sheltered from both the wind and the waves. Being on the water in the rivers and streams at 5am in winter, a highly productive time, also means arriving in the dark. More often than not a large proportion of the day's catch will be taken by 7am, and you can head home for breakfast with your limit just as others are turning up.

Chris Power prepares to release a 3.4kg brown in the Major Jones Pool on the Tongariro River.

Methods and Set-up

All the larger tributaries, such as the Tongariro, Tauranga-Taupo, Kuratau, Waihaha, Hinemaiaia, Waitahanui, and Waikato, fish well at night, as can the canals. Any good daytime location works, but the shallow and tail-end parts of many pools become the favoured lies for trout once darkness has set in. Look for good habitat during the day and, if wading is required, check out the location's suitability for that too.

Most night fishing is done by wetlining with large, dark, bulky patterns such as Woolly Buggers in #2-4, or with luminous patterns. Obviously nymphing in the dark has its challenges – like seeing the indicator and mending the line – but this does not preclude floating-line techniques. Mousing and skating caddis flies are especially effective from dusk until well after dark in summer. They also work well when done from a boat in the lower reaches of the tributaries, and in the right location some very good sport can be had. Spin fishing using dark lures and luminous flies is also deadly where legal, especially in the Waikato River.

BOAT FISHING

It is not widely known that fishing is permitted from an anchored boat, canoe, raft or float tube in many tributaries. Obviously boat fishing in some of these is impractical, but in others a boat is the only way to get to fish certain places because foot access is non-existent. As a result many of those places receive little angling pressure, are usually full of trout and offer superb fishing. Although anchoring while fishing is compulsory, being able to cast from any position is a definite advantage.

A canoe is a useful means of accessing the lower reaches of the Tongariro, Kuratau and (pictured) Waihaha rivers.

Where boat fishing is allowed in the tributaries, fly fishing is the only legal method, except above Lake Kuratau, the Hinemaiaia 'B' dam and the Waikato River below the control gate bridge. The lower reaches of many tributaries are snag-infested, though, and suit dry-fly fishing, but there are also wetlining and nymphing opportunities. Remember to observe the 5-knot speed limit – not just because it is the law but also because the wake of a vessel travelling faster than that is usually detrimental to good fishing.

SAFE WADING TECHNIQUES

Every season a number of anglers get into difficulty when wading in the region's waterways. Most survive the encounter with a wet backside and temporary loss of dignity. Others have not been so lucky and, although drownings are rare, the tragedy of these deaths is that they were often avoidable. And the most common cause? Chest waders, worn to protect against the cold water and keep the angler dry and warm. If they become filled with water they are impossible to remove and are capable of dragging an angler under.

Fortunately, most of Taupo's mouths drop off gradually and do not present a problem to anglers. However, those that drop quickly into deep water can be dangerous. Both the Tongariro and Tauranga-Taupo mouths have claimed wading victims in the past, and the mouth of the Waimarino and the Kuratau Spit are other places to be very careful. If you are planning to fish a deep drop-off from the shore, be sure to stand well back from the edge. No trout is worth losing your life over. Remember that at the mouths of the Tongariro and the Tauranga-Taupo and at the Kuratau Spit it is legal to fly fish from an anchored boat.

It pays to take extra care in the tributaries. Most have sections where it is reasonably safe to cross, but the riverbed can be extremely slippery in places, particularly in the Tongariro, Kuratau and upper Hinemaiaia. Large rocks and boulders compound matters and if there has not been a good fresh for a while, algal growth makes for especially dangerous conditions. On the Tongariro it is the size and width of the river that make it particularly challenging. There are only a few places where it is possible to cross safely in normal flows and even then it is not advisable to do so alone.

Always cross a river near the tail of the pool, where it is usually wider, lower and slower. Before attempting a crossing, check out its suitability,

Crossing a river safely. Use a stout stick for balance, or team up with a buddy.

and always have a back-up plan in case something goes wrong. Always cross on an angle, starting higher up than the point you intend arriving at, and use the pressure of the water to speed up the crossing. Leave yourself a 'bail-out' area – somewhere you could escape to in an emergency. That way, if things start to get difficult, you can immediately turn your body around, face the shore you came from, and make your way back to safety.

An essential piece of equipment for crossing rivers is a wading staff. These can be purchased from good tackle stores but I tend to find mine on the riverbank among the debris from previous floods. A piece of driftwood around 40mm thick and 2 metres long is usually sufficient to act as a third leg and take the weight of an average angler. A wading belt is another excellent item that all anglers should have, especially those who regularly wade out deep. Fitted around the waist, it not only helps to keep your waders from filling with water if you fall in, but turns them into a buoyancy aid. Some anglers are now wearing inflatable life jackets in addition to a wading belt at the deeper mouths. There are several brands now on the market. They are unobtrusive and comfortable to wear when not inflated. Although they are pricey they are worth every dollar in an emergency.

DAVE HART / ©186AD PHOTOGRAPHY

An inflatable life vest, like this one worn by the author, could save your life in an emergency.

9. Fishing the Rivers and Streams: Where to Go

Famous trout fishing pools are just metres from the main highway.

A FAMOUS FISHERY

The fame of the Taupo fishery rests almost solely on the fact that it is one of the few places where you can fly fish for trout during spawning migrations. In the winter months, from June onwards, anglers come from all around New Zealand and all over the world to enjoy some superb fishing.

The winter fisheries of the Tongariro, Waitahanui, Hinemaiaia, Tauranga-Taupo and, to a lesser extent the Waimarino and Waiotaka, all contribute to the reputation the Taupo fishery enjoys. It is possible to venture a short distance off State Highway One, drive your car right up to a number of productive pools, and get out and catch a fat, silver trout weighing an average of 1.7kg. If the fish are not there when you are, it is a simple case of taking a short walk on any of the formed angler access tracks and fishing other pools until you find them. For an angler, it doesn't get much better than this.

However, as good as these eastern catchment rivers and streams are, they are only a small number of the tributaries flowing into the lake, yet many others rarely feature in conversations among anglers. The western tributaries of the lake – the Kuratau, Whanganui, Waihaha and Waihora – experience large runs of trout but their difficulty of access and closed winter season mean they scarcely rate a mention, except perhaps for the fishing at their mouths. But in many of these places the chance to fish alone for large numbers of trout is a real possibility. At the southern end of the lake the Tokaanu tailrace is open all year round, and has plenty of trout – yet you wouldn't know it from counting the number of anglers there. Draining the north end of the lake, the Waikato River is also open 12 months of the year, using all legal methods. It has an incredibly high population of trout and if it were in any other part of the country it would be bank to bank with anglers – but it isn't.

The Taupo fishery has a vast amount of water available to anglers, some of it easy to get to, some of it not. It offers far more diversity of angling than many people realise, which is arguably what makes it so famous.

THE TAUPO CATCHMENT

Three major areas of conservation estate drain into Lake Taupo. Rainfall in the region varies greatly, though, and this is reflected in the size of the rivers and streams flowing into the lake. On the western side of the lake much of the catchment drains the native forest of the Hauhungaroa Range in Pureora Forest Park. The ranges within the park are of moderate terrain, all being less than 1000 metres above sea level, and receive

Where it all begins – the Waikato Stream high up on the Desert Road.

The TPD scheme diverts water from the rivers and streams of the Tongariro National Park, providing valuable extra flows into the lake.

an average annual rainfall of up to 1500mm. Most of the 17 tributaries entering the lake on this side are extremely short – many less than 20km. Consequently many have small flows and most are permanently closed to angling. The waters in the west also have a characteristic slightly stained appearance, due to the leaching of tannins in the upper part of the catchment. While the largest number of tributaries flow into the lake on this side, their combined contribution to Lake Taupo is around only 20 per cent of the total inflow.

On the eastern side of the lake, the main catchment area is in the much larger and steeper terrain of Kaimanawa Forest Park, where the tops of the ranges reach 1500 metres. Because most of the wet weather in the region comes from a north to north-westerly direction, this extra height traps more of the rainfall, which can exceed 2000mm per annum. Although fewer rivers and streams flow into the lake in the east, they carry substantially more water and contribute about 50 per cent of the lake's total input.

The southern end of the region drains the slopes of the Tongariro National Park, where rainfall is over 2500mm per annum. Prior to the construction of the TPD only a fraction of this reached Lake Taupo via the western headwater tributaries of the Tongariro River. However, when the scheme was completed in 1979 it brought in an extra 25 per cent of water into the lake.

It is the volcanic history of the region that has had the greatest effect on the catchment. Substantial layers of pumice and ash are a major feature in the area and, with the top layer of soil less than a few metres thick in most places, erosion is a major problem. This is more evident on the western side of the lake, where farming has meant widespread clearing of the land for pasture, following the introduction of fertilisers to alter the balance of the poor soils in the area. A bare covering of grass is

Intensive land use is degrading previously pristine waterways at an alarming rate.

no match for the ravages of a rainstorm and slips can quickly choke the fragile spawning streams with sediment. The wholesale clear-felling of native bush in this area has meant another problem. With no natural vegetative buffer zone to protect the rivers and streams, the run-off from excessive use of fertilisers, combined with the faeces and urine from intensive dairying practices, has meant inevitable leaching into the waterways. The porous pumice soils beneath the paddocks easily absorb the excess and, although it can take more than 15 years, this leachate eventually reaches the lake through groundwater. Because Lake Taupo is naturally deficient in nitrogen this additional input is already lessening the imbalance in nutrients, with the potential for causing greater plant growth in the lake.

Waterfalls: Natural Barriers

Extensive faulting and subsidence from eruptions have created a large number of impassable waterfalls for trout on 11 of the tributaries. At the south-western end of the lake near Tokaanu, the Waihi Stream lets trout swim about 100m before its beautiful falls halt progress. Further north the Champagne Pool on the Kuratau is the site of possibly the largest natural spring in the region and lies at the base of a normally dry 'waterfall'. A gate was put in above the falls during the formation of Lake Kuratau but during periods of high lake levels and heavy rain this is sometimes opened as a spilling measure, making these falls a spectacular sight.

Right in the heart of the western bays all the tributaries flow over waterfalls. Fishing at the mouth of the Whanganui Stream, you can hear its thundering waterfall less than 1km away. The impressive Tieke Falls on the Waihaha River leave about 5km of river below the falls for running trout to spawn in, while the Waihora has less than 2.5km. Two others, the Waikino and Otupoto, prevent trout from even starting the journey by dropping directly into the lake, with the latter making a spectacular entrance.

In the eastern catchment, the substantial runs of migrating trout in the Tongariro River can only get as far up as the Poutu Intake, just below the Waikato Falls at Beggs Pool, a distance of about 20km from the lake. Lower down the river, one of the main tributaries, the Poutu Stream, also has falls, preventing Lake Taupo trout from reaching Lake Rotoaira. Trout running up the Tauranga-Taupo encounter the impenetrable barrier of a large and impressive 30m waterfall inside Kaimanawa Forest Park, about 22km upstream of the mouth. The most famous of all the waterfalls in the district is Huka Falls on the Waikato River. The falls mark the northern boundary of the fishing district and are also one of New Zealand's most visited tourist locations.

Although not natural, artificial falls exist on the Hinemaiaia River in the form of hydroelectric dams. The 'HB' dam is located barely 5km

The Falls Pool on the Tauranga-Taupo River is always a special place to fish.

from the mouth, which is one of the real disappointments for anglers on what is one of the special fisheries.

Yet despite all the natural and man-made barriers, there is plenty of spawning water available and, as a bonus, all but a few of these tributaries support self-sustaining populations of trout from earlier releases above their falls.

THE EASTERN CATCHMENT

TONGARIRO RIVER

The Tongariro is one of the most famous trout fishing rivers in the world, and its reputation is well deserved. Fishery staff estimate that up to a third of all the trout in Lake Taupo run the Tongariro; regardless of the actual percentage the annual runs of migrating trout number in the tens of thousands. Such a large quantity of fish does not go unnoticed by anglers and when a run of trout is going through the river in the winter the bush telegraph ensures that 100 anglers or more can converge on the river to get a piece of the action. The names of famous pools run off the tongue – the Bridge, Judges, Major Jones, Hydro, Admirals, Cattle Rustlers, the Birches, Red Hut and Whitikau – and these are the ones that tend to attract the most attention.

Before the advent of the Tongariro Power Development scheme in the 1970s, the Tongariro River had the largest single inflow into the lake, with a normal flow of about 45-50m³/sec. This was the domain of the angler fishing a wet fly downstream with a sinking line. With the introduction of the TPD scheme, flows were reduced by about 50 per cent, which saw much of the water become ideal for upstream nymphing, the most commonly practised method on the river today.

The TPD scheme has its critics, but one of its advantages is that during periods of high inflows to the upper catchment it draws off the excess flow to Lake Rotoaira for power generation at Tokaanu, helping to keep the Tongariro fishable when many of the other rivers are flooded.

Although the river is more 'angler friendly' now, it is still a large piece of water and can be extremely difficult to fish successfully. In low and clear conditions trout have plenty of hiding places well away from the reach of anglers. But when the river has good strong flows it can be difficult for trout to find a place out of the current that is safe.

Access Signs

A number of fishing access signs, complete with maps of the tracks, have been erected by DOC. On the lower river they are located at the end of Grace Road at Delatours Pool and on both sides of the river at the main road bridge. In the town area of the river they can be found at the Major Jones swingbridge and in the upper river at the Stag Pool. There is one at

NOTE: The 'true left' or 'true right' bank of a river refers to the left or right side facing downstream.

Interesting and informative signs are placed at strategic points along the river.

the entrance to the anglers' car park at the Tongariro National Trout Centre and upstream there is one located at the Red Hut car park. The last sign is at the access point to the Breakaway Pool.

Anglers' Right-of-Way

The legal anglers' right-of-way is 20 metres wide on both banks from the mouth of the river upstream to the Whitikau Stream junction. Upstream of this point the river lies in the Kaimanawa Forest Park.

The Tongariro Delta

The mouth of the Tongariro River, known as the Delta, is one of New Zealand's most popular locations for fishing from an anchored boat. It sits on a peninsula of sorts, which has been built by thousands of years of sediment being washed into the lake. In years gone by, when there were higher flows, three mouths entered the lake on three sides of this peninsula, hence the name Delta, but today there are only two mouths. Neither is serviced by road and because access is almost impossible on foot now, most if not all anglers arrive by boat. The closest ramps are either Tokaanu or Waihi, about five minutes away in a 90-hp boat. With soft pumice sand underfoot and a very quick, deep drop-off into the lake, wading is not recommended.

Two anchors, one at the bow and the other at the stern, are required when fishing at the Delta. The technique is to drop the stern anchor first in deep water and hold the warp loosely while pushing the bow up the flow and into the river proper. Pull on the stern anchor warp until it comes up tight and then drop the bow anchor over. Let the boat drift back until the stern is just over the drop-off, pull on the bowline to set the anchor and then tie both anchors off.

TURANGI: TROUT FISHING CAPITAL OF THE WORLD

The town of Turangi, which borders the river, was once a small, quiet community catering to the anglers fishing nearby. But the TPD brought an influx of engineers and workers, many from the other side of the world, and a prosperous new town of around 10,000 people grew on the western side of SH1 to house them all. At the end of construction many of these skilled people left to work on
other projects. Today Turangi bills itself as 'the trout fishing capital of the world'. It is also 'Adventure Central', being at the gateway to the Tongariro National Park and catering for the thousands of outdoor adventurers who come to enjoy the region every year. Among them are white-water rafters, canoeists, hunters, trampers and skiers, as well as anglers. There are service stations, restaurants, cafés, a shopping mall, a supermarket, four tackle stores, a chemist and doctor's surgery, along with many fine lodges and other accommodation.

Lower River

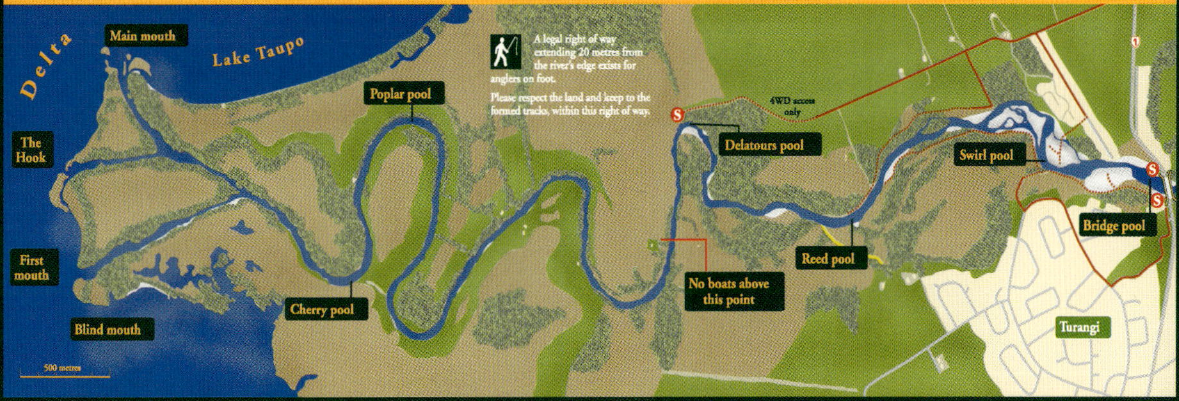

Delta

Lake Taupo

Main mouth

The Hook

First mouth

Blind mouth

Poplar pool

Cherry pool

A legal right of way extending 20 metres from the river's edge exists for anglers on foot.

Please respect the land and keep to the formed tracks, within this right of way.

4WD access only

Delatours pool

Reed pool

No boats above this point

Swirl pool

Bridge pool

Turangi

500 metres

Middle River

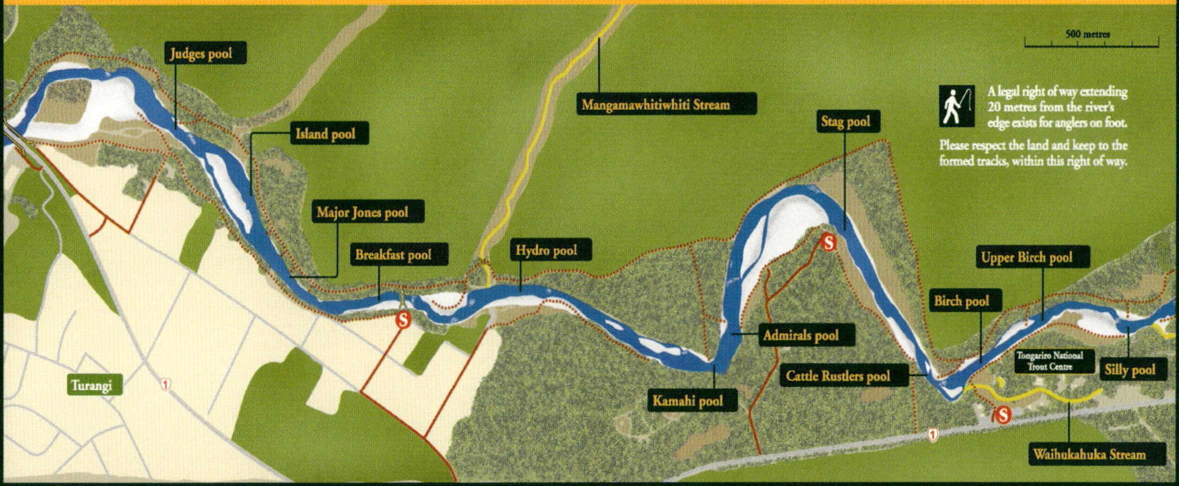

Judges pool

Island pool

Major Jones pool

Breakfast pool

Hydro pool

Turangi

Mangamawhitiwhiti Stream

Stag pool

Admirals pool

Kamahi pool

Cattle Rustlers pool

Upper Birch pool

Birch pool

Tongariro National Trout Centre

Silly pool

Waihukahuka Stream

500 metres

A legal right of way extending 20 metres from the river's edge exists for anglers on foot.

Please respect the land and keep to the formed tracks, within this right of way.

Upper River

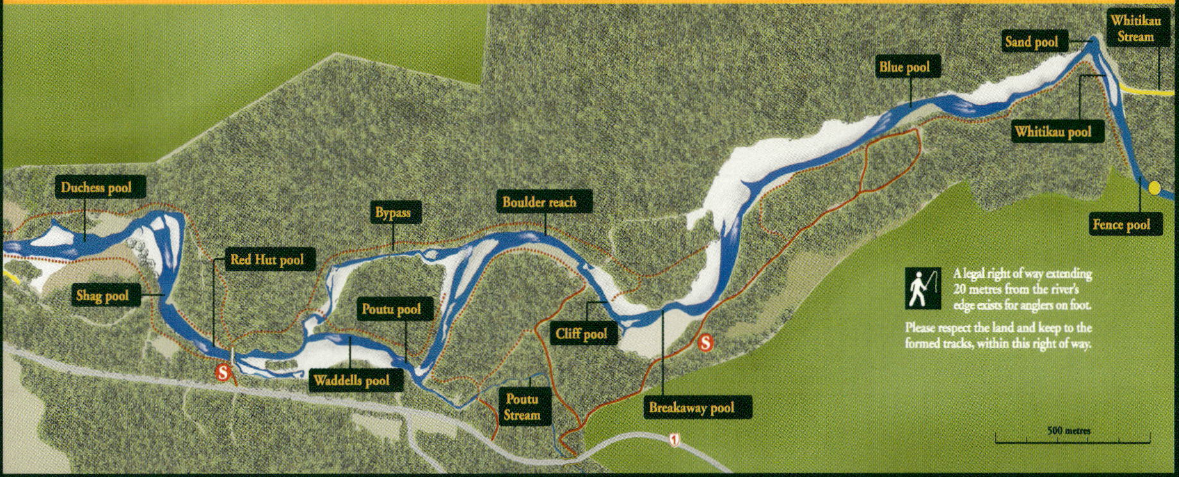

Duchess pool

Shag pool

Red Hut pool

Bypass

Poutu pool

Waddells pool

Poutu Stream

Boulder reach

Cliff pool

Breakaway pool

Blue pool

Sand pool

Whitikau Stream

Whitikau pool

Fence pool

A legal right of way extending 20 metres from the river's edge exists for anglers on foot.

Please respect the land and keep to the formed tracks, within this right of way.

500 metres

  Foot Access

Vehicle Access

 No fishing at any time

 No fishing above this point between 31 May and 1 December

 S Fishing Sign Location

For further information phone Taupo Fishery Area
07 386 8607

Looking over the Tongariro Delta and Stump Bay on a heavily overcast morning.

Fly fishing is the only legal method here and a fast-sinking fly line or shooting head is needed to get the flies down to the trout. Deciding which part of the flow to fish can be difficult sometimes. The river water splits as it flows over the sandy shelf and generally the branch that has the greatest flow seems to have the most fish, although this doesn't mean that it will fish the best. It is often a case of trial and error. There are usually other boats in the vicinity, so it pays to keep a lookout for activity in the area. If things are quiet where you are, it may be worth changing positions.

Lower River (below SH1)

There is a surprisingly large amount of water available in the lower river but, apart from the pools close to Turangi such as the Bridge, Swirl, Reed and Delatours, most of it doesn't appear to offer a lot for anglers. Much of the slower-moving water on the ancient floodplain here is less than 2 metres deep, so there are few actual pools to concentrate the running trout in. Because of this, many fish are found near the only shelter they can find, which is usually behind logjams or under the many willows lining the lower river. The number of potential snags is outrageous, so this part of the river is better suited to dry-fly fishing than nymphing or wetlining. Of course these difficulties still have to be negotiated when you have hooked a trout. There are possibilities for some good fishing, but the size and shape of the river and the hidden presence of underwater obstructions severely restrict opportunities for shore-bound fly anglers.

As well, the prospect of a long walk to access this section puts many people off and the area is devoid of anglers for most of the year. Yet anglers with good stalking skills can experience particularly good fishing in the summer months using imitation and live cicadas during the

Most of the flows come from the Kaimanawa Ranges, and the steep slopes can bring flash floods.

day, and mouse patterns at dusk. Careful anglers can also enjoy great sport with natural nymph patterns such as the Hare's Ear and Pheasant Tail – where a break in the trees and snags allows a cast. If that is possible, long fine leaders and a dry-fly indicator are the only way to achieve consistent success.

During the hotter months from early January, good numbers of large brown trout up to 4.5kg (10lb) or more begin moving into the lower river. They can be a real challenge to catch and will test your stalking skills to the limit. You will need to be very quiet when approaching a likely lie, as these large fish are extremely wary of disturbances. While brown trout may not 'spook' the way a rainbow will, they will move slowly off to the shelter of the deepest part of the river or simply stop feeding. Using summer techniques to catch these monsters can be quite exciting and there are normally plenty of early-running rainbows to add to the action. Juvenile trout also make this part of the river their home and a good part of your catch can be these little trout, which are usually less than 30cm long.

Thankfully, a feature of the Tongariro River fishery is the ability to fish the lower river from an anchored boat. This opens up around 4.5km of the river, from the mouth to the limit sign at the Downs Pool. There are no boat ramps on the river but a shallow-drafted vessel can enter at the main mouth of the Delta. In lake levels below 356.5m boats may need to be pulled through the first 100m until in the river proper. Otherwise a good option is to put a canoe or rigid-hull inflatable boat in below the main road bridge and drift down. Keep in mind that you'll also need a small outboard to get back up the river or across Tokaanu Bay to any of the ramps to be picked up. Either way, you will need to be well organised. The best places to put a small craft into the water are accessed from Grace Road, off SH1 less than 1km north of Turangi.

The Major Jones Pool is one of the most famous trout fishing locations in the world.

Foot Access

The first turn to the left off Grace Road is Herekiekie Street, which has foot access to the **Bridge Pool** from the end of the street. A public accessway for foot traffic only is available outside #50 Herekiekie Street, which leads down to the **Swirl Pool** and **Honey Pot**. Further down Grace Road an unmarked turn to the left, about 1.5km from SH1, leads down to the river at its most braided part in an area known as **The Nursery**. From here there is access to the **Reed Pool** by taking the track to the right at the car park. Access to **Delatours Pool** is by a continuation of Grace Road although only those anglers with a serious 4WD vehicle are able to negotiate this section.

Without a boat it is possible to access the true left bank of the lower river from the end of Awamate Road, which is about 1.5km from the Turangi or Tokaanu end of Hirangi Road. From Turangi it is found by turning off at the Shell/Burger King site on SH1 and then right into Ohuanga Street, which becomes Tautahanga Street (the town loop), and then onto Hirangi Road. At the Tokaanu end Hirangi Road joins SH41 near the Tailrace Bridge. Once on Awamate Road and past the first gate, in dry conditions it is possible to drive down the gravel track for about a kilometre before arriving at another gate. This is just below the upstream boat limit at the **Downs Pool**. There is a legal right-of-way extending 20 metres from the river edge, for licensed foot anglers only, so park here and walk the rest of the way. Always be mindful that you are on private

Late afternoon at the Judges Pool.

property, most of it farmland and you are advised to keep to the tracks in these areas. Vehicle access beyond the first gate is at the discretion and courtesy of the landowner too. Be respectful of the landowner's property, leave farm gates as you find them (open or closed), avoid upsetting the stock and don't litter.

At Turangi the most productive pools of the river below the main road bridge are within a short walk of the town centre. A common sight in winter is a large number of anglers lined up in the **Bridge Pool** on the true left side during a run. The stretch under the bridge beside the Bridge Lodge is also a popular location by virtue of its easy access. Alternatively, drive along the town loop to the Crescent Reserve, through which there is access to the **Swirl Pool** area.

Town Pools (above SH1)

The river above the main road bridge, within a short walking distance of Turangi, contains what is known among the locals as the 'town pools'. It is a popular section of the river and during winter on a typical Saturday you can see more than 100 anglers, all trying to catch a trout. Fortunately there is enough productive fishing water to cope. The **Major Jones Pool** is one such place and at times there can be 15 anglers or more up to their armpits, right up to the head of the pool, with more waiting their turn on the bank. There is always plenty happening and sometimes there are multiple hook-ups as a run comes through the pool. It can be a source of encouragement when other anglers start to catch fish below you, but this can quickly fade to disappointment if you don't hook up and the angler above you does!

The popularity of the town pools has more to do with convenience than the quality of the fishing or the chance to rub shoulders with large numbers of other anglers. Access is easy on both sides of the river, which is served by a very good track network. The Tongariro River Lookout Track starts on the true right bank at the main road bridge and continues upstream for 2km to join the Major Jones swingbridge, before extending a further 5km to the **Breakaway Pool**. The track on the true left is known as the Taupahi Reserve Walk and crossing the river at either bridge makes a good circuit for a morning's angling. Along this circuit there is excellent access to the **Judges**, **Island** and **Major Jones** pools.

At the top end of the town pool area the Major Jones swingbridge can be reached by vehicle at the end of Koura Sreet, off Taupahi Road. There is an easy day's fishing upstream to the **Cattle Rustlers Pool**, and for the more energetic, a full day to the **Red Hut** swingbridge, which is the next and last crossing of the river. Direct access to the **Hydro Pool** and on to the **Neverfail Pool** is also along Taupahi Road. Take the turn at Kotai Street and park at the end, or walk up the true left from Koura Street.

The Neverfail Pool often lives up to its name (but not always).

Upper Pools

A prominent feature of the Tongariro, especially above the SH1 bridge, is that it has a fairly stable but bouldery riverbed, which can make wading and walking on the river's edge difficult. There are two swingbridges over the river, but it can be crossed in a number of places in low flows (under 25m³/sec) by wading. However, it pays to be extremely careful doing so and you should not attempt it if you are alone. Much of the river can be fished from the true right after walking up from the Major Jones swingbridge, but most anglers travel by vehicle and fish from any of the five signposted car parks on the true left that are located along SH1, only a few minutes south of Turangi. These make a useful base from where you can go either upstream or downstream for a good day's fishing. Alternatively, if you are in a group of two or more and have two vehicles, simply leave one at one car park and drive to the next one, so you have a one-way walk only, with no backtracking necessary.

The first car park is located at the **Admirals Pool**, which is less than a couple of minutes' drive from Turangi. This car park also gives access to a track to the **Stag Pool** and **Hill Race**, which ends at the tail of the **Cattle Rustlers Pool**. Foot access above Cattle Rustlers is through the **Tongariro National Trout Centre**, further along SH1. It is a popular parking area and offers excellent access to the **Birches** and **Silly** pools. Above the Birches the bottom of the Silly Pool is easily reached by walking along the riverbed from where a track continues up the true left to the **Duchess Pool** at Kowhai Flat before ending at the **Red Hut Pool**. This makes for a good day's fishing, especially if you can arrange a pick-up at the Red Hut car park.

The last crossing of the river is at the Red Hut swingbridge. Between the car park and the swingbridge is an angler's access sign pointing to the left. This is the track to the Tongariro National Trout Centre, giving access to the true left of the river. Directly under the bridge is the **Red Hut Pool** and a little further down the **Shag Pool**, both reached by crossing the bridge and following a short track immediately to the left. On the true right of the river the Tongariro Walkway track continues another 1.2km to its end at the top of the **Breakaway Pool**. Between those points it gives access to the **By-Pass**, **Boulder** and **Cliff** pools, along with access to the **Waddells** and **Poutu** pools by making a detour and crossing the lower **By-Pass**.

Beyond the Red Hut, the last three access points for anglers to the upper river are in the vicinity of the **Poutu Stream**. The first is less than 100 metres south of the Red Hut car park, where parking is available in the layby on the main road. A track leads down to the river, where good fishing pools at the junction of the main river and the **By-Pass**, the **Waddells** and lower end of the **Poutu** are located. It is also worth walking down the true left and fishing the small offshoot just above the Red Hut swingbridge. Many trout congregate in this part, especially when the river is in flood, and it can offer some spectacular fishing.

Further along SH1 and about 300 metres before the Poutu Stream bridge is another access point, signposted to the **Dreadnought Pool**. After a short drive off the main road it joins the Poutu Loop Track, giving good foot access to the **Poutu Pool** and on to the **Boulder Reach**, ending at the bottom of the **Cliff Pool**. Above the Poutu confluence the

Swingbridge over
the Red Hut Pool.

Tom Watson ponders a change of flies during a break at the Sand Pool.

river has less flow, which makes fishing it a little easier. You won't need to cast as far and the drifts with a floating line can be a lot friendlier to the angler. Combined with some of the best wilderness scenery in the district, fishing on this part of the river can be very enjoyable.

The final river access is at the southern end of the Poutu bridge. Turn left and following the gravel road, which divides in two about 500 metres down, the left branch leading to the Poutu Loop Track. The other option is to veer to the right, which gives access to the **Breakaway** and **Blue** pools. The final car park at the Blue Pool has foot access to the **Sand** and **Whitikau** pools, but the easiest access to the winter fishing limit at the **Fence Pool** is by crossing the bottom of the **Sand Pool**, then the Whitikau Stream and walking up the true right for about 500 metres.

POUTU STREAM

One of the Tongariro's main tributaries in the middle reaches is the Poutu Stream, which joins the river on the true left bank. There is a significant run of fish during the season, but although it is open to fishing all year round it is often ignored in favour of the Tongariro. It is an especially good alternative when the Tongariro is in flood and any effort made to fish this stream could be very rewarding, with lots of trout and few other anglers. The size of the water lends itself to nymphing. Wading is the only way to get to the best spots but the streambed is very rocky and stony and stable flows have encouraged slime growth, making conditions very slippery underfoot. Take care.

A footbridge crosses the stream at the early part of the Poutu Loop Track from the Dreadnought entrance, although it is accessible by wading up from the Poutu Pool to the SH1 bridge. An anglers' right-of-way exists from the Poutu Pool to SH1, but above the bridge the stream flows through private property and access is prohibited.

The Tongariro gorge is trout fishing heaven, but you'll share it with white-water sports enthusiasts.

THE GORGE

Above the winter fishing limit at the Fence Pool the river flows through a gorge, which is virtually impenetrable except by raft or canoe. During the open season (1 December to 31 May) a number of white-water rafting companies specialise in taking anglers through it and it is definitely worth the effort. The scenery is unsurpassed in the region, but with more than 60 large pools it is the very special fishing on offer that is the attraction for anglers. The best time of year to go is during April and May, when the first good early runs of rainbows and a fair number of large browns are in the river. Get a group together, with or without one of the experienced raft/fishing guides and enjoy one of the most stunning parts of New Zealand. It is something any keen angler should do at least once – be sure to take a camera.

Access to the gorge is from Kaimanawa Road, approximately 16km south of Turangi on SH1. The **Waikato Falls** at **Beggs Pool** are signposted about 2km along the road, on the left just before the bridge. Take this turn and once over the Poutu Intake structure turn left again, where a gravel track leads down to the river's edge. It is possible to launch a raft or canoes here, but be warned that the gorge is a formidable part of the river and only people who are experienced in Grade 3 white-water techniques should attempt the journey. Above the Poutu Intake is the very attractive **Beggs Pool**. There are rainbow trout present, although they are typically small in size and number.

Immediately upstream of the falls is the Tree Trunk gorge, which holds no interest to anglers. The tragic rafting deaths of four men in 1985 serve as grim warning not to venture into this part of the river.

RANGIPO INTAKE

The first major part of the TPD scheme affecting the Tongariro River is at the Rangipo Intake Dam. The dam was formed to channel the upper Tongariro River and the contribution from the Moawhango Diversion into a tunnel to feed the underground Rangipo Power Station. Below this point the Tongariro is virtually dry for a small distance, before many small tributaries build up the flows again.

The lake created by the dam fishes well with all methods, but spinning provides a definite advantage. A moderate population of small to medium-sized rainbow trout in the 0.5-1kg range is in residence, and because very few anglers fish here the trout are usually eager to gobble the first available offering. For the more adventurous, it is difficult but not impossible to walk upstream and fish to the Waipakihi Road end – a distance of about 3km. Spin fishing is still useful in the deeper pools but the high water clarity above the Moawhango Outlet means that fly fishing with nymphs and dry flies is generally the most successful method.

The open season runs from 1 December to 31 May and it is always worth giving it a go if you are looking for something different. Access is via Rangipo Intake Road, located 32km south of Turangi on SH1.

WAIPAKIHI RIVER

The Waipakihi is the major headwater tributary of the Tongariro River and flows through the unparalleled scenery of the Kaimanawa Forest Park. Some of Taupo's earliest trout fishing history was made in the vicinity of the Waipakihi. The wild rainbow trout resident here are descended from the first liberations of rainbow trout fry made in the region and have ancestry dating back to 1898. Malcolm and Forrestina Ross are credited with these releases which they made into the Waikato, Mangatoetoenui and Piripiri streams – tributaries of the upper Tongariro and Waipakihi. It was from these initial small and arduous journeys that the first rainbow trout became established in Lake Taupo. But for all its history, stunning location and extremely high water clarity, few anglers make the effort to fish here and those who do tend to be mostly hunters or trampers who are walking through the area.

The river drains a fairly steep catchment area and is subject to large and rapid increases in flow when it rains, which does not do much to help the fishery. Large floods strip the riverbed of insect life and push the trout downstream towards the Rangipo Intake. As such, the upper river tends to hold a few fish in some seasons and virtually none in others. A moderate winter with reasonably settled weather and no major flooding allows the invertebrate community to build up again and the trout to move back up, but this seems to be too rare an occurrence for a good productive fishery. During normal conditions expect the flow to be about 5-8m^3/sec – about the same as the Tauranga-Taupo River.

In addition to facing a sparse trout population and their small average size compared to Lake Taupo fish, anybody contemplating a visit to

The Waipakihi near the road end. It's a great place to visit, but the fishing is disappointing.

the Waipakihi will be faced with trying to tempt some of the wariest trout in the district. Good stalking techniques are essential, as is a careful approach with nymphs and dry flies, although all legal methods are permitted throughout.

A good walking track starts at the end of Waipakihi Rd (37km south of Turangi on SH1) and follows the river for about 13km upstream to the Waipakihi Hut near Thunderbolt Creek. Alternatively, about 3km of water is available downstream to the Rangipo Intake. In line with the rest of the Tongariro upstream of the winter limit at the Fence Pool, the open season runs from 1 December to 31 May.

WAIOTAKA STREAM

The Waiotaka is the first tributary north of the Tongariro River on SH1, and like its 'twin', the Waimarino, it has a flow of 2-3m³/sec. Don't blink when travelling over the SH1 bridge where it crosses the river or you'll miss it! In this part the river is about 2 metres wide and looks more like a large drain than a productive trout fishery. Further upstream it reveals its true shape and size, although the proliferation of willows means a lack of casting room so it is better suited to experienced anglers. Complementing the steady runs of rainbow trout during the winter months is the presence of good numbers of large brown trout running from January onwards. They offer good sport to anglers prepared to stalk them in the summer, but like most small rivers and streams the Waiotaka fishes best when the flows are higher from rain and the water is slightly murky.

The Waiotaka suffers in the popularity stakes by being so close to the Tongariro River, which is a real bonus for committed anglers who want something different.

Having to cast amongst overhanging trees can be a challenge.

WAIOTAKA STREAM

Season: 1 July to 30 June up to winter limit at lower prison boundary. 1 December to 31 May above upper prison boundary.
Methods: Fly fishing only.
Size / Bag Limit: 45cm minimum / 3 trout.
Anglers' right-of-way: 20m wide on both banks from mouth to lower prison boundary. No restriction on access within Kaimanawa State Forest Park.
Map (1:50,000): 260-T19-Tongariro.

N.B. This information is in accordance with the Taupo Fishing Regulations 1984 (incorporating amendments to 30 June 2000).

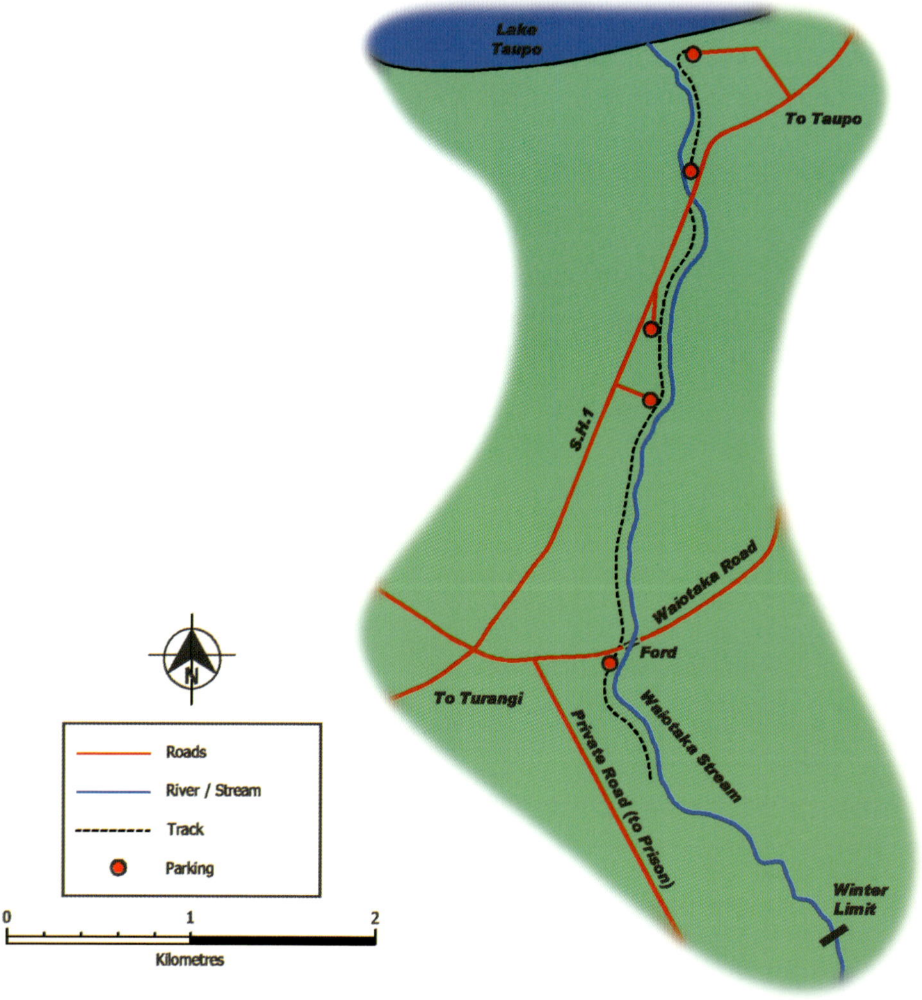

Roads

River / Stream

Track

Parking

0   1   2

Kilometres

Lower Reaches (below SH1) to the Mouth

The stream enters Lake Taupo in a very shallow part of Stump Bay: it is floating-line territory. It can be a fantastic location for smelting trout during the day, and after dark it can be a great place to catch large brown trout when they assemble from January onwards before beginning their slow upstream journey. There is a small drop-off some distance into the lake, requiring a wade of around 100m or more to reach it, but wading out is not usually necessary because the trout can be caught at your feet.

The mouth is reached from SH1 by taking the signposted turn-off at Frethey Drive, 300 metres past the SH1 bridge, which leads to the Turangi Yacht Club in Stump Bay. To the left of the clubrooms is a pumice vehicle track leading down to the mouth. Be careful where you take your vehicle when you reach the end of the track because the pumice sand here is very soft.

The lower section below the main road bridge is very narrow and confined and difficult to fish properly. As it extends only about 500m up from the lake, most trout tend to run through here fairly quickly and into the safety of the shelter further upstream. There is foot and partial vehicle access on the true right from SH1.

Upper Reaches (above SH1)

Around 4km of water are open for angling throughout the year in this section and this is where most of the trout are caught. State Highway One runs alongside the true left of the Waiotaka for about 2km, from the bend past Grace Road to the Waiotaka Bridge. The river is easily accessed by taking either of the vehicle access tracks off to the right, when coming from Turangi. There is plenty of fishing available within a short walk from your vehicle and to fish this section properly would take most of the day. The other access is upstream of the Hautu ford on Waiotaka Road, which contains about 2km of water before the limit at the lower prison boundary. Beyond, the middle reaches of the river flow through a prison farm and access is prohibited at all times.

The section above the upper prison boundary is open from 1 December to 31 May and it provides for some good sport. Unfortunately the road that leads to it is a private prison road and permission to drive on it is required from the Department of Corrections, which is highly unlikely to grant it. The only access is by either helicopter or a long walk in through the Kaimanawa Forest Park from the Waimarino River end. Given the extreme difficulty of access, there are many more places where this type of effort would be better rewarded.

Waiotaka Road is reached from either end by taking Korohe Rd, 7km north of Turangi on SH1, and turning right at the junction, or by turning off SH1 at the Grace Road intersection near Turangi. The Hautu Ford looks fairly tame but be warned that it is for 4WD vehicles only.

WAIMARINO RIVER

The Waimarino River is similar to the Waiotaka Stream in that it has normal flows in the 2-3m³/sec range and enters the lake in Stump Bay. Due to its size and flow, migrating trout tend to just dribble through in low numbers, but large runs of fish enter the river when the water levels rise after rain. The time to catch these otherwise cautious trout is when the river begins to recede following good rainfall in the headwaters. At times like this some very good fishing can be experienced because the extra colour in the river makes it harder for the fish to see the angler. On the flipside, the Waimarino also tends to clear quickly. In low and clear conditions it can be one of the most difficult places to catch a trout, but not impossible.

The Waimarino has a substantially better reputation for fishing at the mouth than it does for fishing in the river, although that does not mean there are no good opportunities for careful anglers. However, overgrown willows and snags dominate sections of the river in its lower reaches, making the fishing so challenging that few anglers ever bother with it, preferring instead to target the larger and more popular rivers in the district.

Lower River (below SH1 to the Mouth)

A signposted vehicle track at the SH1 bridge, about 7.5km north of Turangi, gives access to the mouth on the true left. However, it is not always possible to drive all the way to the mouth and, depending on the

Low flows mean tough fishing at the best of times, but especially on the Waimarino.

WAIMARINO RIVER

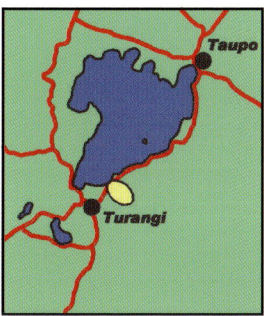

Season: 1 July to 30 June up to winter limit. 1 December to 31 May above winter limit.
Methods: Fly fishing only.
Size / Bag Limit: 45cm minimum / 3 trout.
Anglers' right-of-way: 20m wide on both banks from mouth to source.
Map (1:50,000): 260-T19-Tongariro.

N.B. This information is in accordance with the Taupo Fishing Regulations 1984 (incorporating amendments to 30 June 2000).

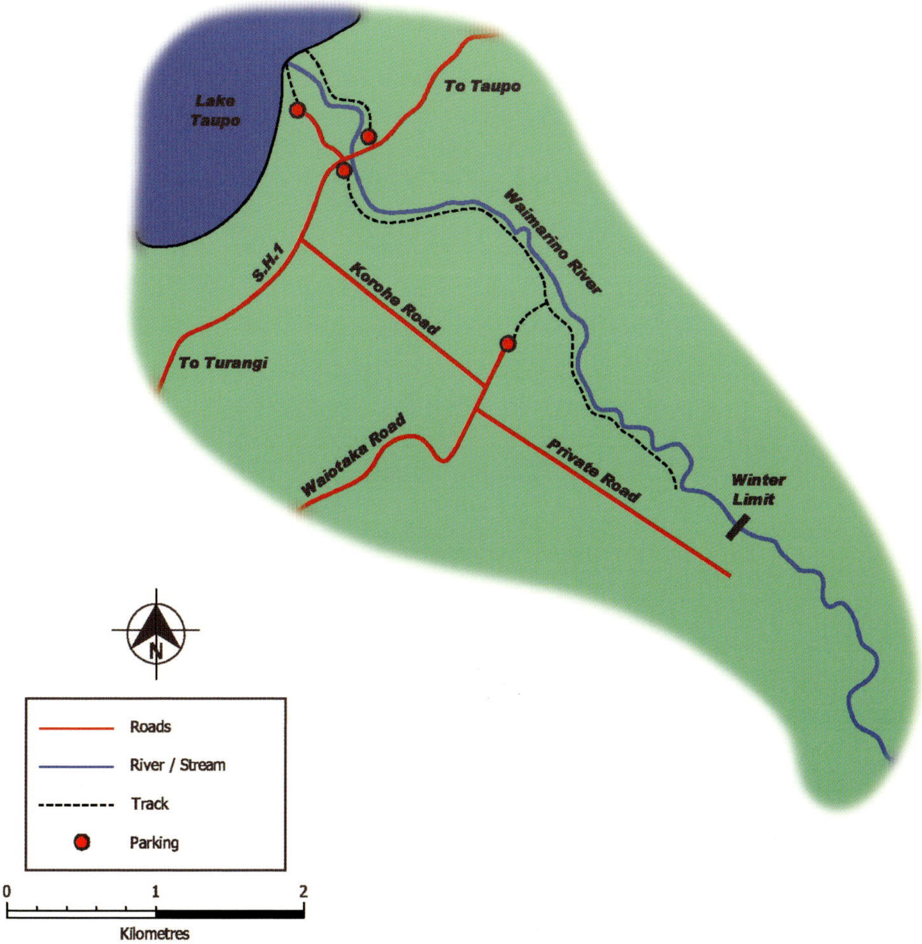

To Taupo

Lake Taupo

Waimarino River

S.H.1

Korohe Road

To Turangi

Waiotaka Road

Private Road

Winter Limit

N

	Roads
	River / Stream
	Track
●	Parking

0   1   2
Kilometres

A fresh-run rainbow from the lower Waimarino.

lake level, sections of the track can be impassable. The usual obstacle is just before you reach the lake, where a small section of the track is frequently under water. If that's the case, leave your vehicle there and walk along the lake edge to the river mouth, which takes only two to three minutes. Otherwise a 4WD vehicle is needed to make the journey along the sandy lake edge and back without getting stuck.

The mouth enters the lake in extremely shallow water, which encourages large numbers of trout to congregate in the deep water over the drop-off, waiting for the flow to increase before they run up the river. Wading is required to reach the drop-off, which is only possible when Lake Taupo is under 356.4m. A fast-sinking line is essential, along with an ability to cast more than 20m. After dark is usually the most productive time, particularly when the barometer is dropping. When it does, the mouth can be very popular, especially during April and May, when it has a reputation for being a good place to catch large rainbows over 3kg.

Most of the section from the mouth to the bridge is overgrown, which severely restricts casting, but it is worth exploring, especially when the barometer is falling and the river is beginning to rise during consistent rain. There are few actual pools to concentrate trout in and the best option is to get in the river near the mouth and wade up to the bridge. Alternatively, park on the true right below the bridge and fish down with a wet fly.

Upper River (above SH1)

During normal flows the Waimarino is low and clear and it can be extremely difficult to fish during the day – successful anglers are usually on the water early in the morning. Stalking likely lies with a careful approach and a good pair of polarised glasses will help you to spot the fish.

Access is on the true left from a parked vehicle above the SH1 bridge, which gives about 3km of river for winter anglers to work with and enough for a good five to six hours of fishing to the limit near the Korohe Crossing. Alternatively, drive up Korohe Road and turn left at the T-junction. After 100 metres the road turns to gravel and is often impassable except by 4WD vehicle.

Beyond the upstream winter limit at Korohe Crossing the river has a more open bed with fewer obstructions and provides some good fishing, particularly during April and May before it closes for the winter on 1 June. It is worth leaving the waders behind if you intend to walk up the river for the day because it is a fairly long walk. To make the most of it, pack a good lunch and make an early start.

TAURANGA-TAUPO RIVER

The Tauranga-Taupo River (or T-T as it is also known) is the second-largest natural tributary of Lake Taupo, with a flow of around 7-9m³/sec.

Peter Haxell battles an energetic fish in the quarry. This was how it looked in 2002.

It forms a vital component of the trout fishery but even on a busy day it often has fewer than 30 per cent of the anglers that the Tongariro River does. This not because it is lacking in trout – far from it – but because it does not offer the convenience of most of the eastern tributaries. Many anglers by-pass this river in favour of easier alternatives. The reduced pressure from anglers, combined with strong runs of trout, means that catch rates can be significantly better here, and the T-T is one of the most productive river fisheries in the region. This is a great advantage to those anglers who do not mind walking up to 45 minutes from their vehicle.

The river is located about 14km north of Turangi on SH1, where the lower 5km flows through a floodplain of alluvial gravels and pumice in much the same way as the lower Tongariro does. This zone covers a fairly wide area of around 35 square kilometres, which extends from the shore of Lake Taupo at Waitetoko in the north to near Motuoapa in the south and for a considerable distance in the east up Kiko Road, the access road to Kaimanawa Forest Park. The size of the floodplain gives away the hidden power of the river when Mother Nature is at her worst. A consistent feature of the river is that it tends to rise rapidly around six to eight hours after rainfall in the headwaters, which lie well back in the steep slopes of the Kaimanawa Range. During heavy rain the river can literally rise in front of your eyes and it has been known to trap anglers who do not see the warning signs. But within 12 hours of peaking the flow and level can be almost back to normal.

The ability of the river to receive large volumes of water in a short space of time, combined with the highly erodeable floodplain, means that huge flows can dramatically change the river in the lower reaches. When the flows return to normal after floods it is not uncommon to find that many of the pools in this section have been altered considerably or disappeared altogether. However, disappointment at the loss of

TAURANGA - TAUPO RIVER

Season: 1 July to 30 June up to winter limit. 1 December to 31 May above winter limit.

Methods: Fly fishing only.

Size / Bag Limit: 45cm minimum / 3 trout.

Anglers' right-of-way: 20m wide on both banks from mouth upstream 4.8km. Beyond this point the landowner has agreed to access as far as the Rangers Pool (Winter Limit).

Map (1:50,000): 260-T19-Tongariro.

N.B. This information is in accordance with the Taupo Fishing Regulations 1984 (incorporating amendments to 30 June 2000).

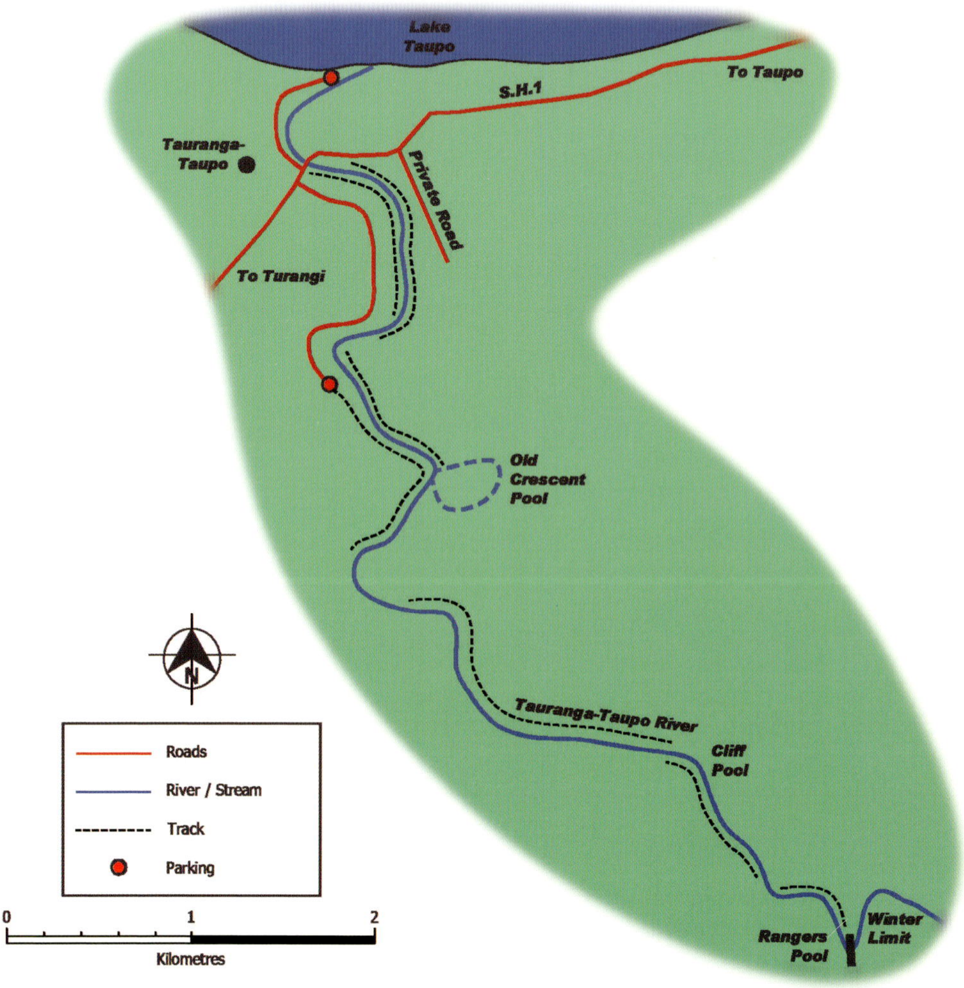

Lake Taupo

To Taupo

S.H.1

Tauranga-Taupo

Private Road

To Turangi

Old Crescent Pool

N

Tauranga-Taupo River

Cliff Pool

Roads	
River / Stream	
Track	
Parking	

Rangers Pool

Winter Limit

0   1   2

Kilometres

one pool often gives way to excitement at finding a new lie that didn't previously exist.

This last happened in a major way during the massive flood in December 2001. At its peak the flow reached 295m^3/sec, which is about 40 times the normal flow. The river broke its banks and changed course less than 1km below the Cliff Pool, flowing through a disused quarry before rejoining the river further down, near the old Crescent Pool. About 2km of river, containing more than a dozen popular pools and many other productive fish-holding areas, were lost, much to the sadness of many anglers who liked this part of the river. It took 16 months, but engineering work to return the river to its old course was completed in March 2003, allowing water to flow down the old riverbed again in time for the winter runs. A similar flood altered the river in October 1998 with the loss of the Crescent Pool. The chance of floods changing the river again is extremely high. Thankfully, although most other rivers in the region are also affected by flooding, they do not normally alter as dramatically or as regularly as the T-T.

In many ways the river has similarities to some of the South Island's East Coast salmon rivers, which are constantly changing with every new round of increased flows. Successful salmon anglers there have adapted to these changes and make a habit of being able to find where the fresh runs of fish are. The same rules apply to the Tauranga-Taupo River.

Despite the floods, and the constant changes in the river, the snags and the walking, the T-T is an extremely productive river and well worth the effort. The short, sharp increases or 'fresh' flows coming into the lake attract good runs of trout and can make for very good fishing – as long as the angler is able to predict correctly where the run is in the river. When you strike everything in your favour and know where to find the fish, it can be very special.

Extensive erosion and the detritus from numerous floods are features of the lower river.

> **ANGLERS BEWARE!**
>
> The erosion of alluvial gravel and pumice assists in adding to the abundance of snags, in particular the trees that are regularly washed into the river with each flood. If you haven't been on the river for a while it is worth taking some time to explore it again – and remember to take plenty of flies! Unfortunately there are some great pools that suffer badly from these snags, which can be very frustrating. You can *see* all the trout, but fishing for them is almost impossible.

Lower River (below SH1) to the Mouth

The mouth is a very popular place and when the conditions are good there can be up to 30 anglers here, many fishing from anchored boats. This is one of only two locations in the lake where fly fishing from an anchored boat is permitted within 300 metres of a river mouth. You will need to use two anchors, as described for the Tongariro Delta.

Like the Delta, the T-T mouth has a rapid drop-off that has claimed the lives of unsuspecting anglers in the past, so it pays to be very careful if fishing from the shore. Depending on the weather and the lake level, the mouth may be split in two, so check where the most flow is concentrated before beginning fishing. The technique is to cast well out with a fast-sinking line before beginning the retrieve. Because of its depth, the mouth can produce well all day, although fishing before dawn or after dusk is usually the most successful. It is also a good place for night fishing on a full moon, because the depth of water appears to provide some cover for the trout and the moon affects the fishing less than it does at shallow mouths.

The mouth is at the end of Heu Heu Parade, which follows the true left of the river for a distance of about 1km from the SH1 bridge,

The short section below the bridge is a great place to fish during a fresh.

enabling easy access to the lake and the first runs of fish in the lower river. Although there is no boat ramp in the river, it is possible to launch a shallow-draft vessel inside the mouth so long as you have a 4WD vehicle with good ground clearance. The river is not very deep in this part and not more than waist height on a good day, so a large fibreglass boat will probably struggle to get out. If that's the case, the best place to launch is at the Oruatua, Motuoapa or Mission Bay ramps, which are less than five minutes away.

A 4WD vehicle is needed when launching and retrieving small craft in the lower Tauranga-Taupo River.

The mouth is very exposed to the wind and waves from a westerly direction and when conditions are rough, migrating trout can be induced into the river, particularly after dark. Fishing in the swell and gales is not a lot of fun, but the first 200m inside the mouth often provides some shelter from the elements.

Wet-fly fishing this section with an intermediate or floating line can be very productive. The fish tend to run up against the far bank where there is more depth and wading is necessary, night or day. During summer large quantities of smelt can congregate in this area, bringing plenty of trout. At times like this they seem to lose all fear and can be successfully stalked and caught, sometimes without getting your feet wet.

The reach below the main road bridge is a popular location for anglers when a run has entered the river following a fresh. It is worth fishing the first few hours of rising or falling levels, colouring or clearing water, when large numbers of trout can be taken with either a wet fly or by nymphing from the embankment. This part of the river is very channelled and the technique is to retrieve or drift the flies as close to the true left bank as possible, since most of the fish will be concentrated there, trying to get shelter from the flow of the river. During low flow conditions and lake levels below 356.5m the river just above the bridge becomes fairly shallow and sometimes you can see hundreds of trout milling around aimlessly as they wait for the next rains to help them on their way. Fishing for them is usually a pointless exercise.

Lower River (above SH 1) to the old Crescent Pool

The lower reaches up to the old Crescent Pool area are often the place to target fresh-run trout within a day of the river dropping again, following rain. However, a lack of good holding water means most trout will usually not stop to rest for long before moving up again. These running trout are known to travel in groups of 30-40 for some way up the river before they pair up and spawn, which means the fishing can be very good when a large group like this is encountered. Sometimes it is possible to take fish on consecutive casts, cast after cast, when the fish have just entered the river system. They tend to move fairly quickly though, but when the strikes dry up you have a chance to get them again in the pool directly above. Chasing them like this means it is possible to keep

The author's wife Rochelle with a good fresh-run rainbow from the lower river.

Almost there: Peter Haxell at the end of the fight with a large rainbow in the middle reaches.

in touch with the fish almost all the way up the river from below the bridge to at least the old Crescent area, but within 24 hours most of the run will have moved further up. Many fish are found in odd places (especially those that most anglers walk straight past) so it pays to fish all the water that could shelter a trout from the current.

Access for anglers with vehicles is limited to a gravel track located at the end of Tuki Road, which leads up the true left bank of the river for a short distance. At the end of the vehicle access is the start of a walking track, and when the river is up during a fresh, the only way to get to the upper reaches is from this side. Tuki Road begins opposite the Tauranga-Taupo Fishing Lodge, 100 metres south of the SH1 bridge.

Foot access to the lower reaches is possible on both banks, starting above the main road bridge. The lower river can be waded in many places, although there are a few deep holes to look out for when considering your crossing point. Remember that the river rises rapidly following rain in the headwaters, so if the conditions are looking doubtful and you are on the opposite side to your vehicle it is advisable to get back across before the water becomes too high. Otherwise it can be a long walk down to the bridge and back up the other side again – something that happens more often than you might think.

Middle Pools (above the old Crescent Pool to the Cliff Pool)

Numerous productive pools and runs lie in the middle section of the river and typically attract most of the angling effort. There is enough fishing for a whole day with about 2.5km of water available if you cover all the likely water thoroughly. The walking track from Tuki Road leads up the true left but it is worth crossing over below **Maniapoto's Pool** and fishing up the true right to **Parke's Reach**. Some of the best water is in this part, where the river makes significant twists and turns and usually holds good numbers of fish, especially in the first 48 hours of a fresh.

Further up, the **Pump Pool**, **The Avenue** and **The Parade** contain shallower but longer stretches that suit both nymphing and wet fly. The wet fly can be very productive, especially at the tail-end of the runs where huge numbers of trout can lie. The time to get them is before the sun is on the water because after that most of the fish take refuge beneath the bankside vegetation or head up to the top of the pool in the fast water where nymphing is more productive. Because this section of the river also offers good backcasting room it is often used by guides offering tuition to new fly anglers. Get on the water early for the best fishing.

Upper Pools (Cliff to Rangers)

The **Cliff Pool** provides a good opportunity to catch some of the hundreds of trout lying deep in it, virtually all year round. Nymphing works, although a very long trace of about 5 metres is needed to get to the bottom and the swirling currents make this difficult to achieve. The currents don't affect a sinking line and using a wet fly can be far more successful. Stand at the head of the pool, feed the line out and let it swing in the currents.

Above the Cliff is a long stretch known as **Ladies' Mile**. This section is very open and shallow, with few places for trout to hide or rest. It is common to see trout digging spawning redds in this part of the river and at times there can be hundreds of fish doing this – almost oblivious to anglers. The fresh running fish are usually found above this long run in the safety of the deep waters in the **Windmill Pool**.

The walking track leads to the WindMill Pool on the true left, where another crossing is required to access the river further up. It is safe to cross in receding floodwaters below 25m^3/sec and is worth the effort, because some of the greatest concentrations of trout are found throughout this section. Try **The Wire** first (it has a flying fox above it and the Environment Waikato river level and flow recorder in it) and then cross over to the true left. Above this point the river swings around a deep bend where the **Boulder Lie** is located, which is the last pool before the winter limit at the **Rangers Pool** is reached: it is about an hour of solid walking from the car park on Tuki Rd. The Rangers Pool is at the confluence with the first major spawning tributary, the **Mangakowhitiwhiti Stream**. Dozens of trout lie in this pool before running up the stream and at times the fishing can be exceptional.

For the effort required, the Cliff to the Rangers section offers some very nice water and, when fished thoroughly, provides about half a day of good sport. Certainly later in the season, from the end of August, the upper pools contain more consistent numbers of trout. They also attract a large number of anglers and there is plenty of competition for the best

The Cliff Pool is a magnet for trout and anglers alike.

TAURANGA - TAUPO RIVER

(Within Kaimanawa State Forest Park to the Falls)

Season: 1 December to 31 May above winter limit.
Methods: Fly fishing only.
Size / Bag Limit: 45cm minimum / 3 trout.
Anglers' right-of-way: No restriction on access.
Map (1:50,000): 260-U19-Kaimanawa.

N.B. This information is in accordance with the Taupo Fishing Regulations 1984 (incorporating amendments to 30 June 2000).

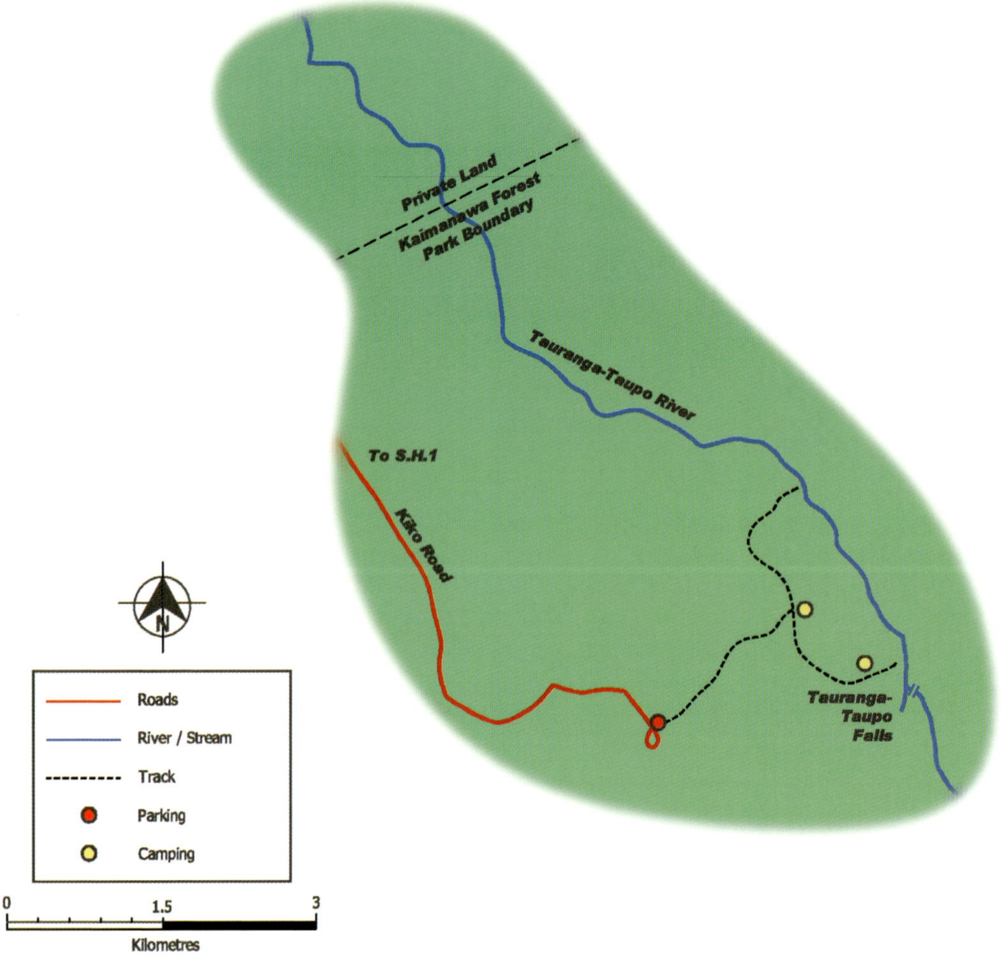

Legend	
Roads	
River / Stream	
Track	
Parking	
Camping	

Private Land

Kaimanawa Forest Park Boundary

Tauranga-Taupo River

To S.H.1

Kiko Road

Tauranga-Taupo Falls

0   1.5   3

Kilometres

pools. It is not uncommon to see half a dozen 4WD vehicles lined up at the Tuki Road car park before dawn, as anglers race to get there first.

The Tauranga-Taupo gorge is in a stunning part of the region.

Upper Gorge to the Falls

About 5km of fishable water lies in the gorge below the falls, within the Kaimanawa Forest Park boundary. This area is open from 1 December to 31 May and is in one of the most stunning parts of the region. It offers superb fishing and is one of the few true wilderness fishing experiences available in the Taupo fishing district. However, the difficult access means that many anglers stay away and head for wilderness fisheries in other parts of the country. Because the spawning season lasts all year round in some form, it is possible to catch fresh-run fish up here all through the open season. Although a greater portion of your catch is likely to be spent or ripening fish, particularly from December to March, it is still well worth the effort.

The riverbed lies in some pretty heavy country and I recommend going in only when the river is below 8m³/sec. This is not normally an issue in the summer months, but it would pay to check the forecast and go in only if the weather looks likely to remain settled for at least a couple of days. Once in the gorge, the boulder-strewn riverbed makes for fairly rugged going but there are plenty of good pools and stretches that hold large numbers of running trout – more than can be comfortably fished in a few days. This is perfect nymphing and dry-fly water and ideally suited to a four-piece, 5/6-weight fly rod. During summer the river can become incredibly clear – with almost spring-creek quality – and this places a premium on your stalking abilities. However, with all the water and trout available, some good sport can be had regardless. At the top end the **Falls Pool** is one of those really special places to catch a trout. Because they can't go any further, hundreds of trout mill around in here before spawning, particularly in May.

Access to the gorge is fairly straightforward, but is not signposted. To find the track take Kiko Road (2km south of Tauranga-Taupo on SH1) to the end and park in a small clearing on the left, which is about 50 metres before the road splits and does a short loop around to the top parking area. If you go past the Kaimanawa Forest Park sign you have gone too far. The track is suitable for two- or four-wheel motorbikes and mountain bikes, otherwise it will take 45 minutes to an hour on foot to the first junction. Here the track to the left gives access to the upper gorge. After about 15 to 20 minutes' walk (ignoring the one small branch to the left), it leads along a ridge above the river before fizzling out. The sound of the river is obvious to the right of the ridge and while there is no well-defined track from here, and it looks like a serious mission, it is possible to make it down to the river in less than 15 minutes. However, a high level of fitness is required, as is some previous bush experience.

Access to the Falls Pool is a simpler and less arduous proposition, by taking the track to the right at the first junction. From here the track to the falls is well marked and takes about an hour. At the first junction there is a good camping spot, which is a handy base for a weekend expedition to fish the entire upper section.

A feature of being in a gorge in such steep country is that the sun rarely reaches the river for long. Be sure to take plenty of sub-alpine warm gear with you because the gorge can be an extremely cold place – even in summer. It also pays to check with DOC about any fire bans that may be in force at the time. A forest fire in here would be uncontrollable and devastating. Last but not least, you also need to be aware that hunters frequent the area and it pays to wear some bright clothing when tramping in and out to avoid being mistaken for a deer.

HINEMAIAIA RIVER

Located 24km south of Taupo at the base of Hatepe Hill on SH1 is one of the region's most reputable and popular river fisheries, the Hinemaiaia River, which has a longstanding reputation for producing very big rainbow trout. There is no evidence yet that points to these being a special breed of trout, but maybe it is the rich feeding grounds of the Horomatangi Reefs only a few nautical miles away from the mouth that help these fish to grow larger. Big trout also occupy the best position in a pool and perhaps because there is less room in the narrow confines of the river for the trout to hide, more of them get caught. It is hard to say, but either

A curious place for a car – over an hour's walk from the end of Kiko Road on the upper gorge track!

The Hinemaiaia River valley from Hatepe Hill.

way it is an extremely popular river with anglers and when the runs are coming through it can get very busy.

While the upper river has well-defined pools and a reasonably stable riverbed, a well-known and undisputed feature of the river is the abundance of snags, which both anglers and trout seem to be well aware of. Floods dislodge any manuka trees seeking a foothold in the bank-side pumice soils that are a dominant feature in this section. Invariably they are washed through the river system and many of them find their way into the lower river below the main road bridge. Various snag-removal operations take place here from time to time but inevitably they reappear next season, much to the frustration of anglers and to the benefit of the trout.

Accordingly it can be an expensive river to fish and when nymphing it is not uncommon to lose up to 30 flies in a day. When the fishing is hot it is annoying to have to leave the water because you have run out of flies, so be prepared to take more than twice as many as you would expect to use in a day's fishing elsewhere. It is one thing to be a sporting angler but you need to have a sporting chance yourself: at times the odds seem to be firmly stacked in the trout's favour here. A number of successful anglers I know use leader material of 5-7kg, together with the heaviest-gauge hooks available, in an effort to stop fish from running into the snags. Sometimes it works and sometimes it doesn't. Such are the charms of fishing for big, strong trout in snag-infested small rivers.

HINEMAIAIA RIVER

Taupo
Turangi

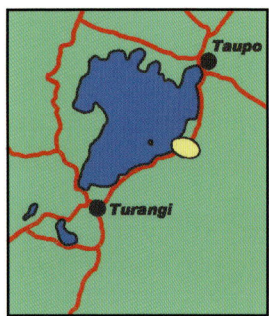

Season: 1 July to 30 June up to winter limit. 1 December to 31 May above winter limit.
Methods: Fly fishing only.
Size / Bag Limit: 45cm minimum / 3 trout.
Anglers' right-of-way: 20m wide on both banks from mouth upstream 4.8km.
Map (1:50,000): 260-U18-Taupo.

N.B. This information is in accordance with the Taupo Fishing Regulations 1984 (incorporating amendments to 30 June 2000).

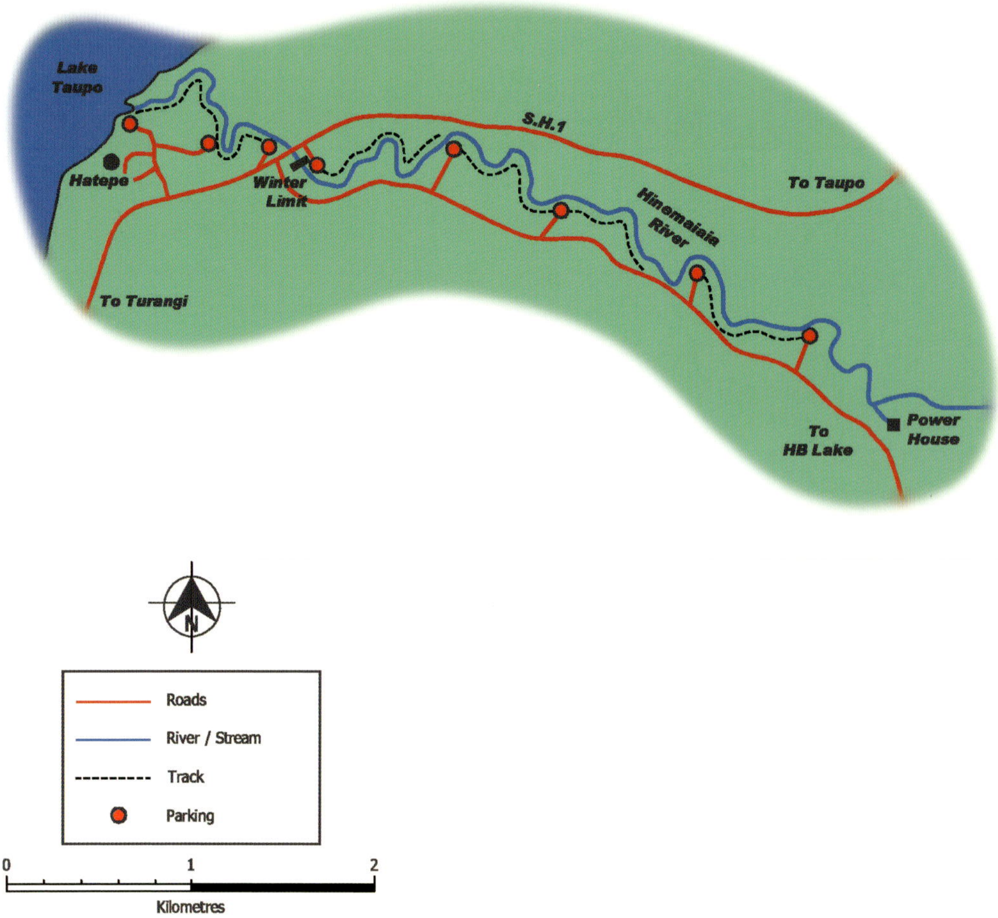
Lake Taupo
Hatepe
Winter Limit
S.H.1
To Taupo
Hinemaiaia River
To Turangi
To HB Lake
Power House
N
Roads
River / Stream
Track
Parking
0
1
2
Kilometres

The Hinemaiaia River is one of a few rivers in the region that bears the effects of hydro-electric generation demands. Migrating trout are blocked by the first of its three dams, which is located less than 5km upstream of the mouth, about 3km above the main road bridge on SH1. Many trout spawn below the dam in the bypass chute and the numbers of fish stacked up here can be amazing. To let the trout spawn in peace there is no fishing for 300m below the powerhouse and a closed season exists above the SH1 bridge from 1 June until 30 November. That leaves a winter season on the river below the bridge to the mouth, a distance of less than 2km.

One of the features of the dams is that they act as a buffer zone during heavy rain. This means the Hinemaiaia is usually the last to colour and can still be fishable for 8-12 hours after the other rivers have flooded. Another is that the daily flow of water fluctuates with generation demands, which are at their greatest around breakfast and dinner time. During the course of a day, whether it has been raining or not, the flows vary between 6m^3/sec and 10m^3/sec. This acts as an artificial fresh that often encourages migrating trout to run up from the lake. The fluctuating water level also means that during low flows the trout will hold in pools below upstream impediments before moving again with the next high flow. Successful anglers find these sorts of fish-holding areas.

The entire fishable length of the Hinemaiaia River is extremely easy to access, with a road leading up the true left and an excellent track system in place. This means anglers can comfortably fish a circuit from any of the car parks and return having seen plenty of the river. The small size of the river and short fishable length belies its strength as a fishery. It produces a hefty run of fish for its limited size and even when taking into account some of the challenges, it is worthy of your efforts.

The extent of the pumice deposits in the region is demonstrated clearly in this steep bank on the Hinemaiaia River.

Lower River (below SH 1) to the Mouth

Getting to the mouth is a simple exercise. Turn into Rereahu Ave, 300 metres south of the main road bridge over the Hinemaiaia, and this takes you down through the baches and holiday homes of the Hatepe settlement to the mouth, where parking is available. The mouth of the Hinemaiaia, like many entering around the lakeshore, is fairly shallow. But it has a good rip that can extend well out into the lake during periods of settled weather and helps keep the trout beyond the reach of most fly anglers. Sometimes, however, strong winds from the south-west bring waves that help to turn the rip and push the flow closer to the shore. When the wind dies down, the mouth fishes well to a slow-sinking line or floating line and sometimes the smelting during summer can be spectacular.

The mouth is very popular with night anglers, too, particularly during March, April and May when the larger rainbows seem to be around in good numbers. Aside from the fishing, the sunsets can be stunning and the view across the vast expanse of the lake towards the western bays is hard to beat.

The lower 2km of river below the SH1 bridge can become overcrowded, particularly from 1 June when the upper river is closed to fishing. The water available is sometimes insufficient to accommodate everyone, especially when good runs are moving into the lower river. To give yourself the best possible chance to catch a trout in this section you need to get to it early during the winter, which is the case on most of the popular parts of the Taupo rivers. By 'early' I mean before first light, which might be too early for some! However, the later you get there the fewer fish you'll catch: it's as simple as that.

The angling access track on the true left bank starts on the downstream side of the SH1 bridge, where a small car park holds three or four cars. You can park here and fish your way towards the mouth or,

Dave Hughes wet-fly fishing the Cliff Pool. Bankside erosion provides plenty of snags for anglers' flies.

alternatively, there is a car park lower down that is accessed from Rereahu Ave. About 400m down turn right into Kahikatoa Lane, then right again into Hinemaiaia Lane and drive to the parking area at the end. From this point you can either walk downstream towards the mouth, or go up to the bridge. The entire walk should take no longer than 10-15 minutes, but there are some good holding areas for running trout in this section – to fish it properly would take two to three hours. The first run inside the mouth can be suitable for wet-fly fishing but nymphing is more effective in the small pockets further up. Sometimes large numbers of fresh-run trout sit in the first few pools and can be caught before anyone else sees them. It is a good place to try when the river is rising or coloured, because the trout can run in large numbers during the day.

Upper River (above SH1)

The upper river is in complete contrast to the lower river in almost every way. You could be mistaken for thinking you were on a different river altogether – but the snags quickly remind you that you're not. It contains about 3km of water before the first dam and some very good fishing is to be had in this stretch. There are many well-defined pools and plenty of good trout-holding water. Nymphing is the usual technique, but further up past the Cliff Pool there are some deep holes and good wet-fly opportunities.

There is easy wading between most of the pools.

The walking track network makes getting to the river in the upper reaches relatively easy. Access to the beginning of the track is from the true right bank, 200m above the bridge. There is parking for about six cars and from here it is an easy morning's fishing. The track follows the river upstream for around 1km before it turns away from the river and goes uphill, back to SH1. Fortunately the river is wadeable at the tail end of most pools, so cross the river where you can and continue up the track on the true left.

If you intend to continue fishing further up it is best to go back to the car, cross the bridge and drive up the road on the true left. Take any of the vehicle tracks leading off to the left, with the exception of the first one. The angler access track is only a few footsteps from the car and it is a relatively easy walk to the pools either up or down the river, which makes for a pleasant day's fishing. Because the river is narrow and confined, it tends to stay well shaded during the day in the upper pools and this can be an advantage when the conditions become low and clear. The trout tend to seek the shelter out of the sun's revealing rays and the shaded areas can fish dramatically better.

Many anglers congregate in the upper section of the river in the last few weeks before closing at the end of May and it can be very busy. This is a good time to fish the lower river, which is virtually devoid of anglers by comparison, and the fishing can be very good.

WAITAHANUI RIVER

Less than 13km south of Taupo on SH1 is the site of one of the most recognised and photographed scenes of the Taupo fishery and possibly anywhere in the world: the famous 'picket fence' of the Waitahanui River mouth. The longstanding nickname was given because of the line of expectant anglers fishing side by side at the mouth, only a stone's throw from the road. Its close proximity to Taupo and the ease of access mean that when the fishing is good there seem to be as many anglers as a picket fence has palings.

While the visible face of the Waitahanui is at the mouth, it is the fishing in the river that is the magnet for most anglers. With most of the flow coming from springs in its headwaters, the Waitahanui is also famed for its crystal-clear water and stable flows, which average about 6-7m³/sec. However, fishing a spring-fed river has both advantages and disadvantages. One advantage is that the river remains relatively clear during substantial rainfall. This is not to say that the river doesn't colour – it does, but some time after the other rivers have come up. It does not usually get the flash floods that the others can be prone to, and because of this it can experience some fairly heavy angling pressure, particularly when the other rivers in the region are high and dirty.

Another advantage is that the minor fluctuation in flow helps to provide a very stable riverbed. This is a welcome rarity in the region and means that the secrets of the river can be learned over a lifetime of angling because the pools remain virtually unchanged year after year. With experience you get to know instinctively where the fish are likely to be and this makes it possible to reduce wasted time and enjoy a better catch rate.

Although the clarity of the water allows for some good stalking, the flipside of this is that it allows the trout to do some spotting of their own. This puts a premium on your stalking techniques and the need for low-visibility tackle if you want to be successful on bright sunny days.

One of the most photographed scenes in trout fishing – part of the world-famous Waitahanui picket fence.

WAITAHANUI RIVER

(incl. Mangamutu Stream)

Season: 1 July to 30 June up to winter limit.
1 December to 31 May above winter limit & Mangamutu Stream.
Methods: Fly fishing only.
Size / Bag Limit: 45cm minimum / 3 trout.
Anglers' right-of-way: 20m wide on both banks from mouth
upstream to source. Mangamutu Stream - 3m wide on both banks
to boundary of Kaingaroa Forest.
Map (1:50,000): 260-U18-Taupo.
*N.B. This information is in accordance with the Taupo Fishing
Regulations 1984 (incorporating amendments to 30 June 2000).*

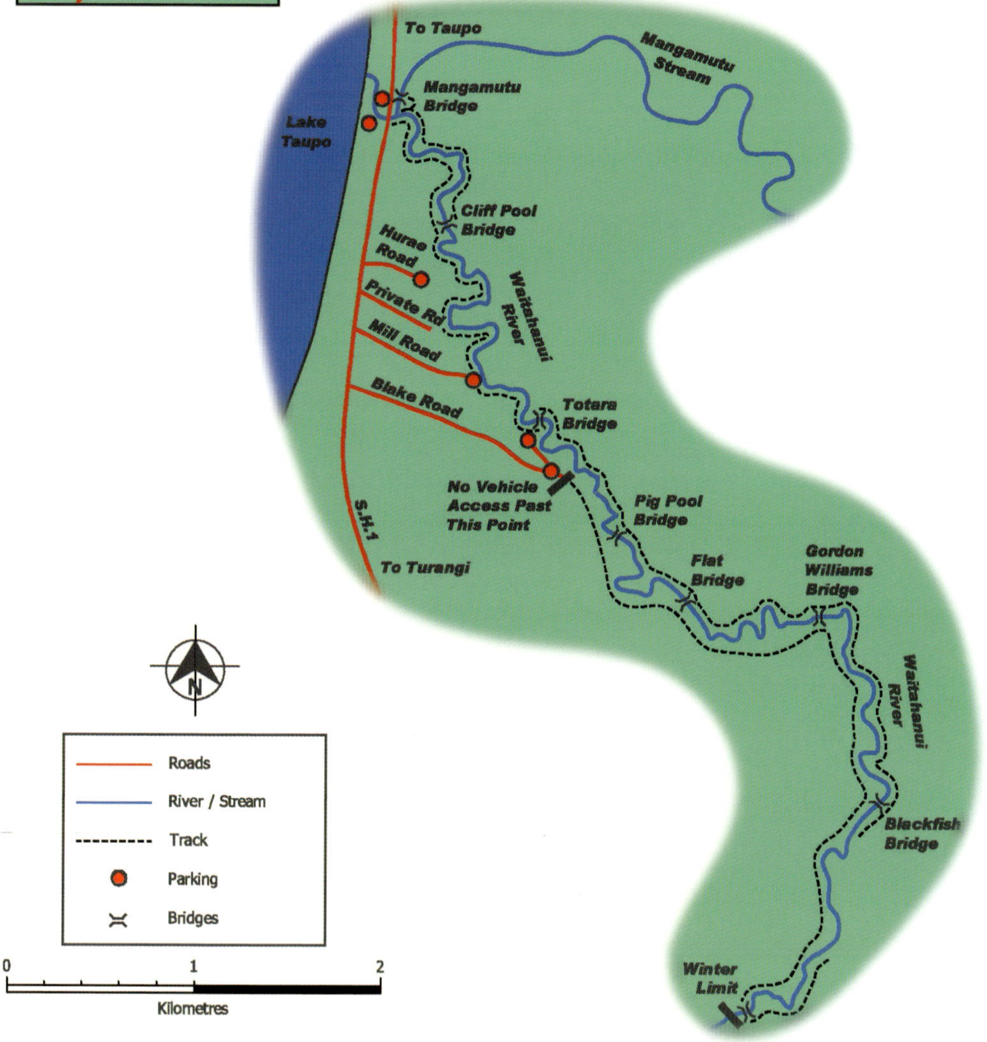

To Taupo

Mangamutu
Stream

Mangamutu
Bridge

Lake
Taupo

Cliff Pool
Bridge

Hurae
Road

Waitahanui
River

Private Rd

Mill Road

Blake Road

Totara
Bridge

No Vehicle
Access Past
This Point

Pig Pool
Bridge

S.H.1

To Turangi

Flat
Bridge

Gordon
Williams
Bridge

Waitahanui
River

Blackfish
Bridge

N

Winter
Limit

——	Roads
——	River / Stream
-----	Track
●	Parking
)(	Bridges

0   1   2

Kilometres

Hooked-up inside the mouth.

Because the river floods infrequently the bankside vegetation is thick and strong, which has encouraged the development of many deep short pools twisting and winding their way down to the lake. Accordingly, wading between pools can be a dangerous undertaking and when a trout is hell-bent on going downstream, following it is not normally an option. On many occasions I have had to give up on a strong fish that has decided to leave the pool, but that's part of the special experience that is the Waitahanui River.

Lower River (below SH1) to the Mouth

The Waitahanui is by far the biggest tributary coming into the northern end of Lake Taupo. Although most of the river has a flow in the 6-7m³/sec range, the total outflow at the mouth is nearer to 9-10m³/sec because of the contribution from the Mangamutu Stream, which joins the main river less than 500 metres up from the mouth. During summer the shallow, wide expanse of Waitahanui Bay becomes very warm and the strong, cool flow of the Waitahanui well out into the lake provides a potent attraction for smelt and trout. In the right conditions, especially following strong west to south-west winds, the rip runs into the lake on a 45° angle. This has the effect of pushing the current well down the beach, sometimes for many hundreds of metres, making it one of the best rips in the region.

From January onwards the mouth has a well-deserved reputation for its night fishing, particularly for trophy brown trout. In overcast and warm conditions, any sort of big black fly retrieved slowly on a floating or sink-tip line cast well away from the main flow can be very successful. Sometimes this could be a long way down the beach but still not far from the shore. Don't wade too far out as the fish can sometimes be in less than 1 metre of water – right at your feet.

The mouth is not just a place to fish in the summer, though. A drop in the barometer and increased flows also attract migrating trout in the winter, and when the lake level is below 356.25m large numbers of fish can congregate here before running the river. At times like this the fishing can be incredible, more so around dusk when large numbers of trout can be caught in a matter of 30 minutes. But just as quickly the action can go deadly quiet and remain that way because the trout have moved into the river en masse.

The next best place to find them is often in The Straight – the shallow 400m section of river below the main road bridge to the mouth. When a significant run of trout has just entered the river there can be 20 anglers or more trying their luck here, and most have a good chance of catching a freshly run trout with either wet fly or nymphing techniques. However, the fish waste no time in getting to the shelter of the deeper pools further upstream and, just like fishing at the mouth, the fun in The Straight may last only a matter of minutes before the fish have moved through.

Anglers wanting to fish at the mouth in the 'picket fence' can park their vehicle on SH1 a few hundred metres north of the main road bridge. From there it is a simple matter of walking through any of the clearings in the bush that lead towards the lake.

Upper River (above SH1)

Hidden by dense vegetation, the Waitahanui River winds its way towards Lake Taupo from the top end of the angling access track at the winter limit pool. It is no more than 5 metres across at its widest and, with no underwater obstructions and stable spring flows, it provides an easy avenue for migrating trout. However, the crystal-clear water, combined with upstream areas of shallow riverbed, help to concentrate trout

The upper river has some superb fish-holding water.

in the safety of the many short, deep pools that are a dominant feature of the river. Both wet-fly and nymphing techniques work well in these locations during the year, and dry or natural flies can be good in the middle and latter part of the summer for the large runs of brown trout making their way slowly upstream.

Access to the river is via an excellent track network put in years ago with the help, funding and foresight of members of the Waitahanui Angling Improvement Association. The track starts on the true left and is easy to walk. If you leave your vehicle at the car parks on SH1, it is possible to walk to the limit pool and back in a day. The river is crossed by a number of footbridges, which take the track up both sides of the river for around 8km. There are many named pools on the river such as **The Parade**, **Totara**, **The Pig**, and **Gordon Williams**, and they are all easily reached from the track. Many little side-tracks veer off in a number of places and it pays to explore these, as some offer good access to areas of nice water that are often overlooked.

Because there is so much water available to both wet-fly and nymphing methods, it can be a nuisance having to constantly change your method to catch the trout. A useful technique some anglers use is to walk up the river nymph fishing all the water suited to that method, while leaving the pools where a sunken lure would be better. On the return journey the pools that were bypassed are covered with a sinking line – this way all the productive water is covered effectively.

In 2001 Blake Road was closed to vehicle access beyond the Totara Bridge turn-off, and this has dramatically lessened the pressure from anglers in this section of the river – a real bonus for those anglers who are prepared to walk. There is a real possibility of excellent fishing and also a good chance that you won't have to share it.

John Cameron in the Totara Bridge Pool.

MANGAMUTU STREAM

The Mangamutu is the major tributary of the Waitahanui and it resembles a miniature version of the main river. After forming from springs back in the foothills of the Kaingaroa Forest, it joins the Waitahanui on the true right at **Delatours Pool**, just above the main road bridge. At first glance the Mangamutu looks insignificant, and although it is less than a fly rod's length wide in most places, its clear spring water flows at about 2-3m³/sec and has a surprisingly good run of trout during the year. Both browns and rainbows use the stream for spawning, but because it has a closed season (open from 1 Dec to 31 May) and no angling access track, most anglers seem to avoid it in preference to the Waitahanui.

During summer many of the big browns that have escaped capture at the mouth run into the Mangamutu, and by exploring the stream where you can, you may see some of these large trout. The low, clear conditions here do not help careless anglers and there is a good chance any fish you do see are likely to have seen you first. With a commando-like approach they will respond to nymphs or a well-presented dry or natural fly from January to March, but the catch rates can make Lake Otamangakau look fantastic.

There are times, though, when the odds are better balanced towards the angler. Although it is spring-fed, the Mangamutu can get a murky tinge during persistent heavy rain, and if this happens during April and May good runs of trout can swim into it, particularly if the Waitahanui is dirty. The colour of the water makes the anglers' lines harder for the fish to see, and fishing can be much more productive.

On one occasion in conditions like this I managed to hook a strong fish 100 metres above the confluence with the Waitahanui. When hooked it turned and made for the main river, and once there it was not content

The Maungamutu and Waitahanui confluence, just above the SH1 bridge.

to stop. Using the extra flow of the river, which was chocolate-coloured following a storm in the back country, the trout bolted under the main road bridge. Having waded under here on numerous occasions I knew it was safe so I followed it around and into The Straight. The trout continued to peel line from my reel and after a bit of a scramble I ended up playing that fish in Lake Taupo, about 500 metres downstream from where it had been hooked. Moments later the line went slack and when I reeled in all I had to show for my efforts was a scale attached to the hook of the Glo Bug. It had obviously been foul-hooked, but the fight was a lot of fun while it lasted. I went back and managed to legally hook and land two fresh-run rainbows, which went some way towards rewarding my previous effort.

WAIKATO RIVER

Lake Taupo has an enormous catchment area and receives inflows of water from over 30 tributaries. This entire contribution leaves via one path – the Waikato River, New Zealand's longest. From the outlet at Taupo its swift, clear blue waters descend quickly into a fairly inaccessible gorge before plunging over the famous Huka Falls less than 5km downstream. The first European settlers recognised the importance of the river well over 100 years ago and built the town of Taupo on the true right bank by the outlet. Back then, paddle-steamers were the main means of access around the lake and the outlet provided a good, natural deepwater anchorage and shelter from the elements. With the introduction of the control gate bridge in 1941, less than 1km from the outlet, and the subsequent raising of the lake level, this area has since been developed into the Taupo boat harbour, where most of the lake's charter boat fleet is moored. Growth in the population of the Taupo borough has been steady since those early years, and today some of its leafy suburbs straddle both sides of the first few kilometres of the river.

With its large and consistent supply from Lake Taupo, the Waikato River is one of New Zealand's most important natural economic assets with large-scale hydro-electric generation at eight dams downstream. Closer to Taupo the river is of significant local economic importance and is the focal point for many tourism-based activities, including bungy jumping, kayaking/canoeing, jet boating, sightseeing, a wildlife park and the world-renowned Huka Lodge. But from an angler's point of view the Waikato River is a virtual paradise. Although the Taupo licence district ends at Huka Falls and a large portion of the river flows through a gorge, there is an enormous population of trout waiting to be caught. Yet, surprisingly, few anglers ever bother with the Waikato, so if there is a place in the Taupo region where you can have a river full of trout to yourself, then this is it.

The Huka Falls have always acted as a natural barrier to upstream-

Taupo Boat Harbour at the Waikato River outlet.

migrating trout, but before the installation of the control gates a huge run of trout from Lake Taupo used this section of river as a highly productive spawning ground. Alan Pye, founder of Huka Lodge, often spoke of the fantastic fishing in this part of the river and the catches of numerous large trout. Although migrating trout do not have access to this section of the river any more, it is still an excellent example of a tailwater fishery. And while the demands for power generation do see wide flow fluctuations during the day, Lake Taupo acts as a buffer zone and protects the river from the worst that the environment can throw at it.

The section down to Huka Falls always runs crystal clear and it never floods like a normal river, which makes it a great place to fish, particularly when the rivers running into Lake Taupo are high and dirty. The relative stability of the riverbed has enabled the trout population to thrive on a reasonably good food supply in the safety of the deep pools in this part of the river. Both rainbow and brown trout are present in huge numbers, and although some of these fish are extremely large, the majority are 35-50cm and weigh 1-1.5kg. With the exception of the section above the control gates bridge, all legal Taupo methods can be used throughout the year, although it is fair to say that there is not a lot of room for a backcast in most places and the preferred method is spinning.

Almost any spinner, lure or fly will take trout in the river, but the key is to make sure you are getting down to the fish in the deep pools. This is achievable when the normal flow is around 100m³/sec, but without adding extra weight it can be difficult when the flow is up to 250m³/sec during peak flow times in the morning, afternoon and evening. In addition, from late January the trout become lethargic during the day, when the flow from the warm upper layer of Lake Taupo begins to exceed 20°C. Then the best time to fish for them is when they are more active, which is either early in the morning or from dusk onwards. Huge hatches of caddis and mayflies occur at dusk and the river can seem to be boiling with rising trout.

Many of the river's best pools are hidden from shore-based anglers and a lightweight boat or canoe is extremely useful. There are numerous places to anchor in the river and fish into some of the otherwise inaccessible pools, or you can get out onto the riverbank on the edge of the gorge and fish some of the best runs in the district. In these places the trout seem to race one another to get at your lures, because in most cases it is the first time any of them have been the target of an angler. The catch rates can be exceptional and when they are, it makes for a very enjoyable experience in a special part of the region.

Outlet to Control Gate Bridge

The section from the lake outlet to the control gates is reserved for fly fishing only, and although fishing is prohibited from the Taupo wharf, further down below the mooring area on the true right there is a good section of riverbank at the motorcamp. There are some enormous brown trout in this area and every summer they get blamed for eating the ducklings, which disappear within a few days of hatching. The definition of natural fly does not extend to a live duckling but I have seen imitation duckling flies designed and developed to catch pike in northern European waters. Perhaps they would work well here too for the big browns.

The boat harbour, early morning.

WAIKATO RIVER

Season: 1 July to 30 June.
Methods: All legal Taupo methods (below S.H.1). Fly fishing only (above S.H.1).
Size / Bag Limit: 35cm minimum / 3 trout (below S.H.1). 45cm minimum / 3 trout (above SH1).
Note: Sections of the river bank are in private ownership therefore an anglers' right-of-way does not exist.
Map (1:50,000): 260-U18-Taupo.

N.B. This information is in accordance with the Taupo Fishing Regulations 1984 (incorporating amendments to 30 June 2000).

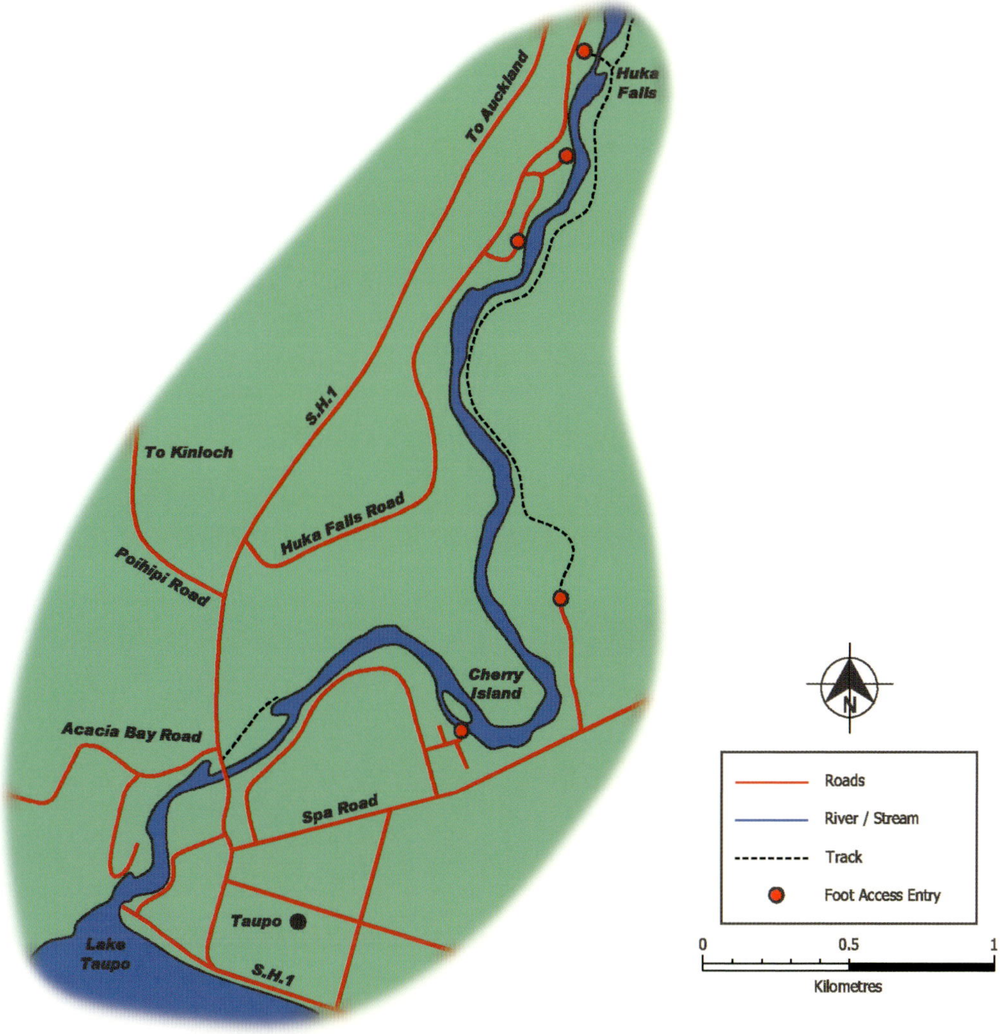

Roads
River / Stream
Track
Foot Access Entry

0   0.5   1

Kilometres

However, fly fishing in this area is a huge challenge and since fishing from a boat is prohibited, it would pay to leave it and fish below the control gates.

Control Gates to Cherry Island

Most of the riverbank is on Taupo District Council reserve land and access is allowed for the general public, but there are few points from which foot anglers can actually get down to the river's edge. The first is on the true left and is reached by a vehicle track starting beside the river on the north side of the control gate bridge. After about 1km the track enters private property but before this, and to the right of the gate, is an area where it is possible to launch a small lightweight craft or canoe from the stopbank. Anglers on foot could enquire at the house for permission to access the riverbank on their property, which is an area of about 400m.

Further down the river the next access point is an area on the true right below Motutahae Island, otherwise known as the Cherry Island Tourist Park. Cherry Island is an animal sanctuary with a café and outdoor eating area from which you can watch people throw themselves off the Taupo bungy site at Hells Gate, less than 300 metres further down. Although fishing is prohibited from the island, there is an area where you can feed wild trout with pellets purchased at the entrance. Naturally there are some very impressive trout around here, and under the cover of darkness many of them drift down the river after the evening release of water from the lake. They can be caught below the island by carefully wading from the river edge and casting a large black spinner or fly where the divided river water joins again. Some of these trout are incredibly strong, and once they are in the powerful main current they can be extremely difficult to land.

There is good fishing around Cherry Island, but fishing is prohibited from the island itself.

To reach Cherry Island take the turn-off signposted from Spa Road in Taupo, near Taupo-Nui-a-Tia College. A car park is adjacent to the island and there is an area where a canoe or small dinghy can be put in.

The Gorge

Below Cherry Island the river enters Hells Gate, a section where the cliffs rise sheer out of the water. Unless you have a boat or canoe the next access to the river is from Huka Falls Road on the true left. The road is signposted 1km north of Taupo on SH1 and gives access to the Reids Farm Reserve where about 500 metres of river bank is available. Free camping is allowed here by the Taupo District Council, which makes it a very popular area during summer.

Further down Huka Falls Road there is a car park area adjacent to the Huka Falls, and on the far side of the footbridge the walking track to Spa Park begins. This gives access to about 750 metres of the true right bank of the river to a point below and across from Huka Lodge, before it climbs above the river.

The section of the Waikato River in the Taupo Fishing District is a big and powerful stretch of water. If you intend to fish it from a boat, be aware that below Reids Farm it is safe for canoes only. Beyond this point the river runs down past Huka Lodge, with one final area on the true left where canoeists must get out. Go any further down and you will find yourself in the channel leading to Huka Falls. A ride over them is likely to be fatal.

Fishing from the river's edge requires some care too, because the river can rise rapidly and trap you before you know it. Choose where you are going to wade carefully, and always have an exit route planned. If you treat the river with the respect it deserves, you can enjoy a special fishing experience in complete safety.

Reids Farm is one of the easiest parts of the river to get to.

Always take care in deciding where to wade and be sure to have an exit option if the need arises. If you treat the river with the respect it deserves, you can enjoy a special fishing experience in complete safety.

TOKAANU TAILRACE

The Tongariro Power Development scheme culminates in generation at the Tokaanu Power Station before the water is carried to Lake Taupo through the Tokaanu Tailrace, a man-made channel. The tailrace is around 3km long, 7m deep and 80m wide and after flowing under the SH41 bridge less than 500 metres downstream of the powerhouse, it makes a left turn behind the volcanic dome of Maunganamu (Tokaanu Hill) before entering Lake Taupo in Tokaanu Bay. This is not one of the most stunningly beautiful places you'll ever fish but it is a good example of a tailwater fishery with some reasonable fishing on offer all year round. All legal Taupo methods are allowed below the main road bridge, although above the bridge to within 110 metres of the powerhouse it is fly fishing only.

The smelt runs in the tailrace are legendary, and from about January onwards these little fish swim up from Lake Taupo in huge numbers. Because the smelt are confined in such a small area, the trout can get at them easily with little energy expenditure and their growth rates can be exceptional. In the 1980s this was one of the places that 4.5kg (10lb) and larger rainbows were often caught at night, and sometimes during the day. Today some huge rainbows are still caught, and there are plenty of browns here too.

During the summer the tailrace offers very good dry-fly and natural-fly fishing, as well as smelting. Trout can be caught in the winter too, when good numbers of trout run up from the lake in an attempt to spawn. Use either wet-fly or nymphing techniques or spinners cast from

The Tokaanu Tailrace: not the prettiest place in the region, but the fishing is not too bad.

Casting is difficult when you are standing on the steep and scrubby bank. A lightweight boat put in above the bridge solves this problem.

the bank. At this time of the year it is rare to see another angler on the tailrace and you could end up with the whole area to yourself.

A bonus of the tailrace fishery is that it is legal to fish from an anchored boat. This makes it much easier to cast to trout without the problem of a restricted backcast caused by the banks of the canal. The only boat ramp is at the Tokaanu Marina near the entrance to Lake Taupo, and while this gives access to the lower tailrace it is impossible to get a craft under the SH41 bridge because of the Tokaanu Stream aqueduct.

The tailrace tends to fish best when there is a current to push the trout to the edge and within the reach of shore-bound anglers. The main flows are during peak generating periods, which normally coincide with morning and evening meal times. Depending on reservoir levels, generation can last for up to three hours at a time, with the flow rates increasing from $30m^3$/sec to $70m^3$/sec or more. (See page 66 for how to find out power generation times at the Tokaanu Power Station.)

The Tokaanu Hole

The Tokaanu Hole is effectively the mouth of the tailrace and a popular fishing location for boat anglers. It enters an area in Tokaanu Bay where the shelf quickly drops away down to about 20 metres, which has the effect of concentrating smelt and trout in substantial numbers, especially when the Tokaanu station is generating. While it can fish consistently throughout the year, it does so particularly well in the summer when the water from the TPD is of a much lower temperature than the rest of the lake.

In the past, fly-fishing techniques were the best way to take trout at The Hole. Now many anglers are reaping the benefits of jigging techniques and this method is quickly becoming the preferred way to catch trout. If you are fly fishing, a fast-sinking line or shooting head will be

TOKAANU TAILRACE

Taupo
Turangi

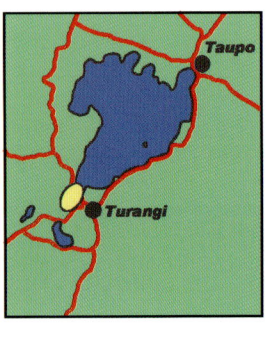

Season: 1 July to 30 June.
Methods: All legal Taupo methods below S.H.41. Fly fishing only above S.H.41.
Size / Bag Limit: 45cm minimum / 3 trout.
Anglers' right-of-way: 20m wide on either side of the canal.
Map (1:50,000): 260-T19-Tongariro.

N.B. This information is in accordance with the Taupo Fishing Regulations 1984 (incorporating amendments to 30 June 2000).

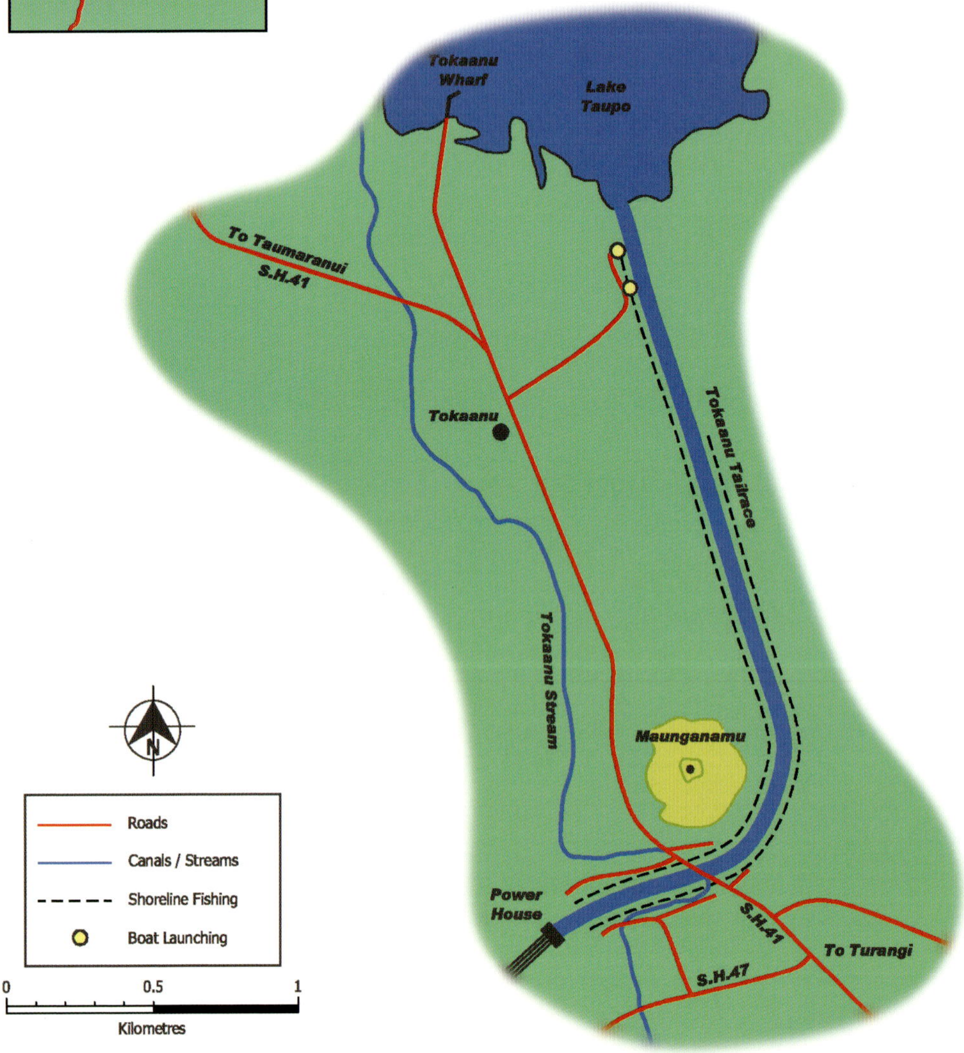

Tokaanu Wharf
Lake Taupo
To Taumaranui
S.H.41
Tokaanu
Tokaanu Tailrace
Tokaanu Stream
Maunganamu
Power House
S.H.41
To Turangi
S.H.47
N
Roads
Canals / Streams
Shoreline Fishing
Boat Launching
0
0.5
1
Kilometres

necessary to reach the bottom from an anchored boat, a slow process that can take more than two minutes depending on the sink rate of the line. Floating flies such as the Booby and Heave 'n' Leave are well suited to this kind of fishing.

Lower Tailrace (below SH41)

The old Tokaanu Steamer Wharf was once a popular fishing spot, but it is now derelict and a new facility built inside the tailrace has effectively replaced it. There are two double boat ramps, a small marina and a wharf. Fishing from the marina wharf is a popular activity, particularly in the summer when the smelt are running. It is a great place to take young anglers or those who have not fly fished before. Nothing is easier than being able to let the current take out a smelt imitation and then leave it swinging there for a hungry trout to snatch. I once saw a boy, who looked no older than seven, hook and land a 5.3kg (11¾lb) brown trout, as well as two fine rainbows, using exactly that technique.

The extensive weed beds in this area restrict the depth of fishable water and a floating or intermediate fly line is recommended. Alternatively, a float bubble with two flies is productive if you are using a spinning rod.

Access to the marina is from SH41 at Tokaanu: take the signposted turn-off opposite the Shell petrol station.

Further up the tailrace at the SH41 bridge there are gravel vehicle tracks on both sides. Foot access is limited to a small part of the steep embankment immediately below the bridge, although with some bush-bashing or careful edge wading it is possible to get access to water for a considerable distance below the bridge. The steep, overgrown bank doesn't lend itself to fly fishing but when the trout are smelting a small, silver, smelt-like spinner with a smelt fly tied above the trace is very effective. Cast across towards the far bank and retrieve the line slowly

The historic Tokaanu Wharf is undergoing restoration, which is due for completion in 2005.

Fishing from the limit fence in the upper tailrace.

back towards your position. It does not pay to stand in one place for long, so try in one area for five minutes before moving down or up 50 metres and repeating. That way you are able to cover all the water and, with luck, find the fish.

Upper Tailrace (above SH41)

The section from above the SH41 bridge to the powerhouse attracts most of the angling effort in the tailrace. Access to the true right is by taking the turn-off for National Park at the junction of SH41 and SH47, then the signposted turn for the Tokaanu Power Station on the right about 300 metres past the intersection. From this short road, you can get to the whole section up to the limit marker 110 metres below the powerhouse. Park by the security fence and walk through the bushes down to the water's edge.

Access to the lower part is by turning hard to the right after crossing the Tokaanu Stream Bridge on the power station road. Once past the bushes, a vehicle track leads down to the concrete causeway of the flood overflow for the Tokaanu Stream. The flood overflow has an abutment jutting into the tailrace below the waterline, which provides a stable and safe ledge to wade along. It is much easier to fly fish here because you can make a reasonable backcast. On the true left a vehicle track leads from above the western end of the SH41 bridge to just below the power-house, but a lack of backcasting room on this side makes it much less attractive.

There are no launching ramps above the SH41 bridge, so anglers wanting to fish from a boat have to carry their vessel down to the water level from the road. There are not many places that are suitable for this, but just past the Tokaanu Stream Bridge on the power station road is a grass area on the right from where a track leads down to the water.

Vessels must be anchored while fishing. Be mindful of the limit sign 110 metres below the powerhouse. It is there for your protection because when the station starts generating you would not want to be any closer to it. The use of a fast-sinking line is required during generating times, otherwise an intermediate line is the preferred option.

THE WESTERN CATCHMENT

KURATAU RIVER

The Kuratau River is one of the largest contributors of water to Lake Taupo, but the flows vary widely during the day, from $5m^3$/sec to $11m^3$/sec because of the demands of the hydro-electric scheme that dammed the upper reaches above the falls. As usual, the peak requirement for energy is normally in the morning and the evening. Generation usually lasts for about two hours during the peak and, as with the Hinemaiaia, the periods of high flow act as an artificial fresh that encourages migrating trout to run. The fluctuating water level also means that during low flows the trout will hold in pools before moving again with the next high flow.

On the face of it, the Kuratau appears to offer little in the way of opportunities for river fly fishing, but there is some good water available in wilderness surroundings. Below the falls at the Champagne Pool the river has about 5km of water available from 1 December to 31 May and it is some of the most scenic and untouched water in the district. In the gorge there are boulder-strewn pools one after the other offering some of the best remote fishing to be found anywhere. But most of it is not easy to get to and you need to make an effort to reach the best water. It can be done, though, and while the lower 1.5km is accessible only by boat, there is foot access to the rest of it. With some good planning a very productive day can be had.

The water from Lake Kuratau is slightly tea-coloured, but when the station is not generating the main source of water in the lower river comes from the spring at the Champagne Pool, which means incredibly clear water in very low conditions. Naturally, the migrating trout are very aware of their surroundings and any aerial cast is seen long before it reaches them. Overcast or rainy conditions are the angler's best friend, as is the fast water at the head of the pools in the gorge section. Here the odds are more evenly distributed between trout and angler. Normal eastern tributary techniques work well but the fishing is best using floating-line methods such as nymphing, dry and natural fly.

The Kuratau River was one of the first two tributaries where brown trout were liberated in the southern end of the lake in the late 1800s. The other was the Whareroa Stream, less than 1.5km north in Te Hape Bay. Today both tributaries continue to see some of the region's most significant runs of brown trout, in addition to sizeable rainbow migrations during the year.

The Mouth

The Kuratau enters Lake Taupo in a small, but very shallow bay covering an area of about 0.5km². Extensive wading is not necessary because it doesn't really get any deeper, no matter how far you go out. If you stand back on the lake edge the trout will come in very close, especially during the summer when they are smelting. The first 100 metres inside the mouth are worth prospecting in late summer and early autumn, when large brown trout can be a regular catch after dark.

Access to the mouth is at the end of Hiuhiuawai Street, which is effectively the continuation of Omori Road, which is signposted from SH41. A small parking area and public toilet is conveniently located only a stone's throw from the mouth.

Kuratau Spit

The Kuratau Spit is about 700 metres south-east of the Kuratau River mouth and the deep drop-off here is less than 30 metres from the shore. There is a 300m fly-fishing-only restriction around the spit, but fly fishing from an anchored boat is also permitted. A boat is not necessary for good fishing, though, because the drop-off is easily waded when the lake level is below 356.5m. When it is, the best time to fish at the spit is after a strong blow from the north, north-east or east has subsided. This has the effect of pushing the current from the Kuratau River along the beach for many hundreds of metres and over the drop-off into the lake at the spit. Because the bay is also shallow, the cool flow helps to concentrate the trout and keep them from entering the bay in large numbers until after dark.

Be prepared to share the Kuratau Spit with fly anglers fishing from an anchored boat.

KURATAU RIVER

(below Lake Kuratau)

Season: 1 December to 31 May.
Methods: Fly Fishing only.
Size / Bag Limit: 45cm minimum / 3 trout.
Anglers' right-of-way: 20m wide on both banks from the mouth upstream 16km from Lake Taupo (incl. Lake Kuratau).
Map (1:50,000): 260-T18-Kuratau.

N.B. This information is in accordance with the Taupo Fishing Regulations 1984 (incorporating amendments to 30 June 2000).

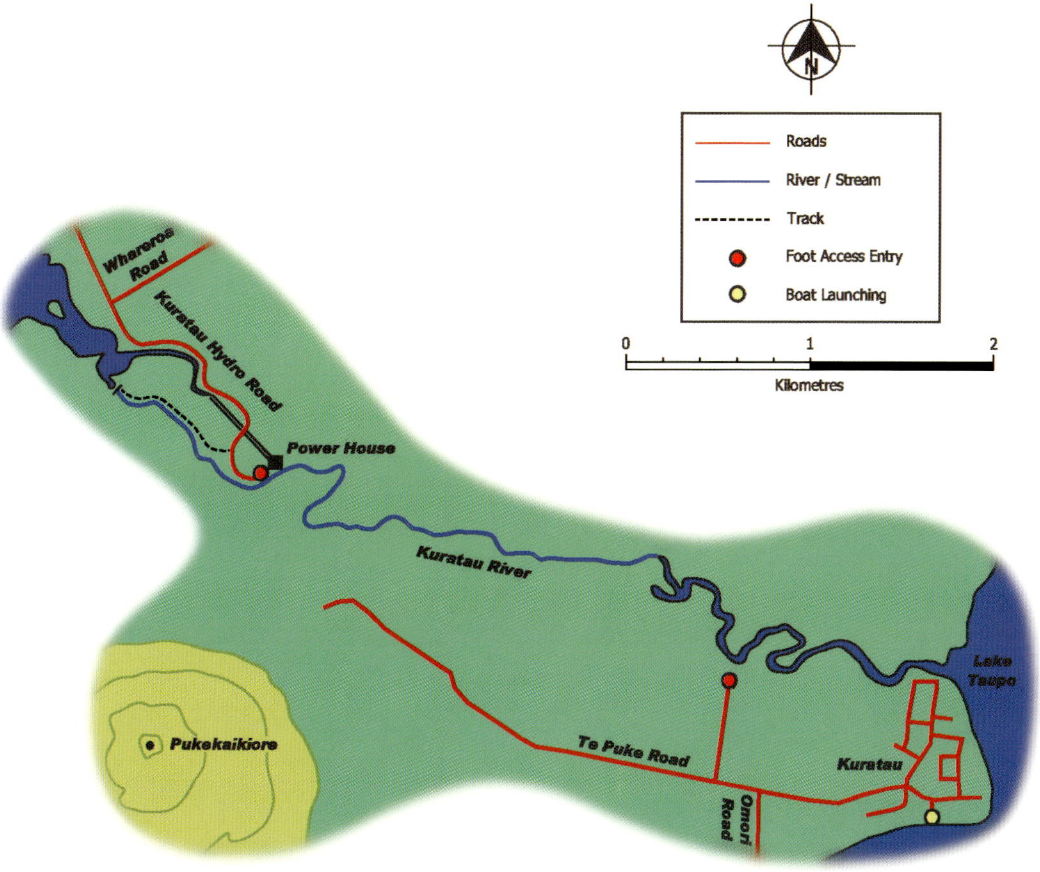

	Legend
Roads	
River / Stream	
Track	
Foot Access Entry	
Boat Launching	

0   1   2
Kilometres

Whareroa Road

Kuratau Hydro Road

Power House

Kuratau River

Pukekaikiore

Te Puke Road

Omori Road

Kuratau

Lake Taupo

During smelting the spit can be very productive, especially once the lake has stratified, but its proximity to the mouth of the river means that recovering fish can make up a high percentage of the catch.

Access to the spit is by turning right onto Waipapa Sreet in Kuratau and following it to the end. On the way you will pass Pihanga Street, which is where the boat ramp and jetty are located.

Lower Reaches

The lower reaches are slow-moving and contain some deep holes. Foot access is non-existent, but the use of a small dinghy or canoe opens up a lot of water. Trout hide in this section during the day, and along with plenty of rainbows there are also good numbers of large browns available during summer. Once the sun is on the water a cicada or beetle can persuade an unsuspecting fish to rise, although the best chance is to locate the trout and come back with a wet fly after dark when they are less wary. The river becomes much shallower in the vicinity of the Kuratau River Park, about 1.5km from the mouth. From here you can walk to the Champagne Pool, a distance of about 4km.

Once in the gorge there is a whole day's fishing for a couple of anglers. Note, however, that the gorge is accessible on foot only when the station is not generating – I recommend you enquire about generation times to avoid being caught by rising river levels. But don't just rely on that: the weather can change in a matter of hours and bring a flood, so check the weather forecast too. It is a good idea to go with a mate and leave a vehicle at each end, saving a long journey back. Park one at the powerhouse and the other at the Kuratau River Park, which is located off Omori Road and then Te Puke Road in Kuratau.

A dominant feature of the gorge is the presence of large, black, slime-covered rocks and boulders, which make for particularly tricky wading. Be very careful and use a wading staff – three 'legs' are better than two and could help prevent a wetting. Be prepared to encounter other challenges in your upstream quest. The going can get a little hairy, to say the least, and some improvisation is required to negotiate the Stag Antlers Pool, at the downstream end of the gorge. Don't give up, though, because once you are past this point the river has numerous well-defined pools and riffles offering some of the region's finest spring creek fishing.

Below the Falls (from Kuratau Hydro Road)

The section below Lake Kuratau is easy to get to. Using the directions previously mentioned in Chapter Seven for Lake Kuratau (see page 111), continue down the gravel road for about 2km to the powerhouse. From here there are some good opportunities for anglers on foot. When the flows are low during the day it is possible to wade downstream and fish some good pools. After crossing above the confluence with the tailrace

The Kuratau has large runs of fish during the season and good fishing in the gorge.

and the spring-fed section, an undefined but useable track bypasses the first major pool and helps to give access to the river below. Crossing the river over to the small island opens up a good pool that can be fished with a wet fly or nymphs. In May, before the winter closing, there can be some huge runs of trout, waiting in this pool until generation starts again before moving further up. Closer to the powerhouse, and when the station is not generating, trout can be caught in the concrete tail-race. Although it is less than a rod-length wide, dozens of trout run up in a vain attempt to get further upstream. They will take a nymph dangled literally below your feet, but landing them can be difficult.

In the section from the powerhouse to the falls at the Champagne Pool there can be a large number of running trout present, which are easily spotted in the crystal-clear waters from the spring. Wading is very rough going, but safe, and it allows nearly 1km of water to be fished. Alternatively, you can gain access to the river from the gravel road about 400m up from the powerhouse, where there is a clearing with room to park a vehicle. The part of the river directly below is the upstream limit for trout in normal spring flows. They can congregate here in large numbers until high levels in Lake Kuratau and heavy rain cause the water to spill over the falls, enabling them to get through to the Champagne Pool. When the spilling stops, hundreds of trout can be seen circling with nowhere to go – one of the most incredible sights in the district.

Spawning trout below the Champagne Pool. Water clarity in this section allows over 20 metres of underwater visibility.

The track to the Champagne Pool starts about 50 metres further up the gravel road from the clearing, but it can be easy to miss. It leads up the true left for about 500 metres.

Above Lake Kuratau

The river above Lake Kuratau has a sizeable catchment, including a significant contribution from the Parakaumanga Stream, which drains the volcanic domes of Kakaramea and Kuharua between Tokaanu and Lake

Otamangakau. The rest comes from Pureora Forest Park in the vicinity of the Waituhi Saddle on SH41, and in heavy rain the flows can increase dramatically in a short space of time. Nearer the lake the Mangaongoki Stream joins the river and it too has its catchment in the Pureora, albeit a slightly different part. These two tributaries and their many small contributors form the main spawning areas for the trout of Lake Kuratau and help to ensure the ongoing productivity of the wild trout fishery. Both have resident fish throughout the open season. Although numbers are high, size is not, but they make for some fun fishing regardless. All legal methods can be used, but fly fishing, especially with dry or natural flies during the summer, is by far the most successful.

Most of the riverbank of both tributaries is overgrown and almost inaccessible on foot, but a canoe put in at the lake gives easy access to a large section of the upper Kuratau for some distance upstream of the SH41 bridge. The Mangaongoki Stream is best accessed by going in at the SH32 bridge and walking in the streambed.

WHANGANUI STREAM

Nestled in the southernmost corner of the western bays is the beautiful Whanganui Bay, accessible to the public only by boat. A small population of Maori inhabit the bay and there are also several leasehold baches along the eastern end. It is a popular summertime destination. Apart from the exceptional angling, Whanganui also has a reputation with rock climbers, who come to tackle the large volcanic ignimbrite bluff at the eastern end of the beach.

Whanganui's remoteness is one of its best assets, helping to keep angling pressure low. With no camping possible in the bay, you'll need to be prepared either to go home in the dark or spend the night on board at the safe anchorage in neighbouring Cherry Bay.

Whanganui regular John Stephenson fishes the rip.

Some of the region's best fishing is to be had at the mouth of the Whanganui Stream, which enters near the middle of the bay. The stream has a good flow of about 2-3m^3/sec and in lake levels below 356.25m it has a good, safe, wadeable rip well out into the shallow bay.

You can only get to Whanganui Bay by boat. It's worth the effort.

The Mouth

Smelting begins earlier at Whanganui Bay than anywhere else in the lake – usually from as early as October and it often continues through to April. At times the whole length of the beach (1.5km) seems to be alive with trout and the fishing can be very exciting, both day and night. Most fishing is done with floating or intermediate lines, but when the mouth is backed up during high lake levels it is sometimes only 3 metres wide and can have a strong current. Be prepared to use a fast-sinking line right inside the mouth when it is like this.

Lower River to the Falls

The walk to the falls is fairly rugged going and a canoe can come in handy. When lake levels are above 356.75m it can be difficult to wade the first 300 metres of the river so it is best to paddle up and get out when it becomes shallower.

With such a small flow there is not much stopping trout from running unimpeded to the falls, but in May they dig redds from just above the mouth and can be all along the stream. In clear conditions you'll need to be careful with your approach and stalk every trout. The streambank is fairly overgrown, which limits casting and suits an in-stream approach best. The size of the water lends itself to floating-line techniques such as dry and natural fly during the summer, and at the falls pool the trout respond readily to a nymph.

The season for fly-fishing anglers runs from 1 December to 31 May.

Anglers' Right-of-Way

20 metres on both banks from the mouth upstream for 1.6km.

WAIHAHA RIVER

Lying between a break in the towering ignimbrite cliffs dominating the heart of the western bays is one of the most famous locations on Lake Taupo – Waihaha. Huge norfolk pines line the remote 1km-long white sandy beach; with no road access they act as a symbol to direct visitors arriving from across the lake by boat. This is the home of the Waihaha Maori, who have a marae in the bay, and it is also the destination for many holidaymakers, who come to the private baches or to camp just back from the lake edge. There are plenty of day-trippers too, and during the summer holidays dozens of pleasure craft venture across from Kinloch and Taupo for a day of water sports, barbecues and fun in the sun.

The attraction for most anglers is the famous fishing at the mouth of the Waihaha River in the northern corner of the bay. In summer the smelting can be very special, as can the night fishing, which is some of the best on offer anywhere in Lake Taupo. However, its popularity as a fishing location is limited to the mouth and bay only. The river has a large run of both brown and rainbow trout during the year and a generous flow from Pureora Forest Park, normally 4-6m³/sec. But getting up the river is not possible without some form of vessel. It is deep and confined within overgrown banks for most of its 5km of fishable water up to Tieke Falls.

The journey to the falls is through one of the most spectacular wilderness areas in the region. The scenery of the Waihaha Valley could well be straight out of a *Jurassic Park* movie, with ancient forest and towering cliffs. This is one of the 'must do' experiences of a lifetime and worth the hassle.

The Mouth

Although Waihaha is remote, a boat is not the only way to get to it. A short but steep walking track allows anglers access from the end of Waihaha Road, which turns off SH32. It takes only about 15 minutes going down, but getting back to the car at the end of the day is not so easy, especially with waders and a limit bag of trout to carry. The effort is worth it, though!

The flow from the river spills over a shallow sandbar, which creates a relatively wide, diffuse rip. It can accommodate a large number of anglers and when the conditions are right most have a good chance at the fish, using floating or intermediate lines. If the mouth is fishing poorly or is too full of anglers, there is also a good opportunity to fish from the rocks at Whakatonga Point, north of the mouth. A short walk around

> It is possible to camp at Waihaha by booking and paying a small fee for one of the 10 camp sites available, but do it early because the sites fill quickly, especially on long weekends and during the summer holidays. To book a camp site or arrange a permit for walking access from Waihaha Rd contact David Chrystall on (07) 347-8515 or alternatively write to The Secretary, Waihaha Maori Lands Trust, P.O.Box 1067, Rotorua.

Waihaha is one of the most popular destinations in the western bays – for day-trippers as well as anglers.

WAIHAHA RIVER

Taupo
Turangi

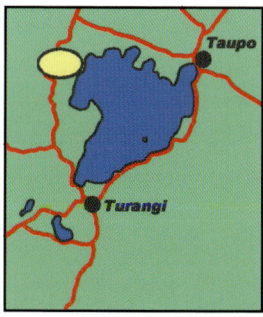

Season: 1 December to 31 May.
Methods: Fly fishing only.
Size / Bag Limit: 45cm minimum / 3 trout.
Anglers' right-of-way: 20m wide on both banks for 9.6km from the mouth upstream to the boundary of Pureora State Forest Park. Above this public access is unrestricted.
Map (1:50,000): 260-T18-Kuratau.

N.B. This information is in accordance with the Taupo Fishing Regulations 1984 (incorporating amendments to 30 June 2000).

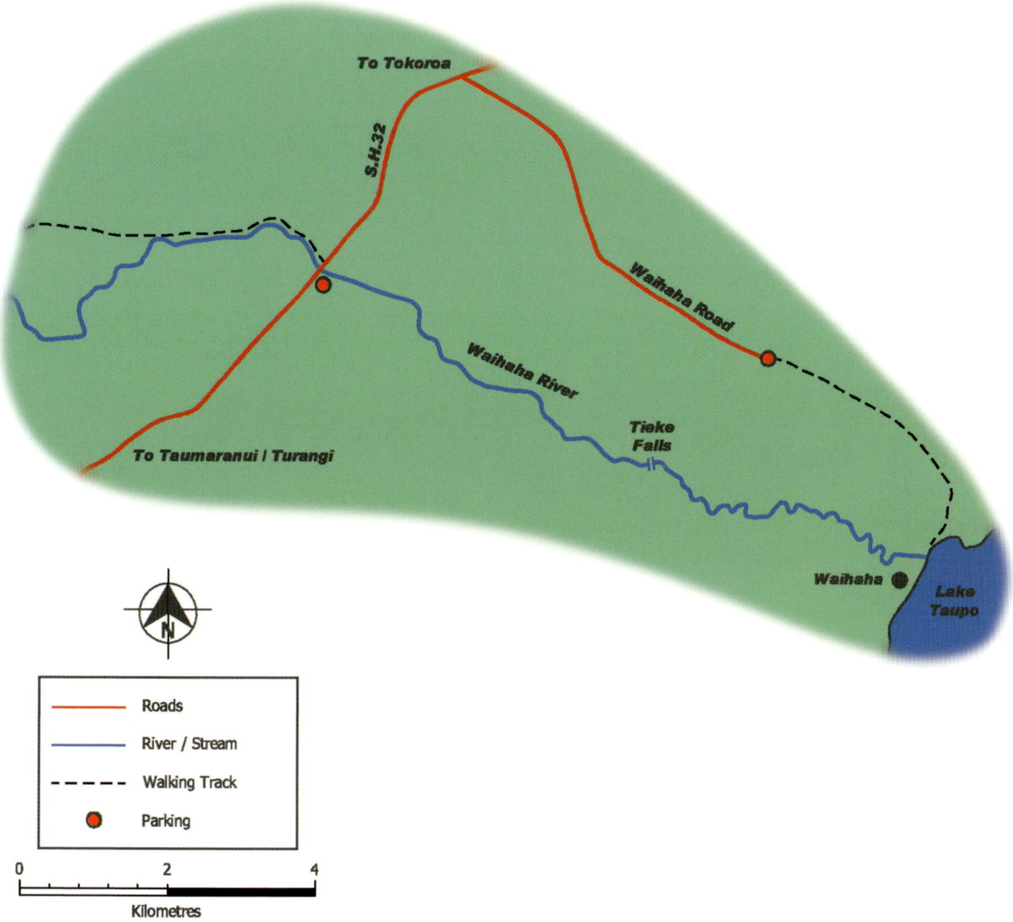

To Tokoroa
S.H.32
Waihaha Road
Waihaha River
Tieke Falls
To Taumaranui / Turangi
Waihaha
Lake Taupo
N
Roads
River / Stream
Walking Track
Parking
0
2
4
Kilometres

the shore past the orange and brown bach leads to the start of the track to the point. Take this for a few hundred metres before turning down to the right through a small opening.

The point has two advantages for anglers, especially at night. First, the flow from the river usually comes directly past the point and many dozens of trout can congregate in the water here because it is slightly deeper than at the mouth. Second, the deep drop-off is less than 50 metres away, which means you are able to target the early movements of prime trout after dusk, before they reach the anglers at the mouth. While fly fishing with an ultra-fast-sinking line can be productive, it also fishes well to spinning methods. This is only allowed if the point is beyond the 300m fly-fishing-only limit, which depends on where the mouth enters the lake. Sometimes the point is beyond it and other times it's not, so that's a judgement call you'll need to make for yourself.

Don't forget the fishing along the beach, especially in summer. It is a wide, shallow bay and with a pair of polarised glasses and a keen eye it is relatively easy to spot trout herding the smelt into the shallows. It pays to walk up and down the beach, watching for the tell-tale signs of splashing fish. When the water is really warm the trout will spend only a few minutes at a time chasing smelt before heading to the comfort of the thermocline or the river mouth area.

Lower River to Tieke Falls

The incomparable Tieke Falls.

When the lake level is above 356.75m it is possible to get a 6m fibreglass boat inside the mouth, but below 356.25m only smaller aluminium boats

can make it by being pulled over the sandbar. Once inside the mouth the trip upstream to Tieke Falls is about 5km – 45 minutes under power. Many big submerged logs infest the riverbed and I recommend having a spotter on the bow with an oar, in case you need to avoid an obstruction in a hurry. Please observe the 5-knot speed restriction. Alternatively, a canoe is a good option – it takes about an hour and a half of paddling to reach the falls. It is certainly not an easy trip and the river takes some skill to fish properly, but the trip is worth it for the amazing scenery alone. Like a number of the Taupo tributaries that require some effort to get to, you should enjoy some good fishing with little competition. Fly fishing is the only method permitted in this section, either from an anchored boat or from the bank in places.

The lower reaches are very deep and slow moving: ideal habitat for huge brown trout. During the summer months a large number of these begin the journey upstream to spawn, and from January to March they outnumber rainbows. They can be caught using dry-fly techniques, most easily during the day with cicada patterns or a natural fly. At night in the summer a properly swum mouse on a floating line at dusk and early evening is a definite winner, as is a slowly retrieved large dark Woolly Bugger pattern. It is a good idea to identify a stretch of snag-free water during the day and come back after dark to fish the Woolly Bugger with a slow-sinking line. Make sure you have a good spotlight to help for the trip back.

Phymatosorus diversifolius, the hound's tongue fern, is a common inhabitant of the New Zealand bush.

The final 2km to the falls contains excellent spawning gravels and in early winter you can see redds of previously spawned trout. Much of the last section is easily wadeable and most of the fishing is to sighted trout. During May there are large numbers present, especially in the pool below the falls, and they can be caught using normal winter nymphing techniques.

Above Tieke Falls (from SH32)

Most of the upper river above the falls lies in Pureora Forest Park. It is characterised by a very slow flow contained by steep vegetated banks and inaccessible gorges. There is plenty of habitat for resident rainbow and brown trout, which average about 1kg, but limited opportunities to catch them. A well-maintained DOC track leads up the true left of the river for a considerable distance, but there are only four sizeable pools you can get to within 1½ hours from the SH32 bridge. Very few anglers ever bother to walk that far to catch a trout, but fly fishing with nymphs, dry and natural flies can be productive with very careful spotting and stalking. If nothing else, the walk is spectacular, with moss-covered trees, an abundance of ferns lining the track, and fantastic views of the gorge.

The long walk is worth it for the scenery alone.

It is accessible only by boat, but the Waihora river mouth is a top brown trout night-fishing spot.

WAIHORA STREAM

Surrounded by plunging ignimbrite cliffs, tucked away in the remote far northern corner of the western bays, Waihora is even more isolated than Waihaha and accessible only by boat. The stream has a flow rate of 1-2m^3/sec and is the last of the tributaries to receive its source from the Pureora Forest Park. Entering the lake in a typically shallow part of the bay at the north end, the mouth is renowned for its brown trout and during the summer a few dedicated anglers come by boat to fish it at night. The smelting can be exceptional, mainly because few anglers ever bother to fish it. During late summer and early autumn, numerous brown trout move into the lower reaches and are joined by good numbers of rainbows. They can't go far, though, because a waterfall about 2.5km upstream prevents any further progress.

The Mouth

The bay is very exposed to southerly winds and it can get extraordinarily rough in less than half an hour. If the lake level is above 356.75m it is usually possible to get a 5-6m vessel inside the mouth, depending on flow through the stream. Here a safe anchorage offers protection from the swells. Most of the bay is less than 2 metres deep and is best fished with a floating or intermediate fly line.

If you are considering fishing the mouth at night then a good option is to camp at one of the two sites available. Camping is free but you need to ring Sam Andrews on (07) 333-9331 to book.

Lower River (below SH32)

The Waihora is open for fly fishing all the way to its source in the Pureora Forest Park between 1 December and 31 May. The section below the falls is narrow and overgrown with vegetation, which makes it difficult to cast a line to the trout available. However, the streambed is wadeable and although bush-bashing is required in many places, with perseverance there are opportunities for some good fishing if you walk up from the mouth. Above the falls, the section below SH32 is bordered by farmland and although there is a resident population of small wild rainbow and brown trout up to 1kg, there are significant difficulties in casting a line to them because of overhanging trees.

They are there all right, but they are not easy to catch. A 4kg-plus brown in the lower Waihora.

Upper River (above SH32)

About 4km south of the Tihoi turn-off on SH32 there is signposted access to the Pureora Forest Park and the headwaters near the Waihora Lagoon. The river is very small in this part and the numbers of trout vary from season to season.

Anglers' Right-of-Way

A right-of-way exists for foot anglers 20 metres wide on both banks from the mouth upstream for 9.6km to the vicinity of SH32 at the border with Pureora Forest Park. In the park access for the general public is unrestricted.

10. Keeping, Eating or Releasing Your Catch

IS IT WORTHY OF THE TABLE?

The Lake Taupo fishery is often referred to as a harvest fishery, meaning that it can sustain a substantial harvest of trout while still maintaining good fish stocks. Lake Taupo trout make excellent eating and can be as good as the salmon available in supermarkets. But like any fish, not all trout are good to eat and obviously it is hard to tell for sure without killing them to find out. Thankfully there are some ways of taking the guesswork out of the decision.

During the early 1990s I lived and worked in the South Island and among my customers was an aquaculture company operating a salmon farm in the Marlborough Sounds. Another made the pellets fed to the fish while they are in their sea cages. It interested me to know how caged salmon got the bright orange flesh they are so famous for, when they were unable to get it from the ocean environment. The answer was fairly simple. The pellets fed to them have the naturally occurring red carotenoid pigment called astaxanthin added to the ingredients during the manufacturing process. Wild salmon get the same pigment from a diet that includes krill and other goodies in the food chain.

A number of studies overseas have shown that this pigment is beneficial to the health of salmonids such as rainbow and brown trout. It may help improve immunity to disease and has strong antioxidant properties along with many other physiological benefits. In Lake Taupo, most healthy maiden trout get their distinctive orange flesh from eating smelt, which in turn have eaten zooplankton – the source of astaxanthin. Koura (freshwater crayfish) also have this pigment

Poles apart. The coloured-up fish is unlikely to make good eating.

and while it doesn't show while the animal is alive, when it is consumed by trout the digestive process releases these pigments into the flesh. Normally only trout over 2.5kg actually prey on these large crustaceans, but nevertheless a trout that has had a diet solely of koura has very impressive, almost red flesh and a swollen backside.

When a trout begins reaching sexual maturity, the distinctive bright silver body colouration typical of a lake fish disappears and is replaced by very dark colours in preparation for spawning. On the inside some major changes are happening too. The high stress trout frequently encounter in the rivers and streams, along with being away from the rich food supply in the lake, takes a major toll on the body. Instead of being firm to touch, the flesh becomes soft and watery, and the orange colouration quickly fades to become very pale, almost white. These fish may still look big and fat but it is often best to return them to the water because they generally do not taste very good. After spawning the survivors, battered and hungry, are particularly easy to catch but they are exceptionally poor in every way. Given the chance of reaching the lake and its high-quality food supply, these trout will often regain condition to be almost indistinguishable to the untrained eye from a maiden fish. But more importantly, they will make a good prize for another angler next year.

If it is a fish to eat that you want, keep only those with small heads, large fat bodies with firm, bright silver flanks, and with no sign of the fin or tail damage commonly seen in previously spawned trout. That does not mean that well-recovered fish do not taste good; but given the choice for a table fish, a maiden trout is a better bet. Even taking all that into account, expect to be fooled by one in every 10 of the fish you take.

A maiden trout (above) and a kelt. Spawning can be exceptionally tough on some trout.

ABOVE: A spike to the brain kills the fish instantly.

ABOVE RIGHT: Bleed the fish immediately.

THE IKE JIME METHOD

One of the best methods of dispatching your catch is to use the Japanese method of ike jime. Basically it involves inserting a metal spike or other suitable instrument into the head of the fish a thumb's width behind the eye, which destroys the brain. The fish dies instantly but the heart will still pump for some minutes. Sever the gills through the neck area, three rows from the back, and hold the fish head-down in the water for a couple of minutes until no more blood is left. The gills turn a light red colour when done, and then you should immediately chill the fish to preserve the eating quality of the flesh. There is nothing wrong with leaving the fish whole for a few hours, but if you are going to be out all day or overnight it pays to gut and clean the fish properly by removing the stomach contents and head.

THE POLYSTYRENE FISH BIN

Once your catch is properly killed, keeping it cool is the most important step in bringing the best eating qualities of a prime Taupo trout to the table. Unfortunately, it is at this stage that most good trout suffer from poor storage by the angler. This can be easily avoided by using an inexpensive polystyrene fish bin and adding a few bags of ice (readily available from any service station or store). It will keep a number of trout icy cool for many hours and also doubles as a handy fridge/freezer once a couple of large, frozen soft-drink bottles of water are added to the ice. The combination lasts for up to three days and is especially handy when camping in the western bays. Of course lugging around a large bin filled with ice is impractical in some situations, such as in the tributaries, but you can leave the bin in the car so that the fish can be put on ice the moment you return.

Cool water in the tributaries acts as an effective temporary fridge.

Temperatures in the tributaries vary during the year from a chilly 7°C to about 15°C so the water can make a reasonably effective temporary fridge to store trout in while you continue to fish. Simply thread a lanyard or any available natural material like flax through the mouth and out the gills to form a loop, then secure it to something solid in the water. A small rock pool serves the purpose well, as does a quiet piece of water on the edge of the river or stream, but still secure the fish properly – they have a habit of floating away otherwise! As long as the sun is kept off the fish, they will usually keep perfectly for some hours.

A common practice among lake-edge anglers is to bury a fish in the sand so that rats and stoats don't eat it first. However, sand contains many bacteria and can also get very warm, especially in the summer. The combination further speeds up the decaying process and can literally spoil a fish in a few hours – even after dark. If you must bury the fish, put it in a plastic bag to keep the moisture in and the extra bacteria out. Without a suitable place to store a fish properly it may be better to release it, because chances are that it won't be worth eating.

CLEANING AND FILLETING

Preparing a trout for eating or storage is a simple task, but they are slippery when wet and can be difficult to control on a plastic or wooden board. Placing a few sheets of newspaper on the board first helps to hold the fish in place.

Cleaning a trout

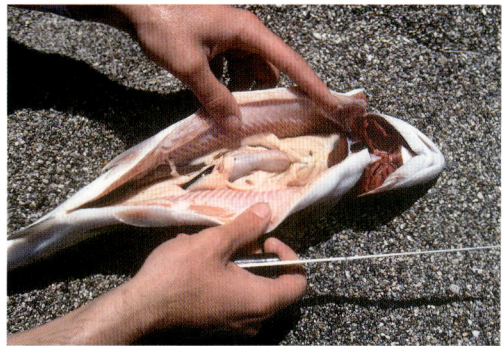

1. Insert the knife at the vent and cut up the middle of the belly.

2. Remove the contents of the gut cavity.

3. Cut a line either side of the dark kidney material that lies against the backbone. Scrape out using a teaspoon or similar implement.
4. Wash off all blood and other unwanted material and pat dry using an old clean towel or cloth.
5. Cut off the head, or if leaving the head on always remove the gills.

To fillet a trout after cleaning it

1. Lay the fish with the gut cavity towards you. Starting at the head end, cut along the backbone, keeping the blade flat to the spine all the way to the tail.

2. Turn the fish over and do the other side.
3. Remove the ribcage and fins.
4. Remove pin bones using culinary tweezers.

The cleaned fish or fillets can be frozen in a sealed, thick plastic bag for up to two months. Remove all excess air or preferably have the fish vacuum-packed.

If you are cleaning a fish while you are on the lake or tributaries ensure that all the offal is retained and disposed of properly in a rubbish bin or composter. Do your part to keep the environment pleasant for the next person to visit.

COOKING AND SMOKING TROUT
Smoking

Most home smoking is done using any of the well-made hot smokers sold in most sports stores. These usually smoke one fish at a time and produce a good result in 20 to 30 minutes. The same thing can be done using hot coals and wood chips with a kettle-style barbecue. With hot smoking, the fish can be put straight into the smoker within minutes of being caught.

Cold smoking does not actually cook the fish and is a more involved process, usually done by commercial smokehouses and some butchers. A mixture of brown sugar and salt (50/50) or a brine is used to cure the flesh overnight. The fish is then flavoured by a slow and cool smoking process that can take up to eight hours. Once vacuum-packed, cold-smoked trout can be kept for three to four months – though it never lasts that long in our house! In the Taupo region there are several licensed operators who will smoke your trout for you, using either hot or cold smoking methods.

I smoke trout by employing a mixture of hot and cold smoking. First I coat the fillets liberally with a brown sugar and salt mix that is a little bit sweeter than normal. I leave the fillets chilled and covered for a few hours until the mix has dissolved. The residue is washed off and the

fillets dried with paper towels. Next, I light the coals in the kettle barbecue and leave them to ash over – a process that usually takes about 30 minutes. Meanwhile the fillets are drying further, before the smoking starts. I apply a simple glaze made from manuka honey and a few squeezes of lemon juice, then sprinkle on cracked pepper and rock salt. I use only four coals per side of the barbecue and pile on plenty of hickory wood chunks that have been pre-soaked in water. The combination keeps the heat down to make the smoking/cooking process last about two hours. When it is done, the pin bones can be easily removed using the sharp edge of a knife or a pair of culinary tweezers.

LEFT: Sprinkle the sugar and salt mix over the fillets and set aside.

RIGHT: The final result. Delicious!

SMOKED TROUT PATÉ

This simple recipe is always well received by guests and makes excellent hors d'oeuvres when served on crusty bread or crackers.

Ingredients
Two hot or cold smoked fillets from a medium-sized 1.7kg trout
250gm each sour cream and cream cheese
2 tablespoons lemon juice
1 teaspoon each freshly ground pepper and salt

Method
Combine all ingredients (leaving aside a small amount of one fillet) in a food processor and blend for about 30 seconds or until the mixture has an even colour. Pulse in some crumbled chunks of the leftover fillet, place in a bowl and set in the refrigerator for an hour.

CAJUN-GLAZED TROUT KEBABS

Summers at Lake Taupo are keenly anticipated in our family. Not only is the fishing more sociable because most of it is done from the boat, but the high-quality trout caught with deeper methods such as downrigger trolling and jigging are excellent to eat. Of the many ways trout can be prepared and cooked, this is one of my favourites. It is especially suitable for larger trout (above 2.5kg) because the thicker fillets make bigger cubes, which are ideal for making chunky kebabs.

Ingredients
1kg trout fillets (with pin bones removed)
1 cup couscous
Sesame seeds for garnish

Glaze
¼ cup each brown sugar, runny honey, soy
 sauce and oyster sauce
2 tablespoons lemon juice
2 teaspoons Cajun spice mix

Salad
10 quartered vine tomatoes
3 cups rocket leaves or mixed-leaf salad
150gm cubed feta cheese
1 large avocado, stoned, peeled and sliced

Salad Dressing
¼ cup extra virgin olive oil
2 tablespoons balsamic vinegar
3 teaspoons lemon juice
Freshly ground pepper and salt

Method
Bring all glaze ingredients to the boil in a small saucepan, then simmer for about 10 minutes or until the mixture thickens. Set the glaze aside for an hour, allowing it to cool and the Cajun spices to release more flavour. Cut the thickest part of the fillet into 3-4cm cubes and push onto 250mm-long kebab skewers. Liberally baste the kebabs with glaze and leave in the refrigerator for 30 minutes. Baste again just prior to cooking under a hot pre-heated grill for 6-7 minutes, turning them after 3-4 minutes. When they're done, apply the last of the glaze and sprinkle with sesame seeds for added effect.

While the kebabs are absorbing the glaze in the refrigerator prepare the salad by placing all the ingredients in a bowl. Make the couscous according to the packet instructions and set aside. Drizzle the dressing on the salad and toss to ensure an even coating. Serve the kebabs on a bed of couscous – and enjoy!

Note: With the widespread popularity of salmon today, there are many good recipes available that suit the excellent eating qualities of a prime Taupo trout. Simply substitute trout for salmon in the ingredient list and follow the directions. Look for recipes in specialist fish cookbooks or try your local supermarket – they often have give-away salmon recipes at the fish counter.

TROPHY TROUT: KEEPING A FISH FOR MOUNTING

Every season trophy fish reaching the magical imperial measure 'double-figure' of 10lb (4.5kg) are taken in the Taupo fishery. In Lake Taupo and its tributaries brown trout reach this mark more often than rainbows, and even though they are outnumbered by about 9 to 1 in the overall population, they virtually own the trophy fish status. Fortunately the staggering numbers of trout in Lake Taupo mean the fishery can sustain a harvest of these enormous fish without any noticeable effect on the angling experience. By comparison, Lake Otamangakau contains just a few dozen trophy-sized trout in a good year, of which most are rainbows, and removing only a few of these can have a detrimental effect on the population of large trout.

For many anglers, catching a trophy trout would be a dream come true, and in the region that dream becomes a reality for dozens of anglers every year. While releasing a large trout after taking a photo can give an immense amount of satisfaction, you may want to have a particularly fine fish mounted. The results of a well-mounted trout look superb, but whatever the skill of the taxidermist, they can only work with what you give them. If you happen to catch a dream fish and wish to have a lasting, tangible reminder of it, there are a few simple steps to ensure that it reaches a taxidermist in the best possible condition for mounting.

WHAT TO DO WITH YOUR TROPHY FISH

Living in Taupo and specialising in trout taxidermy, Richard Abraham has won awards at international and world championship taxidermy competitions. He offers the following advice.

Richard Abraham adds the finishing touches to a 5.4kg trophy rainbow.

1. **Kill the fish immediately, preferably using an ike spike, but do not bleed or gut it.**

2. **Choose the best side of the fish (with no scarring or scale loss) and keep this facing upwards because it will become the show side.**

3. **Do not cover the fish with a damp cloth or towel, because this causes white staining on the skin.**

4. **Keep the fish cool and out of direct sunlight to help set the natural colours in the skin.**

5. **If you cannot get the fish to a taxidermist immediately, place it on a board and freeze it.**

6. **Once the fish is fully frozen, place it carefully in a plastic bag. Keeping it chilled at all times, deliver the fish promptly to the taxidermist.**

Finally, I have some advice on entrusting a taxidermist with your prize fish: if you're unsure of their abilities, ask to see some of their recent work before you give the go-ahead. The job can only be done once, so it pays to choose very carefully.

CATCH AND RELEASE

In the days of ten and eight-bag limits during the 1970s and 80s it was common for anglers to take home every fish caught, regardless of quality, and fill up a deep freeze with them. Inevitably many fish weren't eaten soon enough, developed freezer burn and were thrown out, fed to the cat or buried in the garden. Fortunately, with a daily limit of three fish, such large-scale waste rarely occurs today. Anglers tend to be more selective about the quality of the fish they take home and it is common to release unwanted fish, especially when the fishing is hot.

Releasing a trout is often a very rewarding experience, but some care is needed in handling the fish to ensure that it has the best chance of survival. The trout's gills are made up of tiny filaments, much like small pine needles, and they are easily damaged if you handle the fish around the gills. Keeping it out of the water for any length of time, following the stress of being played and handled, will dramatically reduce the trout's blood oxygen levels, which increases the time it takes to recover and affects its subsequent survival. The following are a few simple, well-proven, catch-and-release guidelines.

Catch and release is an important management tool of the wild trout fishery.

River/stream and lake edge

1. Land the fish quickly, always use a net, and keep the fish in the water if possible. If the fish must be handled, always wet your hands before touching the protective slime coating.
2. Carefully position the fish upside down (this reduces the struggling) and use a pair of needle-nose pliers to remove the hook.
3. Invert the net to release the fish.

Boat

1. Bring the fish alongside.
2. Hold the trace and use a pair of needle-nose pliers to remove the hook.

Note: If you are taking a photograph, ensure that the fish is kept in the water while the camera is being prepared.

11. Protecting the Resource: Conservation and Other Issues

MANAGING THE RESOURCE TOGETHER

The Taupo fishery is probably one of the most heavily managed fresh water regions in New Zealand, recognising its national and international significance as a premier wild trout fishery. While DOC conducts the day-to-day management of the fishery under sections of the Maori Land Amendment and Maori Land Claims Adjustment Act 1926 and Conservation Act 1987, anglers have a large part to play in how the fishery is managed for their benefit.

Most of the regular consultation between anglers and fishery managers is through the Taupo Fishery Advisory Committee. The committee has nine members representing various groups that have a direct interest in the management of the fishery, which include regional angling clubs, those who make a living from the lake, Fish & Game NZ, Ngati Tuwharetoa, DOC and a national fishing interests representative.

Exercise your democratic right and have a say through the appropriate representative on any issue concerning the current or future management of the fishery. The current contact details and a list of the representatives of the Taupo Fishery Advisory Committee are available at DOC, Turangi.

DOC FISHERY SURVEYS

As part of prudent fishery management, a variety of surveys are carried out by DOC fishery staff during the year to gauge current and future angling success, both on the lake and in the tributaries. The most visible

Fishery ranger Dave Hart interviewing anglers on Lake Taupo. Always carry your licence when fishing.

What a beauty! Fishery ranger Brian Taylor prepares to measure and weigh a prime rainbow hen at the Te Whaiau trap upstream of Lake Otamangakau.

of these are 'on the spot' angler surveys that are routinely conducted by DOC fishery rangers. Typically they ask a variety of questions, and will ask to see your current Taupo fishing licence. Any fish you have are weighed and measured and details of the method/s used, along with the number of hours spent fishing, are recorded. These interviews are generally very brief, most lasting only a few minutes. Please be courteous and helpful when talking with the fishery ranger, as the information you provide helps in the ongoing management of the fishery.

Various other studies are undertaken throughout the year to monitor the state of the fishery, none of which directly involve anglers. Drift-dive surveys are done during the winter on the main tributaries, counting the numbers of trout making spawning migrations, while fish traps on three spawning tributaries enable a fairly accurate count of the numbers getting to the spawning grounds. These are located at the Waipa Stream on the Tongariro, and on the Te Whaiau and Waipa streams, upstream of Lake Otamangakau. After the major spawning runs, fishery staff count the numbers of juveniles in sections of the tributaries, gaining a further indication of the spawning success for the season.

Measurements of trout numbers deep in Lake Taupo are done by a thorough acoustic survey using a special depth sounder, and manual counting in the shallows is done using underwater scooters – usually in November or December each year. These surveys help determine the number, size and location of trout in the lake and can give a good indication as to the likely season ahead: for angling success and spawning runs in the tributaries.

REPORTING ILLEGAL ACTIVITIES

Taupo is a truly self-sustaining wild trout fishery, so the success of any given year in terms of the numbers and condition of trout fluctuates as

The regulations are designed to ensure the sustainability of the wild trout fishery.

Mother Nature sees fit. The fishery is tightly managed to ensure that angling success remains as constant as possible from one year to the next, but the process can be severely undermined by the illegal taking or poaching of trout. Although it is impossible to eliminate poaching completely, the fishery's world-class reputation depends on vigilance. DOC spends considerable resources in the area of surveillance of the fishery, compliance and enforcement of the regulations and prosecuting offenders.

People who take part in illegal activities come from all walks of life and while we often think of poaching as something done with nets and spears, some anglers also break the rules. All infringements of the regulations have the potential to reduce the enjoyment of other anglers, but by far the worst include continuing to fish after catching and killing a limit of trout, taking an undersized or foul-hooked fish, and fishing between midnight and 5am. These activities increase the total harvest, which means that the number of trout available for other anglers could diminish – a situation nobody wants.

Information about illegal activities is generally only of use if reported immediately so that staff from DOC have a chance of apprehending the offenders. They can be contacted during office hours on (07) 386-8607, or after hours call 0800 362-468 (0800 DOC HOT) for the duty officer. You can also assist by taking details of suspected offenders, such as what they look like, how many there are and what is happening that makes you suspicious. Other things to note are any vehicles or boats involved, including type, colour and registration numbers where applicable. Anglers with cellphones should enter the numbers above into the memory function so that contact with DOC can be made immediately.

Be aware that approaching suspected offenders yourself may not help the situation and you could face being confronted by people who have a strong desire to remain anonymous. Alerting suspected offenders to your presence could also scare them off and mean that they continue to do damage to the resource elsewhere. Leaving suspected offenders undisturbed usually gives DOC staff a better opportunity to speak to them there and then, and establish whether any law/s are being broken. If an offence is being or has been committed, fishery rangers have a number of powers, including the ability to seize and confiscate property, which may include fishing equipment, vehicles and boats. Penalties for breaches of the regulations can be severe and may include prosecution, fines, forfeiture of personal property, criminal conviction and in the worst cases a jail term.

DOC's staff can't be everywhere all the time. Typically they focus on known poaching hot spots but they also conduct random stings and covert operations at various locations around the district. However, all anglers can take an active role in helping to protect the fishing by being aware of the regulations and reporting those who appear to be ignoring them.

ANGLERS' LORE

Anglers' lore (also called angling etiquette) is a simple set of guidelines for generally agreed good behaviour when fishing. It is not strictly applied, but when you have to share water with others, deviation from it can and will upset other anglers. When the fishing is hot and anglers are in abundance there are times when some people forget their manners. In my experience this is usually an oversight brought on by eagerness or anticipation rather than a blatant disregard for others. It pays to alert the 'unaware' angler to your presence and if possible ask their intentions.

Calm, respectful dialogue often eases any ill-feeling between the parties and is the preferred option if an enjoyable fishing experience is what you were looking forward to.

Good manners make fishing alongside other anglers more enjoyable.

In the Tributaries

1. Always enter a pool behind any angler already fishing. Should you be joined in a pool by another angler it is your duty to keep moving and give everyone a fair go at the fish. A good rule of thumb is to take a step for every one to five casts, depending on the method and the number of anglers in line. Once at the end of the pool simply move to the back of the line and start again.

2. Hogging a position is the fastest way to upset other anglers.

3. 'Shoehorning' yourself into an already congested pool is a sure way to discourage other anglers from taking their step, which means you may not get a turn at the best water.

4. If the pool is full of anglers, wait on the bank or move on to another less crowded location.

5. When an angler hooks a fish leave them plenty of room to play and land it. Don't rush in and take their place in the line while they are away landing the fish!

6. It is common to share a pool with anglers using a technique different from yours and at some stage you will cross paths in the pool, so exercise patience and talk with the other angler about who will do what when the time comes.

At the Mouths

1. The start of the line is usually at the 'rip', which is where the river or stream water meets the lake. Depending on the conditions there could be two lines of anglers coming from the centre of the rip, one either side. Unless there is a large gap between people in the line, your starting point is behind the person furthest from the rip. If in doubt, ask the angler either side of the position you intend to take if it is OK with them.

Be prepared to share popular spots.

2. When an angler near you indicates they have a fish on, immediately wind in your line to avoid a tangle.
3. At night, don't shine lights or torches towards the lake because light on the water can alert the trout to your presence. Turn your back to the lake before switching on.
4. It is not common to move your position as you do in the tributaries because the fish are normally on a beat and there is a reasonable chance that you will have as much opportunity as the next angler to get into them. However, people do leave, so if a gap appears, and it suits, close up the ranks.

On the Lake
1. When harling or trolling, cutting in front of another boat usually results in tangled lines. In particular beware of boats using lead or wire lines, which could be 100 metres or more behind the boat.
2. Don't force the other boat on a head-on bearing to turn in to the shallow water and snag the anglers' lines. Instead make a turn out into the lake and return to the fishing zone when the other vessel is clear.
3. Ensure you stay well clear of the 300m fly-fishing-only radius that is in place around most river and stream mouths. A white marker pole coloured with black and yellow rings usually indicates these. Make yourself familiar with the exceptions on your licence.
4. Remember the regulations regarding proper navigation lighting of your vessel. It is an offence to be on the lake before sunrise or after sunset without the correct navigation lights being shown. The fines are instant and can be very heavy, not to mention the obvious danger you place yourself and others in.
5. When travelling at speed, keep well clear of other boat users. Nobody enjoys rolling through someone else's wake, especially when it is completely avoidable on such a large lake.

Knowledge of the collision regulations is essential – especially when you are in congested parts of the lake.

JOIN A CLUB
There are several angling organisations in the Taupo region that have the common goal of fostering and promoting fishing opportunities for members. All anglers are encouraged to become involved and take an interest in the fishery, and one of the easiest ways to do that is by joining a club.

Tongariro and Lake Taupo Anglers Club (TALTAC)
TALTAC was formed from the amalgamation of two of the region's oldest angling clubs and today it is the largest fishing club in the area, with an active membership of around 600 anglers. The club boasts a range of facilities that financial members are able to use for a small fee, including

Contact
The Secretary/Manager
P.O. Box 149, Turangi
E-mail: taltac@xtra.co.nz

a large anglers' lodge providing accommodation, a modern kitchen, a fish cleaning/smoking room, a clubhouse, hot showers and a drying room. All this, and the lodge is located less than 500 metres from the Major Jones Pool on the Tongariro River – yet another good reason to become a member. TALTAC has a representative on the Taupo Fishery Advisory Committee.

Taupo Fishing Club

The Taupo fishing club began nearly 30 years ago and had some very well-known angler/author founding members, such as Keith Draper, O.S. (Budge) Hintz, John Parsons, Gary Kemsley and Peter Gould. Of those original members, Keith and Budge have passed away and others have left the region, but the club still retains an active membership, along with a seat on the Taupo Fishery Advisory Committee. The club meets informally every Friday evening throughout the year, at its clubrooms in the AC Baths Reserve (off Spa Rd) in Taupo, starting at around 5.30pm.

> **Contact**
> **The Secretary**
> P.O. Box 910, Taupo
> E-mail: r.rountree@xtra.co.nz

Waitahanui Angling Improvement Association

The Waitahanui Angling Improvement Association has a long history with the Waitahanui River. Many years ago they had a major part to play in building the anglers' walkway and many of the footbridges crossing the river. One of their members, local Waitahanui identity the late John Johnson, started twice-yearly rubbish clean-ups of the riverbanks nearly 20 years ago and they continue today. The association went into recess briefly, but has recently become active again. It currently has a representative on the Taupo Fishery Advisory Committee.

> **Contact**
> **The Secretary**
> 7a Waimarie St
> St Heliers, Auckland

Motuoapa Fishing and Boating Association Inc

As one of the region's largest clubs, this is also one of the most active. The Arataha Street clubrooms in the heart of Motuoapa have shower facilities and a bar licence and serve as a base for many organised events during the year, including a two-day fishing competition held over Wellington Anniversary weekend in January every year.

> **Contact**
> **The Secretary**
> P.O. Box 205
> Turangi

THE TONGARIRO NATIONAL TROUT CENTRE

The Tongariro National Trout Centre is on the banks of the Tongariro River, less than 2km south of Turangi on SH1. Run by DOC in association with the Tongariro National Trout Centre Society (TNTCS), it is an interesting place to visit, particularly for first-time visitors to the region, and provides a unique insight into the functions of the Taupo trout fishery. Through the grounds flows an important spawning tributary of the Tongariro, the Waihukahuka (Hatchery) Stream, which features a working fish-trap and an underground viewing chamber where trout can be seen in their natural environment. There is also a hatchery and rearing

Rainbow trout seen from the viewing chamber in the Waihukahuka Stream.

The children's fishing pond at the Tongariro National Trout Centre is always popular.

facility, a children's fishing pond and a new visitor centre (a must see) featuring a range of informative displays. It is open from 10am to 3pm daily and admission is free.

The Trout Centre is a busy place and one of the most popular DOC visitor centres in New Zealand. It is especially popular with school children, some of whom get their first taste of trout fishing during the organised fishing days held regularly at the children's fishing pond. Adult volunteers help children to catch their first trout using a fly rod, and a valuable part of the experience is receiving tuition in fly fishing. During the open days up to 180 children aged between six and fourteen line up to fish. All equipment is supplied and the only other requirement is a current Taupo fishing licence, which can be bought there on the day. Advance bookings for the fishing days are essential. Phone the DOC Turangi office on (07) 386-8607 for details of the next open day.

Operating the Trout Centre is a costly exercise, though, and it is jointly funded by DOC and the Tongariro National Trout Centre Society. The society's main means of revenue-gathering is by fundraising, which helps fund ongoing development for the benefit of visitors. Anglers and visitors can make a valuable contribution by becoming members of the Tongariro National Trout Centre Society or by making a donation.

Membership forms and details for donations can be obtained by writing to:
Tongariro National Trout Centre
**   Society**
P.O. Box 73
Turangi
www.troutcentre.org.nz

FISHING CONTESTS

Three multi-day fishing contests are held in the Lake Taupo basin each year. The first of these is the Motuoapa Fishing and Boating Association's two-day tournament held over Wellington Anniversary weekend in late January every year. It is for boat fishing only and confined to Lake Taupo, but it has a sizeable turnout and plenty of good prizes.

Next is the Lake Taupo International Trout Fishing Tournament, usually held around the third weekend of April every year. It has a wide

The family looks on in anticipation while Dad's fish is weighed in.

appeal, with sections for children, men, women and teams, and categories, including fly, spin and boat fishing based on Lake Taupo and its tributaries.

Later in the year, usually during the third weekend of August, is the Kinloch Fishing Competition. This has a more limited focus, fishing the lake only, either by boat or from the shore, with similar categories and sections as the International.

These events are highly social occasions that are a lot of fun. Year after year many regulars come to 'compete' when really it is just another excuse to go fishing. On top of their social aspect, these events provide valuable information to DOC for the management of the fishery. All competitor information is logged, along with the vital statistics of each trout caught and the method of capture. When combined with the other regular surveys and information gathering, these tournaments help to provide a better picture of the state of the fishery.

With limited numbers of anglers allowed to compete in these events, they usually fill very quickly and it pays to get in early. For the Motuoapa competition, the contact details are in the club section. The Lake Taupo International has an informative tournament website at **www.taupotroutfishingtournament.org.nz** with online entry forms and all the relevant details, including past years' contest statistics.

Details and information about the Kinloch competition can be obtained by writing to:

The Secretary
Kinloch Fishing Competition
  Committee
P.O. Box 879
Taupo

SUMMER ANGLING SEMINARS

DOC holds free summer boat fishing seminars at various holiday locations around the lake in late December and early January. Typically they are held in well-known public outdoors venues near the lake edge, usually reserves, which makes finding them easy. Bookings are not required, so just turn up at one that suits you. These are an excellent opportunity to learn some of the keys to successful boat fishing in Lake Taupo, regardless of the method, from the highly experienced DOC fishery staff. It was after attending one of these some years ago (brought about by my continual poor results) that a light went on in my head, sparking a radical improvement in my fishing success on the lake.

Fishery staff present a wide variety of information on all the popular methods and are able to answer questions during a two-hour session, which begins at 10am. Take something comfortable to sit on and plenty of sun protection. Many people take notes of the good ideas, so a pen and paper can be very useful.

The venue locations and dates vary from year to year, although they are advertised well in advance in *Target Taupo*, the *Taupo Times* and on the Sporting Life website. Otherwise contact the DOC Turangi office on (07) 386-8607.

PROTECTING THE ENVIRONMENT

There's no doubt that the natural values of Lake Taupo are under threat. It is not a situation that's new: the lake has always been up against the vagaries of nature, but in the last 100 years the threats have been increasing at a rate and on a scale not seen before. On top of the risk of volcanic eruption and the potential for a Mt Ruapehu-sourced lahar (a volcanically induced mudflow) in the Tongariro River, hydro-electric development and the introduction of pest fish have changed Lake Taupo for good. However, the greatest environmental issue facing Lake Taupo since colonisation is nutrient enrichment of the lake's water, also called eutrophication.

It is well-documented that Lake Taupo's water is lacking in nitrogen, which is the reason for its clear blue water. Regrettably, humans are quickly altering this, through urbanisation and the run-off from intensive farm-

The risk of lahar from the crater lake on Mt Ruapehu is ongoing.

ing activities – the two largest man-made contributors of nitrogen. The result is that the growth of algae is higher and water clarity is reducing, which is widely expected to affect the trout fishery adversely in the long term. Although the process is slow, it is continuous and over time will irreversibly alter the lake to its detriment if nothing is done to halt the process now.

Surprisingly, there is an alarming amount of apathy about the issue. Fortunately the lake has many friends and guardians, who collectively wish to protect Lake Taupo as a national and international treasure. Local and central government agencies such as the Taupo District Council, NIWA, Environment Waikato and DOC, along with organisations such as the Lakes and Waterways Action Group, are all helping to stop and ultimately reverse eutrophication before it is too late.

Eutrophication of natural waterways is not confined to Taupo but is widespread around New Zealand. Sadly, many farmers appear slow to recognise the urgency of the situation, even when presented with data from numerous studies, reports and environmental monitoring that point directly to the agricultural source of much of the problem. Ironically, the same group of people collectively use New Zealand's perceived pristine environment to promote meat and dairy products on the international market. Modern societies need industry and jobs, but if that involves ruining the environment then nobody wins. Environmentally friendly industries are possible, including dairying, but it will take a concerted effort and a lot of money from those directly benefiting to ensure that no detrimental effects result.

Apart from industry, everybody is responsible for the well-being of the region – and the country as a whole. Michael Drake, author of *The Lake Taupo Boating and Cruising Handbook*, poses the question in the first few pages of that publication: 'If the next 100 people to visit this place

A tropical paradise? No, it's Lake Taupo and it needs protection at any cost.

Farms in the western bays are a major source of nutrient enrichment in Lake Taupo. When you are on the lake, don't add to the problem by urinating in it.

leave it as you are leaving it now, would it be worth coming back to?' Makes you think, doesn't it? I share with others the view that if you ignore litter in the environment you are not much better than those who left it there in the first place. Other people disagree, using the argument that it is not their job to pick up other people's rubbish, but who will come and do it if you don't? Many people are now taking an active role by making a regular habit of picking up rubbish. Anglers can play their part by, for instance, retaining used nylon and leader material instead of leaving it on the riverbank. It does not biodegrade and needs proper disposal.

Even urinating in the lake, which may seem insignificant, provides urea, exactly what the nutrient-deficient water needs to help plant life grow. In the height of summer up to 400 boats or more can be on the lake in any day, so this could mean that hundreds of litres of untreated urine enter the lake daily. Lake Taupo is one of the best wild trout fisheries in the world, not a large toilet, so we should treat it with the respect it deserves. If getting ashore is not possible then have a reliable method of collection and dispose of it properly when back on shore.

With encouragement, those using the great outdoors will take a more active role in being the guardians of it for the benefit of everybody. Do your part to protect the environment: it is the only one we have and with your help it will remain enjoyable for many generations to come.

12. General Information

VISITOR INFORMATION CENTRES

Visitors wanting up-to-date information on virtually anything should call in to one of the region's **i-SITE** visitor information centres or look them up at **www.visitorinfo.net.nz** before you arrive. They have all the very latest information on activities, attractions, free regional touring maps and can even make bookings for accommodation and travel.

ACCOMMODATION

The visiting angler has plenty of options when it comes to accommodation in the region. There are camping facilities, backpacker hostels, homestays and bed-and-breakfasts, budget and executive motels, 4-star hotels, luxury lodges and rental holiday homes. Many of these are located near the most popular fishing locations so you do not have to stay in either Taupo or Turangi if that is not where you are planning to fish. Contact the **i-SITE** visitor information centres or, for motel, hotel and lodge listings in the area log on to:

www.jasons.com

www.nz-accommodation.co.nz *or*

www.nzmotels.co.nz.

If you want something for a longer period or for the family, choose from the many holiday homes that are available for short-term rental. In Whangamata Bay the Kinloch Store arranges rental bookings and they can be contacted by phone/fax on (07) 378-7836. In the southern part of the lake, Tongariro First National has dozens of homes for short-term rental in all the popular locations including Kuratau, Omori and Motuoapa. Contact them online at **www.laketaupoproperties.co.nz** for a look at what is on offer, or phone (07) 386-0030 for more information.

EATING OUT, SHOPPING AND BANKING

Taupo has a vibrant local restaurant and café scene that will cater for virtually any visitor. From simple takeaways through to award-winning silver service, there is plenty of choice. Contact the Taupo **i-SITE** for a listing or walk the town centre streets. Turangi has a number of good eating establishments too, some of them located at fishing lodges. The Turangi **i-SITE** has an up-to-date listing.

There are shops of all types catering to the local population and the visitor alike. Most large national supermarket chains and department stores have a branch in Taupo. Turangi has fewer shops, but it does have a well-stocked supermarket handily located in the mall, along with a small selection of other businesses serving the local community.

---

i-SITE TAUPO
Tongariro St
P.O. Box 865, Taupo
Phone (07) 376-0027 or
Fax (07) 378-9003
E-mail: taupovc@laketauponz.com

I-SITE TURANGI
Ngawaka Place
P.O. Box 34, Turangi
Phone (07) 386-8999 or
Fax (07) 386-0074
E-mail: turangivc@laketauponz.com

DESTINATION LAKE TAUPO
This is the promotional arm of the Taupo District Council, and their website provides an excellent overview of what to expect before you arrive in the region.
Private Bag 2005, Taupo
Phone (07) 376-0400 or
Fax (07) 376-0410
E-mail: info@laketauponz.com
www.laketauponz.com

A handy publication to have is the *Baches and Holiday Homes to Rent* guide, which is an annual national directory. With more than 40 listings in the region and growing by the year, it is available from most bookshops and is good value for around $20.
Look up the website:
www.holidayhomes.co.nz
or e-mail:
info@holidayhomes.co.nz
P.O. Box 3107
Richmond, Nelson
Phone/fax (03) 544-4799

Bank hours are typically 9am to 5pm from Monday to Friday and although most branches are in Taupo, 24-hour ATMs are located in Turangi outside the National Bank in the mall and in the Shell/Burger King on the corner of Pihanga Street and SH1.

VEHICLE HIRE AND TRANSPORT

A number of local and major international rental car companies such as Avis, Budget and Hertz have offices in Taupo. Contact the **i-SITE** visitor information centres for the contact details or look up the companies on the Internet. For short journeys around the district, two taxi companies operate in Taupo. Taupo Taxis has a depot in Gascoigne Street and can be contacted on (07) 378-5100 and Taupo's Top Cab Company is in Roberts Street on (07) 378-9250.

SECURITY

The Taupo region is a great destination, but like anywhere there are criminal elements at work and they will take advantage of any opportunity that presents itself. Unfortunately thieves are active in the region, with the main targets being the car parks located at popular sites, especially on the tributaries and many of the famous walking tracks. They are attracted to these places because there is an abundance of easily stolen, valuable items left in unattended vehicles. Within a few moments a window is broken and the items removed, irrespective of alarms. Vehicles are not usually taken: most of the offences are simple theft, but an experience like this can spoil your visit to the region and leave a very sour taste in your mouth.

The risk of theft from vehicles is avoidable if you take some simple precautions. The most basic of these is to lock the vehicle, but also make sure you never leave valuable items in view if the vehicle is going to be unattended – even for a moment.

A registered professional guide can improve the odds and provide that vital bit of local knowledge.

FISHING GUIDES AND CHARTER SERVICES

There is no doubt that local knowledge can make the difference between an OK and a highly successful trip: both are remembered for different reasons. It makes sense to employ the services of a professional guide, even for half a day, especially if you are new to the region. A good professional guide knows the local conditions and where the best chance of catching a fish is likely to be. Not only can this be a great kick-start to a Taupo fishing trip, but it can also be a quick way to learn the local techniques first hand from an expert.

More than 50 fly fishing guides and 30 commercial charter operators are active in the region. Not all offer the same quality of service, yet most have similar fees. Ensuring a quality experience is made easier by dealing with a registered guide or charter operator, who in the most part make fishing their living and breathing passion. These people belong to an administrative body overseeing a strict code of conduct, which is your only recourse if you are not satisfied with your experience.

The Taupo Launchmen's Association is one such organisation. It has a booking office located at the Taupo Boat Harbour in Redoubt St and can be contacted by phone on (07) 378-3444. The **i-SITE** visitor information centres also have a listing of the local guides, although I recommend logging on to the New Zealand Professional Fishing Guides Association website at **www.nzpfga.com** for a list of Taupo registered guides.

Lake Taupo is serviced by a sizeable charter boat fleet. If you don't have your own boat it is an ideal way to get out on the lake and experience some of its magic.

Taupo's famous floating 'Hole in One'. Divers retrieve the balls regularly from the lake bed.

OTHER OUTDOORS AND RECREATIONAL ACTIVITIES

The Taupo region is one of New Zealand's busiest recreational playgrounds and offers something for virtually everyone. Many anglers will also be pleased to know that the region is a golfer's dream, with a number of courses including the internationally recognised Wairakei Golf Course. The Taupo Golf Club arguably has more to offer, with two courses: the championship-length Centennial and the club-length Tauhara. At the southern end of the lake Turangi Golf Club has one of the finest 'country' courses in the North Island, and a new international-standard resort course is being constructed at Kinloch, which will be in addition to the odd-sized, but pleasant 10-hole course currently in the village. For less serious golfers there is always Taupo's famous 'Hole in One' located along the main foreshore.

Other land-based activities on offer include 4WD motorbikes, horse trekking, walking and tramping, deer hunting and mountain biking. On-the-water activities other than trout fishing include white-water rafting on the Tongariro, canoeing, kayaking and jet boating, eco-tours at the southern end of the lake, and relaxing cruises.

Many activities take place above the ground, such as the Taupo Bungy at Hells Gate on the Waikato River, tandem skydiving, and scenic flights over the lake and central volcanoes. At the end of a tiring day there are hot springs and spas at both Tokaanu and Taupo to soothe weary bodies.

Bookings can be made at the office of motels and hotels, or by contacting the **i-SITE** visitor information centres in Taupo or Turangi.

Appendix: A Note on Trout Fishing Photography

New Zealand's natural landscape is incredibly beautiful, and anglers are fortunate in seeing more of it than most. Often just getting out of the car and walking to the water's edge can open up a completely new world, unseen and unimaginable from the roadside. Making a special effort to venture into the unknown has its own rewards; as does catching the trout of a lifetime and releasing it rather than killing and eating it. Memories fade, but capturing the moment with photography can be very satisfying. Faithful recording requires good equipment and film, planning, a degree of technical ability and some luck. Of course luck is only opportunity and timing coming together, but there are times when it can turn an otherwise good image into something very special.

Rafting the Tongariro Gorge. Keeping camera equipment dry while you are getting right in amongst the action is a challenge in this environment.

The camera used to take most of the images in this book is a Canon 35mm EOS 33 SLR fitted with a variety of professional lenses, from a wide-angle 24mm to a long-range 400mm zoom. Close-up work was mostly done with the 24mm lens, which has an incredible close macro-focusing capability, and the mysterious world of night fishing was brought into the daylight with a Speedlight (flash). Carrying this expensive camera equipment around in a damp environment is risky and places added importance on waterproofing, particularly when you are trying to be right in the action and keep everything dry at the same time. I take extreme care, especially when crossing rivers, and double plastic rubbish sacks inside my camera backpack help prevent a disaster.

Publishers prefer colour reversal (slide) film for high-quality print reproduction and my personal preference is the Fujichrome range of films. Many of the images that appear in this book were taken with Fujichrome Velvia because of the outstanding reproduction of colour and detail it offers. However, it is very slow (ISO50), which means using a tripod in nearly every situation where sharp images and good depth of field are needed – even in bright daylight. Weighing over 2kg alone, the tripod is religiously packed along with all of the other equipment I take fishing.

Although Velvia is a superb film, the long exposures necessary to get good-quality images mean that it is not always suitable for people or other subjects that are capable of sudden movement. Fujichrome Provia and Astia (ISO100) filled any gaps very nicely and although they don't have the beautiful colour rendition of Velvia, they do offer excellent image quality without the steadying influence of a tripod. Faster film also allows the use of a polarising filter to reduce the problematic reflections and glare that can be a common feature of water-based images. Apart from that, and a lens-protecting UV filter, I rely on the vagaries of natural light to provide the colours to an image, so what you see is what I saw through the lens.

Another day in paradise. The author photographs Rob Hood fishing for smelting trout.

In the end, just as good equipment enhances the success of an angler, good photographic gear is limited only by the person using it. Photography is not an exact science, though, and at times it can be downright frustrating. Sometimes a 36-shot film contains only a handful of usable images conveying the message or accurately portraying what anglers are likely to see when they venture out in search of trout. However, 'capturing the moment' is what it is all about and is the essence of many photographs in this book. It is my belief that good images can inspire others to go in search of their own memories, and I hope that some of these achieve that aim.

I wish you all the very best in that pursuit.

Brendon Mathews

Recommended Reading and References

I credit my angling success to years of fishing, a lot of it not as successful as I would like, and to a number of instructional books and sources of valuable information from which all anglers can benefit. The books listed below and others like them are an investment, especially if your goal is to become a proficient and successful angler. Understanding and putting into practice the information contained within them can have an enormous impact on your fishing success, usually for the better – something that all anglers aspire to, whether they like to admit it or not.

Catching Trout (1991), Les Hill and Graeme Marshall, The Halcyon Press, Auckland, New Zealand

Choose the Right Fly! (1997), Keith Draper, Shoal Bay Press, Christchurch, New Zealand

The Lake Taupo Boating and Cruising Handbook (1978), Michael Drake, W.N. Drake, Taupo, New Zealand

Nymph Fishing for Larger Trout (1976), Charles E. Brooks, Lyons & Burford Publishers, New York, USA

Salmon Fever (1997), Ross Millichamp, Shoal Bay Press, Christhurch, New Zealand

Stalking Still Waters (1997), Les Hill, Halcyon Press, Auckland, New Zealand

Stalking Trout (1985), Les Hill & Graeme Marshall, The Halcyon Press and SeTo Publishing, Auckland, New Zealand

Target Taupo. This newsletter for anglers and hunters is an excellent magazine published three times a year by DOC Turangi and is free to full-season licence holders.

REFERENCES

Forsyth, D.J and Howard-Williams, C. (1983), *Lake Taupo – Ecology of a New Zealand Lake*, Department of Scientific and Industrial Research, Wellington, New Zealand

Wilson, C.J.N and Houghton, B.F. (1993), *Taupo the Volcano*, Information Series No. 13, Institute of Geological and Nuclear Sciences Ltd. Wairakei Research Centre, Wairakei, New Zealand

Williams, K. (2001), *Volcanoes of the South Wind*, Tongariro Natural History Society, Turangi, New Zealand

The Taupo Fishing Regulations 1984 (incorporating amendments to 30 June 2000), Department of Conservation, Tongariro/Taupo Conservancy, Turangi, New Zealand

Taupo Volcanic Centre, Institute of Geological and Nuclear Sciences Ltd, Booklet No. 7, Wairakei, New Zealand.